The
PLUM TREES

ALSO BY VICTORIA SHORR

Midnight: Three Women at the Hour of Reckoning

Backlands: A Novel

The
PLUM TREES

A Novel

VICTORIA SHORR

W. W. NORTON & COMPANY
Independent Publishers Since 1923

The Plum Trees is a work of historical fiction. Apart from the well-known actual people, events, and locales that figure in the narrative, all names, characters, places, and incidents are the products of the author's imagination or are used fictitiously. Any resemblance to current events or locales, or to living persons, is entirely coincidental.

For information about permission to reproduce selections from this book, write to Permissions, W. W. Norton & Company, Inc., 500 Fifth Avenue, New York, NY 10110

For information about special discounts for bulk purchases, please contact W. W. Norton Special Sales at specialsales@wwnorton.com or 800-233-4830

Manufacturing by Sheridan
Production manager: Anna Oler

Library of Congress Cataloging-in-Publication Data

Names: Shorr, Victoria, author.
Title: The plum trees : a novel / Victoria Shorr.
Description: First Edition. | New York, N.Y. : W. W. Norton & Company, [2021] | Includes bibliographical references.
Identifiers: LCCN 2020042617 | ISBN 9780393540857 (hardcover) | ISBN 9780393540864 (epub)
Subjects: GSAFD: Historical fiction.
Classification: LCC PS3619.H667 P68 2021 | DDC 813/.6—dc23
LC record available at https://lccn.loc.gov/2020042617

W. W. Norton & Company, Inc., 500 Fifth Avenue, New York, N.Y. 10110
www.wwnorton.com

W. W. Norton & Company Ltd., 15 Carlisle Street, London W1D 3BS

1 2 3 4 5 6 7 8 9 0

To Isabelle, Olympia, and Beatrice Perkins
with love

Commoner: Maybe goodness is just make believe.
Monk: But without goodness, life would be hell!
Commoner (*laughing*): Life *is* hell!

> *Rashomon*,
> 羅生門, Akira Kurosawa

THE LETTER

1

"SOMETHING TO DRINK?" asked the bartender.

Gin, Consie was thinking, or maybe something warming, since it was cold, and not just cold, but Ohio cold. Bleak midwinter, though not even Thanksgiving yet, with all the rest to go.

"Bourbon," she said.

But "No bourbon," said the bartender.

Fine, what did they drink here? She tried to remember the bottles from when they were children. Canadian something? Seven and seven—what was the seven? Schenley's? It didn't matter. "Whatever you've got," she said.

But it turned out there was no liquor at all here, not even old-lady sherry. Her aunt didn't think alcohol was appropriate for a funeral.

But when was it more appropriate? She wanted to slug someone. And deconstructing the thing, what *was* appropriate for a funeral? Bitters? Dirty water? Lukewarm tea?

And what about all the little cakes then, the sweets, the sandwiches they were passing? If they were to mourn, then let them bring out the ashes, cover the mirrors, tear their clothes. They had just put her oldest uncle in the ground. The worms whose dirt he'd taken would just be thinking about moving back in.

Unless they were frozen. It was sleeting outside, not even snowing. At the cemetery, they'd been hit in the face with freezing rain. It had been grim, blowing, and the trees stood stark and lonely.

She had tried to get here before he died; she'd wanted to get here. When she got the call that he was failing, she'd booked the first flight out, cost be damned, since weren't distances supposed to be nothing in this postmodern world? And compared to the old days, what was a five-hour flight across the country?

But in the end, it proved too much, the same too much as two hundred years ago, when the news would have come months late, by tattered letter, rather than over the phone in real time. Though two hundred years ago, she wouldn't have lived in California, or even survived childbirth for that matter, and if she had, then the Spanish flu would have gotten her by now, or whatever people died from. She too would be lying out there, under the sleet and the freezing rain.

She walked over to the window and looked out over what was left of the trees. Melville had once called the woods around here "the holy of holies," but they'd been despoiled long ago in the service of an industry that hadn't held up either, and now they were both gone, the forests and the mills. In their place was this remnant of some third-growth wetland, turned by recent development into another outpost of Nowhere, complete with the usual mall.

"Dust to dust"—had they said that at the funeral? She didn't remember hearing it. Maybe it wasn't part of this particular drill, maybe its clear-eyed assessment was considered somewhat harsh. They'd stood instead for the Twenty-Third Psalm, but wasn't that a young man's song, victorious in God's good graces? Walking through "the valley of the shadow of death," fearing no evil—but what did that have to do with her uncle?

He was ashes, dust. "Worms' meat," as Shakespeare put it. "Gone." "Passed away," "Passed"—when did people start saying that? And what good was it supposed to do? Make it all sound light, like a guru on his way to life as a butterfly?

Her uncle had been a father to her for most of her life. She'd loved him. She took a deep breath. Her head was already starting to hurt, but just then a cousin appeared with a flask, which, when poured into her paper cup, did wonders for the ginger ale.

"The good stuff," he muttered. "Too bad we have to mix it."

Not that there was anything the matter with bourbon and ginger. Consie drank—and then again. She'd made a mistake at the cemetery, one of those confoundings that have a name in the philosophy she used to study with such excitement, such belief, in college. When you mistake the whole for one of its parts; or was it the opposite? Anyway, the point here was that she'd wanted to see her uncle one more time, so that when a man in black asked if she'd like to "view the deceased," she'd said yes.

Wherein lay the flaw, because what she'd wanted was one more glimpse of her uncle alive, the pink cheeks and lovely gray eyes that had from her earliest days graced her world. But what she'd gotten was her uncle's hair cut a way he'd have never abided, and his pink cheeks a strange orange—self-tanner, she realized with horror. The undertaker having his way with a dead man.

After that, the rest of it had passed in a blur. There was a service during which they'd sat or stood as commanded, and then they filed out into the graveyard itself. She had grown up here, but had forgotten Ohio in the sleet, and the way the freezing rain hits you full in the face. There had been snow in the nice old neighborhood where they were staying, but here there was no snow, only half-frozen mud. As they lowered the coffin slowly, she'd wanted to cry out. Were they really going to leave him out here, in this cold, under the stark, leafless trees? What about waiting a day, or just till it snowed, which people said made a blanket. People who'd been caught out in what they called "the elements" and survived.

But there was no stopping any of it, the slow lowering of the coffin on some sort of machine these days, by Spanish-speaking workmen in jeans and hoodies, for what was this to them? Still, couldn't there be some sort of uniform, couldn't they at least be clad in black, out of respect?

And then, people stepped forward and threw shovels of dirt into the gaping hole on top of the coffin—how could they have done that to her uncle? And why? To make sure? But she was sure already. She had "viewed" him. Someone offered her a shovel, but she just shook her head.

THE APARTMENT WAS GETTING CROWDED. "We're so sorry," people were saying. Paying "condolences," as they used to call it, maybe still do. They didn't seem to have death like this in California, not normal death, that is, of old age, where nice people in wool gather to drink ginger ale and eat a cookie. There was instead sudden, shocking death of the young—a suicide, a crazy crash on Sunset. Where people afterwards aren't drinking much of anything, just standing stunned and drugged amongst the teddy bears and flowers.

She took another drink and remembered a scene in Rilke—some half-crazed old aunt sitting at the table, having dinner with her dead. The strange thing being that it seemed less voodoo than custom, just life going on as it always had, the same places set with the same silver, the candles, the "Yes, please," and "No, thank you," only no one there.

Not a bad way to do it, all things considered, or even a few things considered, because what else was there? A world of sadness? Nothing but loss? Alcohol? And even with that, even if you went out there, crazed or drunk or tripping, could you ever hear their voices again, saying your name just the way they used to, which was what she realized she wanted? More than anything.

Her uncle saying her name, "Cons"—that, and some air. Some sleet, or maybe snow by now, in her face. She headed for the door. She'd left her scarf on the plane, and forgotten her boots altogether, but that was fine. The worse now, the better.

"So sorry about your uncle—" A woman took her arm. Had she met her before? She couldn't quite place her. Foreign, but with one of those bad Cleveland haircuts. Long in the front, short in the back. Sassoon meets the Midwest.

"I helped your aunt go through his papers—"

Yes, yes. Was she a friend or secretary? Her aunt had come into the marriage with money of her own, so there was that possibility.

"Before the telephone," the woman was saying, and "so many letters," and so on. The point was to get away and outside. But the woman was going on, about something. Said she'd been so moved since she herself had come from there as well.

Yes, exactly—or from where? Whatever. It was getting darker. Consie wanted to, had to, get out, to catch the last of the light.

"So interesting," said the woman.

Yes, in their way, interesting, her uncle's letters—she'd seen some of them herself. The sweet formal notes to her aunt, asking her to dances. An account of hitchhiking home from college once, when he'd found himself in a small Ohio town at dusk, knocked on a random door, and was invited in for dinner and given a bed, as in the Greek myths or the Bible.

The past. Nice, but over. As opposed to the sleet outside, and the freezing air, which would fix her pounding head.

"Still, to read it now—" the woman was saying.

"Yes, amazing—" Consie could see the door, over the woman's shoulder. Ten steps, but the woman had her arm.

"So you've read it?"

They exchanged a look.

"Since you're a writer."

Was she? Unpublished?

"Your uncle told me."

Had he?

"He loved your stories. The ones about Brazil."

Checkmate. Consie took a breath. "Read what?"

It was six pages, single-spaced, from her uncle, dated *"August 31, 1945. Biggin Hill, Kent, England."*

So—her uncle's war. That part she knew. There was a photo of him on the coffee table when she was a child, in a kilt and tam-o'-shanter, with a nice smile. It looked like it had been fun for him there, in Merry England. He was twenty-five then, the war was over. She even remembered meeting some elderly English-women who'd come to visit her grandmother, years ago. They'd befriended him over there, invited him to suppers and tea.

"Dear Mother and Dad," it started, *"This letter has been on my mind for a long time and now I am determined to write."*

An ominous tone for a salutation, though we all owe letters. Used to, when we wrote them, all of which we were "determined to write." And sure enough, soon her uncle was talking about the weather. *"Hot . . . terrible,"* still, he was, *"as always, glad to be back."*

In England, presumably. He mentions a side trip to Paris, where he went to a *"semi-cabaret,"* whatever that was, ate *"iced tomatoes,"* and *"almost dropped through the floor"* when an army buddy opened a bottle of *"vine blanc,"* as he wrote it.

"But," he confessed, *"we drank it!"* And not only drank it but danced afterwards and listened to *"another Yank"* with a *"trained voice"* sing a few songs.

Funny, those old touches. The "semi-cabaret," the dropping through the floor over white wine. The "trained voice"—did that mean church choir or Carnegie Hall? Either way, she would have liked to have been there for the dancing that night.

He went on to say he'd spent the night in Paris—he mentions "Villa Coublay," which must have been somewhere posh, or formerly, since six years of war, which would have meant either Nazi occupation or hardly any coal and strictly rationed food, probably both, would have taken its toll on any villa—and the next morning arrived early for his plane. He did a little work for the army while he waited, *"signed a few passengers through."* It sounded almost like fun.

But *"So much for that."* Now he came to *"the real purpose of this letter."* He had been *"procrastinating,"* he wrote. *"But now that you expect the worst, I guess I can begin."*

SHE COULD ALMOST HEAR his voice here. The flight he was early for turned out to be to Frankfurt, which was as close as he could get to the town of Starnberg, in Germany, where there was a holding camp for "displaced persons," as they were calling people who'd survived the Nazi death camps. He was seeking two girls, cousins, who he'd heard from someone—he doesn't say who or how—might still be alive.

From Frankfurt, he hitched in his US Army uniform to Starnberg, about 150 miles, picked up by *"any and every German car,"* he wrote, which were on the road strictly with Allied permission, and afraid to *"brown off"* an American. The first car was a '37 Buick, with a rich man and a driver; next came a small bus carrying *"a GI and a German girl seeking work as an interpreter."* The driver was *"the typical Nazi type,"* and when her uncle mentioned that he was going to Feldafing, the DP camp, *"the girl claimed innocence of the place, but the driver shut up like a clam."*

They rode to the town of Starnberg in uneasy silence, and then her uncle got a ride the few kilometers out to the camp in an ambulance. It was a lovely place that had been an elite Hitler Youth school, set in a group of charming villas with a view of the lake. Now it served as a sort of halfway house for about four thousand men, women, and children who'd somehow eluded the gas and the chimneys, and found themselves on the other side of the nightmare, blinking and, for the most part, alone.

Her uncle was let out at the gate. When he walked in, *"everyone looked at me. I was a strange face and carrying a musette bag, and these poor people must have wondered what the devil I was doing there. I walked into the main building, and it was a rather depressing experience. For some silly reason, it had a peculiar odor."*

She looked up. What did people know, in August of 1945? Enough to make even Bavaria smell "peculiar"? Of human flesh?

And why "silly"? Still, it sounded somehow like her uncle, and she read on.

THERE WAS A "VERY NICE" Danish girl in charge. She looked in the register for the names he gave her, and told him the good news was the girls had been there; but since they'd come in *"from Auswetz Camp,"* as he wrote it, they were in need of medical care and had been taken over to a nearby sanitarium, at St. Ottilien. It was close by, and he could get there easily enough, but only in the morning. The roads around there were still deserted after dark. They would put him up for the night, the Dane said.

He was invited to share in the displaced persons' dinner, in one of the men's rooms—bread and butter, a bit of cheese. In his honor, they opened a tin of anchovies and another of tuna fish. *"I felt like two cents taking it,"* he wrote, *"but I was hungry."* And so were they—there was a shocking paucity of food at the camp. These survivors, as they weren't really called yet, were on nobody's list. While the Nazi POWs were receiving the same food as American soldiers, *"these poor people must exist on meager rations, and they are meager,"* her uncle wrote.

As they were having their scant dinner, *"Some of the neighbors came in, a few middle-aged women who really looked very nice. You might think it was a cottage and this was a vacation,"* he wrote, *"until they started talking."*

He had heard some of the stories coming out, and seen some of the first pictures, but *"it doesn't really strike you as thoroughly and completely as when you're with these people."* It was one thing to see all the corpses and the living skeletons in black and white, but what of these "very nice-looking" young women, who found themselves alive somehow?

And how? They didn't know, after what they'd seen—how had they lived? What did it mean, what could it mean? They didn't know yet. In June of 1945, it seemed to mean that they were still half-starving, still in a camp, albeit a nice one. Not like the ones they had only recently departed, camps designed by the best engineers in all of Germany for the express purpose of killing them with the least amount of muss and fuss to their friends and neighbors.

Former friends and neighbors—it had been hard for them to believe at first, these people said. Not that they hadn't read their history in school, hadn't studied the various pillages and massacres, the Mongols, the Goths, the Turks, the Huns, but all that had been done with passion, in the heat of battle, and weren't the conquered people enslaved afterwards and at least given a chance to live? The women and children?

"But this—"

"It's over," he tried to soothe them, and they agreed, yes, it was over, and they had lived instead of died for one reason or another, all of them, each one with a different twist to the tale. One could sew and got on a work detail, one knew the girl who ladled out the soup and got a little extra to eat, one was a gymnast and strong enough to walk through her typhoid fever. One could draw, but her sister could draw better and they sent her to the gas anyway, along with her mother, her father, her brothers, all their mothers and fathers and sisters and brothers, along with grandparents, aunts, uncles, and cousins, and what they seemed to be asking that evening was less how to get on with their lives than why.

WHICH WAS RATHER A PROBLEM for Lieutenant Smith too, the camp commander, who invited her uncle to stay with him in his beautiful house that night. It was built in "a *circular manner*," and had previously served as the Nazi headmaster's quarters. The Nazi books were still on the shelves—*Mein Kampf, SS Women*. Before that it had apparently belonged to a rich, cultured family who had vanished into the camps with no trace. Her uncle sat with Lieutenant Smith in the library, "*a fire burn-*

ing in the fireplace, everything serene and really nice. The house is just
above Lake Wurm, and of course the Bavarian country is, and I say
unfortunately for such a bestial people, heavenly.

"*We spoke of many things, the lieutenant's troubles, both short*
term—getting more food—and long term—what to do with the
inmates. Many of these people have no places to return to, and no rea-
son to, either. He's hoping that Palestine will be open to them.

"*Also, the next day, he was sending back to Romania about eight*
hundred people" —

What? To survive Auschwitz and then end up in the Romania heading straight for Ceausescu, and the worst police state in
what would soon be the Communist bloc? Hardly seemed fair.

And why Romania? Because it would take them?

But maybe why not Romania if you'd been through the
camps. Everyone was dead, everyone. If you spoke Romanian,
knew the streets, knew the black hearts of your fellows there
as well as anywhere, maybe the idea was why bother with anywhere else?

Still, *What about Brazil?* she almost said out loud.

But Stefan Zweig had fled to Brazil and taken poison in
despair, so who knew? Certainly not her uncle and Lieutenant
Smith in June of 1945, as they sat smoking and speculating in
front of the fire that night, concluding that Palestine was the
most expedient solution; an easy gift of some scrub acres in the
Middle East—what was it called then? Arabia?

And looking back on that too, one could see that if, instead,
they'd bought them all, every one of those survivors of the death
camps, lovely old mansions in Oyster Bay, or beach houses in
Malibu, with full-time maid service and regular junkets to, say,
Monte Carlo, all expenses paid, it would have been cheap at the
price compared to the cost of "Palestine."

But what concerned her uncle that night was less the fate of nations than how to get over to the sanitarium called St. Ottilien in the morning; and he wrote that he was greatly relieved when, after a few more cups of the Nazis' very good brandy, Lieutenant Smith offered to requisition him a car.

THE CAR TURNED OUT TO BE a small truck, painted white with a huge red cross, complete with a corporal as driver. St. Ottilien had been a monastery, founded in an old castle, with the white walls and red roofs of this Bavarian countryside, so begrudged its "beastly" inhabitants by her uncle. It was "suppressed," say the histories, whatever that means, "by the Gestapo," but reopened in 1945 to care for former death camp prisoners, informally at first.

So informally that, when her uncle rode up in the white truck with the red cross, they greeted him with relief and flowers, thinking that finally an American soldier had come to run the place. When he finally clarified his mission—that he'd come looking for some cousins—one of the nuns looked more closely at his face.

"Yes, of course, you look exactly like her," she said.

Like whom? he asked. He didn't know these girls.

"Like Alice," the nun smiled.

This uncle had been fair, the fairest in the family, with his pink cheeks and delicate nose, delicate build—it had always been the tennis team for him, never football. He left that for his two robust brothers, half brothers in fact. His own mother, delicate also, had died in childbirth. His grief-stricken father had married her grief-stricken sister. A very different girl from the first one he had chosen, but life ran along different lines in those days.

Still, this Alice must have been lovely if she looked like

this uncle. She must have had the light eyes, too, and the fine features.

But he doesn't describe her, just goes on:

"When the girls entered the room, I asked them if they had any relatives in the States. They told me yes, and told me your name, Dad, and Cleveland, Ohio. I told them in my German that I was their cousin. Somehow or other, they were so stunned that it made very little impression on them."

How had he said it? His German must have been rudimentary at best, learned as it was in an Ohio high school from a normal-school spinster whose closest encounter with the spoken language was likely Pennsylvania Dutch. Maybe instead of "cousin," which is *Vetter*, he had said *"Vater*," which meant father, and maybe the girls who'd survived Auschwitz weren't up to guessing games that morning.

But then, *"After about five minutes of conversation, Klara suddenly turned to me and asked me my name."* And when he answered—their mother's last name, the last name of their grandparents—when he said that lost, beloved name, *"they just started bawling and crying like a newborn babe."*

Which was *"wonderful,"* he wrote—even miraculous, considering what these girls must have known by then about tears. How they stopped nothing, not the sewing on of the first yellow stars, which must have been shocking in itself, though not compared to what was to come. And as it came, relentlessly, stopped by no tears, not mothers', not babies' whom these girls had seen tossed alive into burning pits, they must have thought, after that, there were no tears left. Not for anything on earth.

Until her uncle walked in that day, triumphant in his US Army uniform, with the news that he was their cousin, that they still had a cousin. They had come to almost believe the redefinition of themselves that had started with the yellow stars—that they were people apart, with no home, no place on earth, no cousins.

But here was their cousin, their victorious cousin no less, and not only had he beaten their enemy, but they could see their mother in his eyes, and that's when the tears came back.

"*They started to kiss me again and again,*" her uncle wrote, "*and caress me and hug me. Just knowing that they hadn't been altogether forgotten.*" Klara was in her early twenties, Alice just seventeen. She was fifteen when she was taken.

"*They were dressed nicely, but it was all they had. It was a blue print dress, the goods of which they'd managed to save. We went out and the weather was beautiful. We sat around and talked. They told me the same stories I had heard the night before from the other refugees. I had to listen to them again, but the fact that they got it off their chest was something.*

"*Then we went up to their barracks, which isn't nice, but at the same time was clean, mildly clean that is, and they showed me off to everyone. I was doing fairly well with the language, but of course had some difficulty. There was a boy, though, who had just been operated on about a week or so ago. He spoke English very well, and so he acted as our interpreter. Klara then again told me the very sad news.*

"*They had worked night turn, making munitions. Twelve hours daily. They had their numbers tattooed on their arms. Their food was terrible, that is, the little they had. The prisoners lived like pigs and slept practically like them. They had every bit of their hair shaved off their entire body from head to foot, to prevent lice from breaking out.*

"*Terrible, yet they once heard Radio London. While working one night, they heard some wonderful jazz music on the radio. Being in a corridor away from the main part, they explored and found that the Nazi overlord had left the radio on in his room, and it was tuned to London. The news and courage they got from that one broadcast was something. Naturally, it spread through the camp.*"

He went on then to say that Klara introduced him to her fiancé. She had met him in the DP camp, and wasn't sure if she should marry him. She turned to her new cousin and asked him his opinion.

"*Well, I was put on the spot,*" he wrote. "*But I said that as neither of them now have anything, why I thought that at least they could have each other. Again, she hugged me and kissed me. From no one else alive could she have got such advice.*"

Alice told him she wanted to go to the States, not back to their home—their former home—in Hungary. She was afraid she'd see people she knew, "*and they would ask her about her parents and she couldn't face it.*" Seventeen. She started to cry again.

Klara thought maybe they should go back, just to see. There was a chance. No one had thought to talk about "afterwards," where to meet and so on. It had all happened so suddenly, they'd been separated on a train platform in the camp, with no chance for even a word of farewell. The girls had been sent in a different direction from their parents, and told they'd be together again "right after the shower."

Her uncle, an American boy who'd only nights before drunk his first white wine, found himself hard pressed to advise them. He knew the truth about their chances for a visa to the States. "*I told them the family would do all we could, but didn't want to build up false hope.*" He explained that if they went back to the displaced persons camp, "*they'd at least have food, a bed, and some clothes to get through the winter. But if they tried to go home, they wouldn't know what they'd have. I told them how bad things were there, and also that it was hoped that many of the camp personnel would go to Palestine.*

"*But these girls definitely don't want to go to Palestine.*"

They were, after all, European, born and bred. Maybe they'd start, they said, by going to Romania with Klara's fiancé. That's where he was from, and he wanted to take them back there with him. Consie's uncle told them he would help them, the whole family in America would help them, once civilian mail opened up. Meanwhile, he gave them what he'd managed to bring from England—"*a dozen candy bars, four bars of soap, toothpaste, gum, lifesavers, three undershirts, a half dozen handkerchiefs, and socks, and a carton of cigarettes,*" which you could trade for anything. Her uncle wanted to give them some money, but they told him that "*money here is practically worthless.*" What they really needed were shoes, which her uncle promised to send.

It was hard to leave, he wrote. There were more tears, and the girls told him that though they were grateful for what he had brought them, "*despite their need, they didn't want those few things as much as knowing that they had really met me. They told me of a picture they have of us.*"

"Had," they should have said. Maybe they saw it in their minds, still in a silver frame, gleaming on a sideboard, behind a sofa in a living room they forgot was no longer there.

"*I had forgotten it,*" he wrote, "*but I do remember the one taken many, many years ago.*" Consie knew it, too—taken in a photographer's studio, the usual affair, a Victorian palm, an art deco sofa. Her grandfather with a half-smile she'd never seen as a child. Her grandmother's hair still dark, her uncles in short pants, her mother, a tomboy, stuck in a dress, with an oversized ribbon in her hair.

Did Klara and Alice's parents know that it was set in a studio? Did they think that palms and récamiers graced Middle American parlors in those days? Especially the parlors of men like her grandfather who'd left behind all that the rest of his family had held on to, in his quest for something new?

Who knew what any of them made of any of it? America hadn't attracted these people. Her uncle shook hands with the

Romanian fiancé, who explained through the English-speaking boy that they were leaving within the next few days. *"So I caught them just in time,"* he wrote. *"Lucky, wasn't I?"*

Lucky, yes, indeed, a nice story. Good weather, a fortuitous meeting of young survivors, one of the battlefield, the others of the camps. But then came a *"Now"*—and she could almost hear the dead man take a breath.

"Now to a more serious and sad truth which I must tell you. Here are the worst facts I can tell you, so prepare yourself for the shock which you've been dreading so long, because the worst has happened.

"These girls know nothing about their parents. They do know that most of the family have not escaped the fate, not even the children. They also said that your brother, Hermann, was at Auswetz Concentration Camp with them, and as he was very strong and healthy, they have hopes that he may be alive. They do know that he escaped from the Concentration Camp.

"So there may be some ray of hope. Not much, but maybe a thread. Please, Dad, try to take this hard news as easy as you possibly can. I could tell from your voice over the phone how anxious you were."

Then a few words about God's will, a brief reference to his happy return to England, an appropriate reminder that *"it is for those who still live that we must cry,"* and then, *"All my love."*

Her uncle.

CONSIE LOOKED UP. The light was finally fading on the gloom outside. How long had she been reading? The doorbell was still ringing with new guests. She held on to the letter with great care now—it had been pecked out on an old-fashioned typewriter, on crinkly thin paper, onionskin, they called it, and maybe it was. Anyway, it seemed altogether more akin to an illuminated manuscript at the Getty than to a cold computer printout.

She tried not to imagine it arriving, tried not to see her grandfather, a reserved and formal man, walking in the door, taking off his summer jacket—the date said August—"washing up," as he used to say, taking a drink of water, then maybe his schnapps, and then, as he sat to read the evening paper, being handed the letter.

The letter would have been opened already, ripped open even, for her grandmother would have seen that it was from their boy in the army and read it. So definitely the drink for her grandfather, and the radio off, and silence from the two teenage boys who were still at home, as her grandfather sat to read "*the worst news possible.*"

She got up, stiff now, and went back to the window. This apartment was new, built in the ex-urbs, on what had only recently been wetlands—who had allowed it? Though who didn't allow it, in America these days?

There was a flock of Canada geese on the lawn. She used to like the sight of them, but someone had told her that now they were just another sign of the whole imbalance, like deer.

They were brave, though, out there in November.

Did her grandfather know all that had happened when he read that letter? How his brothers and sisters, nieces and nephews had been killed? Everyone was used to it now; it was everywhere, the museums, the Academy Awards. All that "Never Again," till you open the paper and read the news.

But when did people start knowing? Her grandfather had never mentioned it, once, during her own childhood. Never said a word about his brothers and sisters, just told her of a horse that had once carried him across a flooded river, and the geese that had nipped at his heels, even when he fed them. A grandmother who would slice a raw potato and put it on his temples when his head ached.

She had tried that once, when her own head ached. It had worked, as well as anything worked. The truth is, you can't stop a headache, not a real one. She turned back to the letter.

Who were these sweet girls dressed in blue, this Klara and Alice? She'd never heard their names before. They were young—Alice only seventeen. *"Sometimes so old, and sometimes so young,"* wrote her uncle. Did they go into Romania after all, with Klara's fiancé? Were they caught again then, a few years later, when the Russians lowered the Iron Curtain?

A terrible thought, though maybe they'd lived perfectly nice lives there, as most people do, most places, with husbands, children in school, work of some sort. Poverty at first, but then perhaps some measure of comfort, even relative prosperity. Had they ever written to her uncle after that, or her grandfather? She tried now to remember if her grandfather had ever mentioned them—had he? He wasn't talking much anymore, by the time she'd gotten old enough to understand.

"Clinically depressed," she was told, years later. Apparently they'd even tried electric shock.

But why hadn't he said anything? It must have seemed unspeakable to him, but wouldn't it have helped? Was he trying to spare her, to spare himself, from actually seeing it all? There were a few photos in an old album of his sisters, tall, elegant girls in silk, with their chic twenties hairstyles, and his brother, Hermann, who looked very much like her grandfather. A finer version, perhaps, but with that same half-smile.

He had lived in Czechoslovakia, which he called "a democracy, a Little America," in a letter he'd written in response to some sort of papers that her grandfather had sent, which he could have taken to the US consulate in Prague, and used to get a visa to America. That was in 1938, when he still could have sold his house and businesses—for a loss, granted—and bought passage on whatever boat was leaving, and brought his wife and daughters, his mother-in-law even, to America, right then.

But "we are Czechs," he wrote, "we love our country," and then that door slammed shut, and she knew the rest of the story, or thought she did. Hermann had died in a concentration camp.

Contradicted, though, by the letter. Which claimed that Hermann had escaped from Auschwitz—"*They do know*," said the letter.

She rifled through the papers, trying to find that bit, but the letter was long.

"One for the road?" The cousin was back with the bourbon.

"I don't think so—" She had an early flight back.

Although, on second thought, why not? It was dark outside, finally. No more spindly birches, no further surfeit of geese.

She took the drink and sipped. If she had read the letter a month ago, or even last week, she could have asked her uncle. Now, the whole thing lay out there with him, six feet under, in the graveyard.

Ironic. But life. The reason for the drink. She drank it down quickly, and slipped the letter into her bag. Maybe she'd read it again.

Or not. The past. Over. She walked out into the freezing night.

2

THE SLEET HAD TURNED to snow, and they were digging their cars out the next morning as she rode to the airport, and even so, she had a momentary thought to tell the taxi to stop, turn back. Not that she could say what she would be staying for, but there is only one place in this world that is home.

And this was it for her, the place that looked—not good exactly, but intensely familiar to her. The crumbling brick factories, the boarded-up old wooden houses with the porches half off. She knew it was blighted, miserable, decaying, but none of that could stop the chord that it still struck in her heart.

And there was that moment in the cab when she was thinking to stay, even just a little longer, doing the math of how much *Adbusters* or maybe even *Rolling Stone* would pay her for a piece on the decline and fall of the industrial heartland. But once she put in the cost of a rental car, the thing fell apart.

Despite the fact that hanging around a bit might have eased the loss of her uncle. A visit to the cemetery, maybe alone, and a few more nights under the covers with the out-of-date sleeping pills she'd found in a cousin's guest room. A deep winter's sleep going back—back, back—to the formal old dining room where they would all still be sitting, her grandparents, and her uncle, too, coming for the night.

BUT UP AGAINST ALL THAT was the simple fact that any flight across the country is good if you've got a window.

"Please have the courtesy to close your shutter so that your neighbors can watch their monitors," they were saying over the speaker. Which she didn't have—that "courtesy," not even when they came in person to bug her.

What—close her blind on the view that Icarus had died for, so that her so-called neighbors could binge-watch *Friends*?

"It's against my religion," she'd finally taken to saying, and that seemed to work, even with the most militant of the flight attendants.

Not that they cared much anymore, not like they used to, and she was left to wonder, as they flew over the part of the Midwest where the fields get round, did people escape from Auschwitz?

She'd never heard anything about that. She'd read her share in the past—who hadn't? Drawn to that half-pornographic cult of cruelty, those tall blond Nazis with their boots and whips and dogs—they even wore the skull and crossbones on their collars, she'd read somewhere. Death in person, and Auschwitz was their Acropolis, their Rome. As far as she knew, you went in on the train and out through the chimney. You only survived if you somehow lived it out.

But—she pulled out the letter and read it again.

"They also know nothing of Hermann, but he was at Auswetz Concentration Camp with them, and as he was very strong and healthy, they have hopes that he may be alive."

That was spoken, and then written, in August of 1945, when

hope was still a possibility. People were still creeping out of the camps, or even the woods. She'd met a German in Brazil, an officer on the Eastern Front, who'd taken three years to limp back from Russia. Clutching a crust of bread that he didn't let out of his sight for a full year, even in the bath, till they got on the boat to Brazil.

"They do know that he escaped from the Concentration Camp."

What did that mean? How did they know? Primo Levi hadn't said anything about escape from Auschwitz. There wasn't any escape in *Life Is Beautiful* or *Schindler's List*. Of course those were all constructs, and even the brilliant Levi was writing with hindsight and a story, but these girls were telling it the way it was, right then and there, in 1945, to a man who didn't even know how to spell the name yet.

So did Hermann escape? And who would know? Why hadn't she read this letter before? That is, maybe she had, years ago, but why hadn't she been interested? Does it take a death? Does it take a voice from the grave to toll like a summons?

If she'd paid attention before, she could at least have asked her uncle the girls' last names. Or if he ever saw them again? And what happened to Hermann? Did anyone know?

She closed her eyes on all that brown down below on the ground, all that gray. It was late November in America, coast to coast, though not in California. That was the thing about the place. It was never November. The sun would be shining when she got there, and the bougainvillea flowering, pink, orange, magenta. No one has to go to sea. Jump off a bridge, maybe, only they don't have bridges out there either. Only a freeway overpass, and how do you get there, and where do you leave your car?

Because it wasn't as if she hadn't thought about it. Life has a way of going to seed out there. All those ideas, all that time, all

those screenplays, in every waiter's back pocket, not just yours—
and then, statistically, nothing in the end. Not even seasons to
mark it. You lie down by the pool, as someone put it, and wake
up old.

They were in the West now, flying over—where? New Mex-
ico? The pilots used to tell you, but now no one wants their
screen time interrupted. But something was sparkling down
there, not just a frozen river, which would have been lovely
enough, but something pink, red, like crystal. It looked like a
city, lost in the wastes.

Something still undiscovered in this world? Something still
to be found? Was it possible?

And then came the flat-out sand of Nevada, and finally the
artificial green of profligate water use, which meant first Vegas,
then Palm Springs, and finally LA. The always half-desperate
touchdown, funneling them into the truly bad airport, the
crowds, confusion, traffic, and finally, mismarked but welcome,
the road to the beach, through the strip mall slums on Lincoln she'd come to know so well. The cheapest gas stations and
car washes, the good fish taco stand with its lines of gardeners
and bricklayers interspersed with hipsters out from New York.
The half-lit, expansive fabric store still trying to sell gold bro-
cades from the forties. The old Fox Theatre where her husband
had once shown his Brazilian film, now a permanent "swap
meet," filled with China's worst toys and the oversized flannels
the Mexican kids seemed to like. Then the discount shoe place
where, every once in a while, she could get the children the
shoes they actually wanted. Now being remodeled into a Whole
Foods, so that's what was happening to the back side of Venice
these days.

And then finally, the turnoff, marked by a giant penguin
offering cheap dentistry—why, though? A penguin?

And yet, over the years, it had come to make its own sense, it promised calm and cool, and more to the point for her, led to the ramp away from it all, down to the Pacific Coast Highway, where, with one simple turn, you left all the grubby commerce behind you and confronted instead the great vast blue.

There were even dolphins, some days, right off the road, as if all was well. And maybe it was for them, it was her fondest hope, and the sun was shining, the surf was up, but who in the whole round world were Klara and Alice? She called her mother as soon as she got home, but all she could say was that she thought they'd written once from Vienna, in the fifties.

Still, Consie had kept her grandmother's old address book, and now she dug it out. A lot of the numbers were archaic. Some had only five digits, others names instead of area codes. Riverside 7. Trafalgar 9. But finally, she found one, scrawled in blue ink in the margins, that looked possible. She dialed and got a distant cousin who vaguely remembered her name.

Life had worked out well for this cousin. She was married, with children, a good job, or maybe no job, no need for a job. Consie didn't remember afterwards. She wasn't really listening, until the talk turned to the dead.

Yes, this cousin had heard of Klara and Alice, but had no idea where they were now, or even if they were still alive. She confirmed that they were Hermann's nieces, and had been in Auschwitz. She mentioned a few last names, but no cities or even continents. Anyone who might have known was likely "gone," she said.

"By the way, though," she added, "speaking of Hermann, did you see the videotape that his daughter Magda made?"

3

It CAME IN THE MAIL, no longer a videotape, but a small, thin DVD. Consie slipped it into the player with trembling fingers. She'd known Magda, as a poor relative from Canada, who came with her sister every year or so, to see Consie's grandparents. "Uncle and Auntie," they called them.

They were hairdressers and dry cleaners in their new lives, these women. They would rumble in, with their Eastern European husbands and old cars. They had children—Canadian children, who didn't play baseball—and numbers on their arms. It was their own fault in a way, though, she'd vaguely gathered. They could have gotten out in time, but refused—"*We are Czechs. We love our country.*" Magda had been studying music in Vienna when the Nazis marched in. She and her sisters spoke several languages, Consie's mother had told her, and that's what had saved them. She grew up thinking that only the uneducated died at Auschwitz.

Magda and her sisters cried every time they saw her grandfather. "Uncle!" They would embrace the stiff old man with tears rolling down their faces. That was in the fifties, the early sixties. They were all dead now, and it brought Consie a shock of pleasure to see Magda again, alive and well, sitting on a chair—

presumably in her apartment in Toronto, in front of some pictures, her grandchildren, she told the interviewer. She had nine.

She looked lovely, with her hair done in an elaborate bouffant, dressed in a vaguely European suit, with plenty of jewelry, rings, bracelets, necklaces, perhaps to make a point. She had not just survived: she had prevailed. Behind her on the wall was a modern painting, school of Mondrian, it looked like, or maybe Klee—had it belonged to her parents? Had she brought it from Europe?

It turned out she had, but as the camera pulled focus, Consie saw not an avant-garde abstract, but a sort of Renoir girl.

Still, it was art. *"Are you ready?"* asked the interviewer, off-screen, in one of those therapy voices. Her hand came into view, proffering Kleenex.

But Magda shook her head—Magda! No Kleenex for her. And then she started to talk.

"Ve had a beautiful childhood"—what did they call that in drama class? Hollywood has a good name for that. The setup? You make it so terrific that it's clear you're heading for a fall.

Too clear—which was the case here. Consie almost didn't want to hear about the loving grandparents, the aunties and uncles, the cousins, the lunches, the dinners, the sleigh rides. The friends all over town, all over everywhere, all religions—everyone was happy. Magda grew up in the village where they'd all been born, in a big house, with nice neighbors. Everything was fine.

Except that the strangely hypnotic voice was already screaming on the radio in the background by then, and they'd seen the newsreels at the movies—"Heil Hitler!" Everyone shouting, singing, marching, arms raised together. Thousands and thousands, soldiers, girls in dirndls, boys in lederhosen, people lining the streets.

"Ridiculous!" Magda's father—the Hermann of the letter—concluded. "Look at that mustache—preposterous! He looks like Charlie Chaplin, he's a joke, the Germans will never put up with him, he'll be gone in a month."

Which made sense—much more sense than what in fact came to pass. But Hermann had read Kant, not Nietzsche, nor was he a man of storm and wind. The breezes he felt in those days were still the gentle ones that blew in from Prague, the capital of his own country, a democracy that had sprung from the ashes of the Austro-Hungarian Empire, young and new, a sort of dream place, a democracy like America, as he would write his brother, but with culture.

Music, art, and to back it all up, the businesses, which for Hermann and his family were thriving. There is mention of grand houses on both sides of the shifting Hungarian border. As for Hermann himself, it was farms, orchards, and a grain dealership. He and his wife would, upon occasion, travel to Baden to take the waters. His daughters were studying music in Vienna.

Though what they should have been doing—but how do you fast-forward? Either that or play it back and change everything—how easy it could be. A few bullets, well placed, or even a sustained and organized campaign to get people out of there, to Uganda or Nevada, the top of a mountain or a valley where the sun never shines. It would have been better, but instead, life went on, Magda was saying, 1936, 1937.

Eventually 1938. Hitler was still shouting in Germany, but still dismissible in Czechoslovakia. She and her sister were home from Vienna for spring holidays when her father received the "affidavit," as they called it, from the States, from Consie's grandfather, Hermann's brother, guaranteeing a million dollars' backing for him in America.

Whatever that meant, the million dollars, which her grand-father, a prosperous merchant in a small Ohio town, could not have mustered. Still, he had one of those nice old rambling Midwest houses that would hold his brother and family, and more, any of them who could get out, and he could feed, even employ them, and his congressman knew it and must have filled in the papers with whatever figure it took. And Hermann could have sold his house and his businesses right then, and booked passage, first class even, on one of the ships that was sailing that spring.

But instead, he went walking in his orchards with his eldest daughter. It had moved him greatly, he told her, that his brother in America had gone to such trouble for him. Magda was sixteen then, it was a Sunday, and they'd driven out in a taxi to visit his farms outside of town, as was their custom, and the sun was shining. The fruit trees, apples, pears, but mainly plums were snowy with blossoms. Amid the flowers, white, pink, and that incomparable plum purple, he'd turned to her.

"Look how beautiful it is!" he said. "Nothing bad could ever happen here, you'll see."

And he folded his affidavit away.

And she and her sister Gabi went back to Vienna the next day, and resumed their study of piano and violin. They lived in Dr. Krugerheim's pension, along with other *comme il faut* young ladies from the provinces. They loved Vienna, loved their studies, the music, the art. The daily strolls along the Danube, the *Kaffe* and Sachertorte at the Hotel Sacher itself. They had friends, girls like them with well-off papas and pretty moth-ers in Prague, in Budapest, in Bucharest. Life was beautiful, except that while they'd been home, strolling with their fathers amongst their fruit trees, the prime minister of Austria had resigned, and Hitler had annexed Austria. That was Austria's natural state, he'd stated. Now it too would be part of the glorious Thousand-Year Reich.

Which was fine with most Austrians, even better, at least at first. After World War I, they'd been living in a state of almost suspended animation. Their old Austro-Hungarian Empire had been dismembered, and though there was a general agreement that the structure had been obsolete, there was also a sense that history had passed them by.

Which was nothing, however, to the unemployment. It hit twenty, then thirty percent—one out of three men not working. Men who'd fought in the war, lost their brothers, their friends, their limbs, and come home with the shakes, to no jobs.

It made no sense to them then, all that fighting, all that dying, until they went out into the streets and heard the cheers and the singing. "One People, One Nation, One Leader!"— why not? Hitler was one of theirs, he'd been born and raised in Austria, and his dream was, on the face of it, beautiful. A Thousand-Year Reign of the strong and the brave, a complete regeneration, a whole new world that would be theirs if they had the will to seize it. True, he had forced their elected leader from office and sent in the Wehrmacht—but on the other hand, there were already new jobs, lots of jobs, as the shuttered steel and iron works threw open their doors and cranked up their machines to fill German orders for tanks and guns.

It was a new beginning, a new destiny; but firmly based in tradition, so even the old folks were happy. It came from deep within, who they were, and had always been. Only now, the true extent of their latent grandeur would be reached. It would not be easy, and there would be blood. But that was the price, and the blood required seemed, especially at first, to belong to other people, people who were already taking more than their share—

"Look around you!" cried Hitler. "See how rich they are," the very people who "betrayed you" at the end of the last war. It was "they" who had pushed the good Germans and Austrians into the untenable Treaty of Versailles, according to Hitler. "Behind our backs!" he shouted.

But this time would be different, he promised. This time the good clean people would be vigilant, and do it themselves, their way. The pure old way, when the Norse ruled the land and the war god Wotan still stormed through their hills. And the girls in Vienna braided their hair and shook out their mothers' dirndls, the boys took down their hunting horns and killed lambs in the woods, draped their decadent Beaux-Arts monuments in Hitler's red and black, strengthened the coat of arms on their flag with his swastika, and joined their Austrian voices to his "Horst-Wessel-Lied," which filled their streets, too, now, and seemed to swell to the very stars that spring.

Hermann's daughters sang along, too, at first. This new song wasn't as beautiful as the Haydn it replaced; but it promised freedom and bread, and the young officers in the street, in their black and gray, were not, as Magda put it, "a bad sight either." She and her sister weren't immune to the calls for renewal; down with the old, in with the new! Young girls in springtime, they too were thrilled by the sound of the horns in the hills.

But then, one morning in May, three German SS officers knocked on the door of Dr. Krugerheim's pension and regretted to inform its residents that the establishment was as of that moment closed. They had come to escort the foreign students to the station. The girls had—the officers tapped their watches—half an hour to pack their bags, so as to catch the next train east.

A few years later, and those same SS men might have just taken the girls out and shot them, and saved the Fatherland some money. What with the cost of the transports, and striped pajamas, not to mention all that gas, the Zyklon B, for which IG Farben was paid 300,000 marks, over the years.

But all that was just evolving, and in that May of 1938, the Reich was still feeling its oats. The Austrian sun was shining and the birds were singing Wagner. The officers were young, and they waved to Hermann's daughters as they put them on the train.

"Tell your countrymen in the Sudetenland," they called, "that we send our regards to them, and that we'll be there soon ourselves, to convey them in person."

Then a whistle, another wave, and the train was off. East, out of Austria, in and out of Hungary, and then back into Czechoslovakia, the girls' republic, their democracy, their home.

THERE WAS STILL TIME THEN for Hermann to leave, but only a little, as we know but he didn't. Hermann's daughters traveled the four hundred kilometers from Vienna east to their village, Trebišov, in May of 1938, with some misgivings, but no real fear. Their father met them at the train.

"A bunch of thugs," said Hermann. The Nazis were no longer comical, but still beneath contempt.

The girls reported the comment about the Sudetenland.

"Impossible!" snorted their father. "We are a sovereign country! The English and Americans will never allow it!"

Which still made perfect sense at the time. The borders were still open, and Hermann probably still could have taken his affidavit to the US embassy in Prague and gotten a visa. And had it been November then, with his trees standing stark and the snows blowing in off the Carpathians, maybe he would have boarded a warm train or even taken a taxi. Prague was about one hundred and sixty kilometers farther than Vienna, but as long as you could still travel, it wasn't so far. An easy trip, one he'd taken before. He could go anytime, he figured.

Which was true, until one day it wasn't; and by the time the fruit had set on his trees that year, it was already too late. The America that would "never allow it" had problems of its own. Henry Ford himself was publishing *The Protocols of the Sages of Zion*, a half-cracked czarist hate tract; Charles Lindbergh, still a hero, was traveling the country, speaking darkly of "their" ownership of "our motion pictures, our press, our radio, our government." And forty million Americans were tuning in, three times a week, to hear Father Coughlin, a Catholic priest, on CBS Radio, ranting coast to coast about "New York capitalists," who were also Communists, and you-know-what religion, and the true enemy to boot. It was they who were mongering war with Christian Germany, when the real Satan was atheist Russia, and in the meantime, Father Coughlin wasn't so sure Hitler was wrong. At a rally in the Bronx in 1938, he gave the Nazi salute.

Roosevelt eventually turned to Joseph Kennedy and even the future Pope Pius XII to try to silence Coughlin, but it took Pearl Harbor to shut him down. And that wasn't till the end of 1941, and in the meantime, in 1938, 1939, 1940, years so crucial to Hermann and his kind in Europe, America didn't—couldn't—do a thing.

But who knew that in the summer of '38? Especially since life went on at home as it always had, or almost. Hermann's daughters were still nice girls, rich girls, though nice, rich girls who'd been tossed out of Vienna. No one said it out loud—on the contrary, they didn't say it. Which turned out to be very much like always saying it, since it was always there. On the radio, even on the BBC, there was either Hitler himself, with his strange, high-pitched raving, or someone else, nonstop, raving about him.

Even the plum harvest, the best time of the year, with all the work and celebration, took place under a shadow. The same workmen as always were building the same fires, just so, under the plum trees; and their sturdy wives were stirring the same sweet blue plums into jams and liqueurs in the ancient copper kettles as always; but instead of the usual laughter and joking, there seemed to be a strained silence—or was Hermann imagining it?

But his wife felt it, too—or felt something. The people hadn't brought their small children to play under the trees, she realized. When she asked about them—"They're not sick?"—the women mumbled excuses, but didn't meet her eye.

Yes, that was it, said Hermann. No one looked him in the face anymore. Men he'd known for years, men whose fathers he'd known—he couldn't understand it. He had always treated people well, he was known for it. "Pay as much as you can, not as little," he'd taught his daughters. People flocked to work for him. They named their firstborns Hermann, or Aneta, for his wife.

But now, when he walked among them, they fell silent. Turned and looked the other way. And inside the house, among friends, it was not much better. Women who'd come to discuss plums and sugar, to pick up the eternal argument over proportions and how long sugar should "stand" on fruit before cooking, would suddenly, apropos of nothing, blurt out that the Nazis were taking people's houses in Berlin.

Or launch into a recital of who'd already left—Thomas Mann, Bertolt Brecht, finally Freud. Were they thinking of nothing else, then? Even Hermann himself, one afternoon, as they sat in the shade of the trees, drinking tea from the old tin cups and eating the first plum tarts—even he had looked up and said, as if he were continuing a conversation, that life in America wouldn't agree with them.

His daughters turned.

"There's no music there that we would like," he said.

"There's jazz!" cried Gabi.

"Jazz, but no Beethoven! No Mendelssohn! No Vienna."

And none of them spoke English, they would have no friends, no land, no plum trees—he waved his arm around him. Everyone fell silent.

"It's so beautiful here!" He turned to his wife, almost in tears. "How can it be finished?"

His wife had grown up on this land. So had her parents. She had been born an Austro-Hungarian, but now was proud to be Czech.

"Of course it's not finished." she summoned a smile. And it was still warm enough for a wade in the pond, if they finished their tea in time. It would be lovely in the water in the late-summer afternoon sun.

But autumn comes early in eastern Czechoslovakia. And even as the last of the old kettles were being scrubbed down with ash and hauled on carts back to the barns where they slept through the seasons, the ethnic Germans among their compatriots, who lived mainly in the western part of the country, were joining the Nazi Party in percentages surpassing even the Germans at home. Their allegiance, they insisted, was to Germany. Despite the accident of having been born in what was temporarily part of Czechoslovakia—again the betrayal, the treacherous treaty! Versailles!—they had always been Germans, not Czechs.

Walter Runciman, an English envoy on a fact-finding mission, reported back to London on the logic of their position.

The Germans' descendants there did, after all, speak German. They looked German. Maybe they were German. Maybe Hitler had a point.

Plus this was all he wanted, Runciman assured his government. Give him those parts of the country, their so-called Sudetenland, and then he'd leave everything else alone.

The Czechs protested—Hitler's "Sudetenland" was where their coal, their iron and steel works, their electrical plants were. Its mountains, wrapping around the provinces of Bohemia and Moravia, provided the only natural defenses. Without them, the country would not be viable.

But to the rest of the world, the sacrifice of Czechoslovakia offered the chance for "peace in our time," and the English prime minister, Neville Chamberlain, took it. His name lives in infamy for that.

But there were, in his defense, other names, long lists of them, in every village church in England, the World War I dead, hanging down the walls. Appalling lists—so many names from such small places, lost in "the War to End All Wars," as they still called it in 1938.

But if it wasn't that, after all? What if another war was to be fought, a mere twenty years later? Meaningless, then, all those dead, and presumably Chamberlain felt that, and was trying to stop more writing on those walls when he and the French left Czechoslovakia to its fate in Munich that September.

It was a popular move, at the time. Chamberlain was greeted upon his return by cheering crowds lining the streets of London. He had, he told the English, looked into Hitler's face and seen there "a man who could be relied upon when he had given his word."

It might have helped, though, had he read *Mein Kampf.* "Peace in his time" was not on Hitler's agenda.

As would be seen, but these things happen as they happen, one by one. And what happened first, under the folded arms and misty eye of the English and French, was that the Nazis marched into the western edges of Hermann's country, his "Little America," and that was the end of that.

4

THIS WAS IN THE FALL OF 1938. The trees were bare by then, and there was a growing sense among Hermann and his family that they should have left the day they got the affidavit from America. But visas to America were no longer possible, and travel even within the country was becoming increasingly problematic. It seemed they now needed special permits on the trains.

Special permits that Hermann feared might be refused to him. This was something he very much wanted to avoid—an actual out-and-out confrontation with the authorities, his friends till now, his compatriots, that might put him on the other side. The outside, in fact. No longer recognized as a Czech, somehow.

As long as this didn't happen in black and white, he could still maintain both the fiction of his dignity and some hope. But it was hard—the cold came fast and early that year, and the news from Germany was always worse. There was a rampage there, they heard, in November. The papers blamed a young Polish boy whose parents had been killed by the Nazis and who in turn had shot a German diplomat in Paris. The German people, outraged, had risen up spontaneously and broken shopwindows and set houses of worship on fire. They called it *Kristallnacht*, "Night of Crystal," for all the broken glass.

Bad news, Hermann and his friends shook their heads over the newspaper accounts, but at least explicable. The killing of the German diplomat, and then a hooligan rampage that had gotten out of hand. Nothing that hadn't happened before.

But that wasn't how it was, it was far worse than that, said a young woman who had been there. She was passing through their village, hopping from train to train, heading east, and Hermann's wife had invited her to dinner. After a few glasses of plum brandy, she started to talk.

She was a student, studying philosophy at the University of Bonn, in Germany, and had been visiting an elderly aunt, in the nearby town of Cochem, on the Moselle River—

"Cochem?" said Hermann's wife. It was famous for its wines. They'd been there once on holiday. "A nice town," she said.

"Nice?" The girl gave a short laugh. She lifted her glass, drank it down. They saw that her hand was trembling.

"Go on," Hermann urged her. She took a deep breath.

Of course it had already been getting difficult, she said. You understand.

They understood, or were starting to. The increasing possibility of harassment in the streets, the new, ever-changing restrictions, even some imprisonments. Pitfalls that were starting to be set along their daily paths there too, these days.

Well, so it was in Germany, though perhaps a little more *advanced*, a little more *refined*—and here Hermann could hear the university in her voice—"since it was the epicenter of the—*activity*, and home to its *avant-garde.*"

Hermann refilled her glass. She drank again, and went on.

And unless you were blind, as she had been—had to be!

How else do you continue your studies, or try to continue, because there were restrictions there too! But she'd managed to get around them, had gotten dispensations, that sort of thing, and had been thinking that, with a little cleverness, she would be able to work through this thing, wait it out, but that sort of delusion was impossible now, after Kristallnacht.

Granted they'd had their pretext—the shooting of the diplomat in Paris. But as for it being 'a spontaneous uprising of the offended German people," as Hitler claimed, it was nothing of the sort. The whole thing had been plotted and orchestrated by the SS, a new kind of Special Forces, who had dressed in civilian clothes for the operation, and launched a wild spree of destruction and killing that swept all of Germany, every city, every town.

But once it got going, the girl said, it no longer needed the SS. It was as if the whole population had gone mad together.

It started on the night of the ninth of November. She and her aunt were already asleep in their beds. When she heard the first shouting, very close, she thought she was dreaming. Her aunt lived in a very quiet neighborhood, prosperous and solid, no place for an uproar of any sort. But then there came more shouting, followed by a scream, a shot, and a woman's voice very close: "My God, he's dead!"

Who? She jumped from her bed. A distinguished doctor lived next door. Had thieves broken into his house and killed him? The girl ran into the hall, to the telephone, to call the police, but the line was first busy, and then dead. And the noise from the street was getting worse.

Was it a whole gang of thieves, then? But didn't thieves act in silence? She'd been frightened at the thought of thieves, but more frightened still if it wasn't thieves. She went softly into her aunt's room, so as not to wake her if she still slept—she was old, with a bad heart, but her aunt was already sitting straight upright in her bed, her face white, her hand on her heart. From the street came more shots, more shouting, and then the sounds of glass breaking, cars screeching, a crash, and then another, of what might have been a wall falling down. They could smell fire, and her aunt thought that it must be an invading army, or even a natural disaster of some sort—an earthquake or a thunderbolt, though there'd been no rain.

But as the shouts came closer, they started to make out the Nazi language, the name-calling, and then the nature of the disaster became clear. She said nothing to her aunt, but they could hear—couldn't not hear—the cries and pleas of their neighbors being dragged from their houses and beaten. They waited for police sirens, but heard none.

Her aunt's husband had been a judge in the town, a decorated veteran of World War I. He had believed in twentieth-century Germany. "Our Fatherland," he'd called it.

"Where are the police?" her aunt kept asking.

The girl didn't tell her her worst fears—that this was the police. The elderly housekeeper appeared in the doorway, and the three women groped their way downstairs to the kitchen, and sat in the dark at the table in their nightgowns, waiting for the Nazis to smash in their door.

Outside the shouting and crashing ebbed and flowed around them, coming closer and then moving away, "but never far enough." At dawn, the frail housekeeper got to her feet and made coffee. The girl said she put two lumps of sugar in each cup, which was not her way.

But why not, she must have been thinking, if this was to be their last cup of coffee? The girl herself was a student of philosophy, studying a highly complicated system of mathematical probability, but the mystery of life had come clear to her that night. It was even elegant in its simplicity: If some random boy in the street scratched his head and shot her, then even the most abstract and intricate systems would be, as far as she was concerned and in one fell swoop, solved. Over. If he scratched his back and shot the man next door instead, all the permutations and combinations would dance themselves on. That was all the logic there was to it. Her whole three-hundred-page thesis could be reduced to a simple if-then.

She was through with her studies, she'd said aloud then. Her aunt and the housekeeper had nodded together, as if they already knew. None of them moved. If there was any safety at all for them, it was there, in the middle of the kitchen. The table had become a life raft, and the coffee an invisibility draught.

Occasionally the housekeeper rose to make more, but that activity seemed to fall within the sphere of safety. Anything else might break the spell. The three women sat and drank into the morning. It was a gray day, November, and the light outside seemed all of one tone, early and late. There was still the screaming and the crashing from outside, and they still hadn't moved when, sometime after noon, there came a knock on the door.

They sat terrified, but then a voice called her aunt's name politely, in the sort of tone not generally associated with the Nazis, and it turned out to be one of her late uncle's colleagues, a young man he'd helped along, now a judge himself. He'd come to get them out, he called, to his wife's mother's villa, outside of town.

Her aunt rose to pack a few things, but he said no, there was no time. He had a taxi waiting, and when they'd finally gotten her aunt into the car in her nightgown, he urged the man to drive fast and then faster. They had to take a circuitous route out of town, because of all the fires. Shops, houses, old places of worship—all blazing, but with no attempt to put out the fires.

"Have they no water?" her aunt asked.

But there was water, you could see it, the girl said, for the buildings nearby. It was only selected targets that were left burning. The firemen were standing in front of them, arms folded, watching them burn.

All alike, said the girl, as if they'd been trained in the art of not putting out fires: "You fold your arms just so."

She was joking—the university again, thought Hermann. It was a shame this girl hadn't been allowed to keep studying. She would have made a good logician, Wittgenstein-style.

Her poor aunt couldn't comprehend, though. "Why can't they do anything?" she kept asking. "Is something the matter with the water?"

Yes, yes, they told her, but she must have understood, because finally she lay back and closed her eyes. Which was good, because what would they have told her when they passed the children, laughing and throwing stones through stained-glass windows, and the men tossing leather-bound books onto bonfires already sky high?

The worst part, she said, were the well-dressed women, really fashionably dressed, people who looked like her friends, or her parents' friends, people she could have known—it was hard to see them shouting and cheering on the destruction, holding up their babies to see. Hard to have to face the truth that it wasn't just the rabble on this rampage. It was everyone.

The taxi had to detour down an elegant street, where men were throwing china and crystal out of the windows of some of the houses, crashing it down into the streets below. Things that they could have used, things of value—even a grand piano. This she saw with her own eyes, saw men pushing a grand piano, a Bechstein, over a balcony. It caught by one leg in the ironwork and hung there, in midair, to the wild cheering of the crowd below.

The girl fell silent for a moment—her listeners, too, sat stunned. To kill a man seemed easy these days, but to destroy a Bechstein piano, built by hand over years, with great art for great artists—finally from Hermann, a hoarse "Who?"

The girl shrugged—that was the point. Anyone, everyone, the ticket-taker on the bus, the postman, the butcher's boy, the countess. Nice women with their children—but all out of their heads, raving like lunatics, all of them. Like something out of the Greek myths, the Furies, or the witch burnings, right there, in Germany, five centuries before. No one knew to this day how many women they burned, but some sources claimed hundreds of thousands. Some said a million. Whole villages were left without one woman, she had read somewhere.

She'd taken that as wild hyperbole at the time, but now she knew that whole towns could go mad. She had seen it, and seen, too, the way it unhinged its victims. Now she understood the bizarre confessions the accused witches had made. That they'd turned men into black cats and forced them into unspeakable acts on their broomsticks—she could understand that now. "You are no longer part of God's ordered universe." She herself had looked fearfully at the birds in the trees that day, half fearing that they might fly at her and peck out her eyes. When they drove across the gentle Moselle River, she was surprised it wasn't raging. Actually surprised that it too hadn't joined the madness.

Her aunt was still asleep when they finally got to the villa, and in fact she never really woke up. Which was a mercy, since a few days later, when the rampage had subsided and the girl crept back to the apartment, she found the place destroyed. Not so much robbed as wrecked, like what she'd seen in the streets. The crystal and china smashed, the piano hacked to pieces, dirty oil poured over the lovely old rugs. Paintings slashed, even her aunt's Nolde, which was ironic, since wasn't he a Nazi himself? Her own books had been pulled off the shelves and seemed to have been kicked around a bit, but not burned. Maybe they'd run out of petrol.

It had come to her then, she said, looking around that room in the aftermath, that this chaos, this insane destruction, was a perfect portrait of postwar Germany. The chaos in people's lives, the unemployment, the insane inflation, wheelbarrows full of their own good marks worth nothing, and the crippled veterans, home from a war they hadn't realized they'd lost, with their lives in ruins. They had struggled with it for ten years, the German people, each in their own private abstract desperation, but then Hitler had flung open their doors and taken them out of their dark rooms, into the streets, with someone real to chase down, to hate, to blame. Someone whose windows they could take the great pleasure of shattering with impunity now.

She got to her feet—anyway, she was through with all that, with trying to make sense, to understand. She was on her way to Romania, where she heard you could still get out. She had a cousin in America, but that was hopeless; there was said to be a line three-deep surrounding the US consulate in Bucharest, and people who managed to get inside the palings were sleeping on the steps.

But the British Consulate was still giving a few visas, and she had a sister in England, and could speak the language. She was hoping to find work as a governess there.

"And then perhaps study?" asked Hermann.

She laughed—a sort of cackle.

How old are you? he asked her.

Twenty, she said. "Old."

AFTER THAT, HERMANN STOPPED talking about "the twentieth century." Still, they had grown up on German culture, Goethe and Schiller, Kant and Hegel, Mozart and Beethoven, and couldn't comprehend what was going on in their land. What was the madness? Where had it come from? There were only about 600,000 "undesirables" in Germany all told, in a population of 65 million. To be obsessed like that, even if it was hard, even if they'd lost the war—the girl was right, they'd gone mad.

"Maybe it's the bread," his wife suggested. Bad rye was known to make people see things. And they'd always gone a bit mad with their Walpurgis Night, when the ancient demons rode down from the mountains—but didn't people light bonfires then to keep them away? A sort of protection?

But these bonfires had been part of the general madness, which meant what? Who knew? The only thing now, though, would be for someone to step in and stop them. Restore the rule of reason. Hermann still had faith in America. They heard that Roosevelt recalled his ambassador from Germany after *Kristallnacht*. This he took as a good sign.

Anyway, the year was turning. People would surely come to their senses soon. It was 1939—"A better year!" They clinked their glasses and drank the last of their plum brandy, the last for them anyway.

Because in March of that year, Hitler marched east from the Sudetenland and took the rest of their country.

"AND RIGHT AWAY, *you could feel the Hitler atmosphere*," said Magda. It started with the posters on the walls, warning the populace of subversive elements in their midst. You would know them henceforward by the yellow stars they would be required to wear on their clothing. What that star meant was that those persons were no longer Czechs, or Hungarians or Poles or whatever else they might have been or thought they were before. Now they were foreigners, a different race in fact, even if they had blond hair and blue eyes.

As for the "subversives" themselves, they were to report to the police station for their stars, and Hermann complied. For one thing, it would have been beneath his dignity as a leading citizen to flout the law. For another, there was the strong belief, general among the law-abiding populace, that compliance would afford them protection.

So in 1939, Hermann and his wife and daughters sewed on their stars. Their town had a prewar population of ten thousand, of whom seven hundred and fifty were now required to walk around with yellow stars on their coats. Just a piece of cloth, they told each other, a small thing, but now when they walked into a shop, silence fell. People stared or looked away, people they knew. Friends and neighbors crossed to the other side of the street.

Why, though, was the question. What had they done? Had some strange planet risen in the sky? Someone they knew went to a nearby town to consult an astrologer, but nothing clear seemed to be written. A psychic had visions of fire and drowned herself in a pond.

But she had been half-mad anyway, Hermann assured his wife and daughters, and anyway, this couldn't go on much longer. Not with England poised for action, and America in the wings.

STILL, "THIS," AS HERMANN CALLED IT, was steadily closing in around them. *And the truth was, it all happened so fast,* said Magda. First one right revoked, not so bad in itself, but then another, still leaving room, though, for some hope, some belief in an ultimate rationality, offstage perhaps, but somehow there, somewhere.

But every week brought more scrawls on the walls, ugly faces, caricatures—big noses, bags of money—and posters calling them names—VERMIN! PIGS!—and further restrictions. People with stars were no longer allowed out at night, or into shops, even groceries, except during certain inconvenient hours. Nor were they permitted in public places—first the restaurants, then the movies, then the parks.

NOW THE PARKS ARE JUST FOR US! proclaimed the posters.

"*It was ridiculous,*" said Magda. A childish game, "them" and "us," which even as a small girl she'd grown out of. But people she knew and liked—used to like—were starting to walk around with swastikas on their arms, "*proud as peacocks,*" she said. Her father scoffed, but still it was painful.

And is the park so much more fun now, without us? she wanted to ask them. Or the schools? Because that's what came next, and once the thrill of expelling a hundred children had passed, what were they left with? A hundred empty desks, along with a few faces gone from the staff room? But someone must have missed those faces, maybe even most people missed them. She agreed with her father—it was all too infantile, too stupid, to last. People would come to their senses.

Though it was taking longer than they'd expected, and next came the order to turn in their bicycles, which is when she started feeling less scorn than fear. Not that anyone was imagining a wild bike ride over the border at night, but the thought that someone wanted their movement restricted yet further was unsettling. Still, the bicycles were duly turned in.

But then came the demand for the radios. And this was when Hermann stopped and considered. The girls loved their radio, it

was their only music these days; and more important, their con-
nection to the world beyond, the real world, as they called it.
They couldn't, of course, ride their bicycles to London, but they
could tune their radio into the BBC and hear the voice of reason,
even if they couldn't quite catch or understand all that it said.

"Should we comply?" the people of the town stopped and
asked each other. Should they continue, as the staunch citizens
they'd always been, to do as the law commanded, or draw the
line here and reconstitute themselves as outlaws?

For this, surely, was the way they were being treated, the
young men among them were starting to argue.

But it's a big step from law-abiding, upstanding business-
man to even passive resistance, a step that Hermann, as a pillar
of the community, a payer of taxes and supporter of the arts and
the poor, found he couldn't bring himself to take. There was
still the belief that if they complied with the law, no matter how
harsh, how outlandish, if they complied to the letter, sewed on
the ridiculous stars, turned in their bicycles, if they did everything right, then they were still somehow *inside*. Still entitled to
the law's protection.

But to keep their radio, hidden in a back room, under the
bed, only to be played very softly after dark, the BBC and the
station from Vienna that still played Mozart every evening—
"Who would that hurt?" his daughters were begging.

"Me," Hermann concluded. He had always obeyed the law.
He was a Czech, a good citizen. Hitler wouldn't take that from
him, he said. He'd turn in the radio, and once the English and
Americans stopped this thing, he'd buy a new one, a better one.
Even if the whole German nation was eating bad rye bread, this
was still the twentieth century, not the Middle Ages. This kind
of madness could not be allowed to go much further, Hermann
still believed.

5

BUT HE WAS WRONG, because right after that, they were forced from their house.

"No longer permitted to live on principal streets," was how the edict put it. They were given a few days to be gone.

And what had happened to the Czech constitution? Hermann asked the officials who came to inform him—local police, not even Nazis.

But they didn't answer because, for them, the loss or not of their constitution wasn't much of an issue. Nor did it seem to matter that their duly elected president Edvard Beneš was in exile, or that the country had been dismembered into a pathetic group of "protectorates." What mattered were the good-looking new gray and black uniforms they'd been given, and the furnished houses that would soon be available to them free of charge, or so they'd been told.

"*We had no time to pack more than a few necessities*," said Magda, some pots and pans, a few mattresses, a suitcase or two. They found a small apartment nearby, on one of the back streets, "and when it's over, we'll be back," Hermann swore to his daughters, and despite orders to the contrary, locked the door. He pinned his own war medals on his coat, beneath the yellow star, and then they were escorted away "*like criminals*," Magda said.

A man Hermann knew took over their house, lock, stock, and barrel—their silver still on the sideboard, the carpets still on their floors. "*They came before we left, and stood there watching, like vultures, with swastika armbands and pins on their coats.*" One hundred and fifty houses in their small town changed hands that way in one weekend. The neighbors watched from their windows, but no one came out to say good-bye.

"*People who were so close to us, people who'd lived next door for thirty years, suddenly just stopped talking to us. The whole world turned upside down.*"

Although she didn't really blame them. The posters plastered to the walls warned of the consequences in big red letters: ANYONE SEEN HELPING THEM WILL BE TREATED LIKE THEM. A clergyman who'd sewn a yellow cross on his robe was taken in and beaten. People heard the screams on the street outside.

"*They too were petrified for their lives*," said Magda. Not that it wasn't painful when old friends crossed the road so as not to have to risk a smile; but on the other hand, no one could deny the opportunities that the situation afforded.

Because after people's houses came their businesses, which were also now available, virtually free of charge, to former managers, partners, even junior salesmen, trained and trusted by the displaced owners. In Hermann's case, his farms went to his manager, an ethnic German named Goodmann. He wouldn't forget Hermann's kindnesses over the years, Goodmann called as he drove back out to the farm, on Hermann's sleigh, pulled by Hermann's horses. Goodmann's now.

As for the grain business, a young man Hermann had hired was now the owner. He was a nice fellow, which was why Hermann had hired him, given him his big chance in life, and he actually asked Hermann's forgiveness, even paid him something under the table, and "hired" him back, to keep running the business, though at a subminimum wage. It was all he dared pay, the young man said.

ANYONE SEEN HELPING THEM WILL BE TREATED LIKE THEM— Hermann told his wife he thought the man had been decent enough, considering.

Though considering what? He had thought this—this nightmare would be contained, would be one of those things that happen, history, a coup d'état, a change of government, even of borders, something you struggle against but then move on from, and go about your life, with a reconfigured sense of friend and foe, perhaps.

But it had already gone on much longer than anyone could possibly have expected, and who knew anymore what the so-called civilized world would do about it, if anything? Hermann was trying to make sense of it, even as it shifted under his feet, trying to find a way to protect his wife, his family. He wasn't worried particularly about being poor. He was smart, and lucky in business, he knew that. He would always find a way.

If they let him—when they let him. But when would that be? Each day seemed to bring another law, another street he couldn't cross or store he couldn't enter. Next it would be the very air they breathed, he laughed—tried to laugh.

But there was something here that confused him, seemed to go beyond the garden-variety hate he'd thought belonged to the past. He'd thought, growing up, that they'd left that behind, along with the dark clothes, the beards, the closed world of their grandfathers. They'd been born into the light of a new century, and they'd embraced it; they had friends of all religions, all walks of life, they sang carols at Christmas. He'd risked his life in the last war.

"Their war!" some people had called it, but he had begged to differ. It was his war too, and he would fight for his country, die for it if he had to; but what would he be dying for now, if it pleased one of these thugs in uniform to shoot him in the street in front of his family, as they'd done to one of his friends the week before?

Had he been fooling himself all along? he wondered. And what about those so-called friends—had it always been there, behind the cheer, behind the smiles? He had loved them, stood godfather to their children, cried with them in the graveyards when their parents died. And yet, not one of them had stepped out once to greet his wife when she passed, proud head in the air, yellow star on her coat.

He knew the risks they too ran—told himself that maybe, probably, he wouldn't have had the courage, either. The local Nazis were brutal enough, and there were German SS in town now as well. Still, would he have moved into another man's house like that, or taken another man's business, no questions asked?

Because that was part of it, too. No one seemed to be asking any questions. Wouldn't he have at least gone to the prefecture and made a little inquiry?

But no one did—it was almost as if they blamed the people walking around with the stars. A kindhearted countrywoman in the grocery had asked his wife what they'd done. When she'd answered, "Nothing," the woman had shrugged and said, "Well, but they don't treat people like this for nothing."

"That's how they see us now!" his wife had cried that evening. "As criminals!"

"They're the criminals," he said, but whom did he mean? The woman in the store? The friends and neighbors who'd kept silent when at least they might have asked?

AND THERE WAS HIS OWN silence as well, the way he'd pushed it aside when he still could, when the stories he was hearing were still about someone else. People in Germany, people in Poland—how different had he been, from his neighbors here, who, though they'd had to watch their neighbors leave their lifelong homes with pots and pans banging in a mule cart, were still snug inside their own nice houses? And what if they had spoken out and then landed in the street themselves? How would that have helped Hermann?

Unless they'd all spoken out together—that would have been the thing. Not to let the monsters pick them off, one by one. It would happen one day, he assured his wife and daughters. Good people would come together. After all, the Nazis' dream of oneness, of unity, could be remade to include them all.

All they had to do was take the hate out, and there could be something good there. He too would like a purification, a renewal, reaching back to old virtues. Wagner's horns stirred something in his blood as well, and he remembered, as a boy, that feeling of singing all together in the school hall. And in the army too, marching all together. We are invincible, and one.

That had been attractive, almost irresistible, and as for the Germans who'd had no jobs after the war, and no money, Hitler, with all his yelling and thumping, was both offering work and bringing people together, with all that singing, all that marching, arms in the air, with the shouts, echoing off the walls, "Heil Hitler!" Appealing, he knew. Immensely appealing.

Especially when one could turn a blind eye to the dark side of the thing that was putting relatively small numbers of people in difficulty. Easy enough, as Hermann said, to look away as other people packed and left, or were shipped off to somewhere—few enough so you might not even notice.

Not at first, anyway, though there would come the time, he felt almost certain, when the Germans, highly civilized people after all, would surely take a breath and call a halt to the hatred. And in the meantime, he and his wife and daughters put their mattresses in one corner, their pots and pans in the other, and created order in the dark apartment where they'd landed, taking turns going down to the cellar at dawn for coal to make their ever-weaker tea.

Quite a change from the strong dark coffee with freshly baked rolls they used to have in the morning, "before," but still it was something—he'd heard that people were going hungry in Poland. And there was something nice, too, about all sleeping in one room, where he could hear the comforting sounds of his daughters' breathing. There were worse things in the world, much worse, than losing one's house.

And before long, a sort of routine took form for them again, and became their life. Teachers, excluded from the public schools, started organizing classes for the excluded children, and Hermann's daughters helped out, teaching music and French. Hermann himself was still working part time at his old business, and still had some savings in a bank box—Magda couldn't remember afterwards how it had worked; maybe the bank hadn't reported him. He had also buried some gold and silver in glass jars among the more distant fruit trees. With this, they should be able to eke out a life till the world came to its senses again.

———————

WHICH SEEMED TO HERMANN to be happening the next fall, in September of 1939, when Hitler marched into Poland, and the French and English declared war at last. America would follow suit shortly, he was certain, and even confided to Magda that he thought there was a chance that they'd be back in their own house by Christmas.

Though it was around then that the first stories started coming out of Poland. Two small boys had somehow made it over the mountains, alone and on foot, and had emerged from the woods not far from there, like sylphs with horror in their eyes and the news that the Nazis in Poland were shooting people into mass graves.

They'd rounded up everyone in their village, the boys said, and marched them into the woods, where they shot them all into a big hole, their parents, their sister and two brothers, their grandparents, uncles, aunts, teachers, and friends. These two boys fell under some bodies, which saved them, and when it got dark they managed to crawl out and escape through the deep Polish woods.

"Is it possible?" whispered Hermann's wife, later that night. "The Germans shooting people into mass graves?" No one had ever heard of anything like that before.

They knew that Hitler was insisting on more "living room" for the German people, which was why he had gone into Poland, or so he claimed. But that was a far cry from depopulating Poland, as some people were saying, in order to turn the whole place into a breadbasket for Germany—preposterous!

And how would you depopulate Poland anyway? There were thirty-five million people living there. Was Hitler planning to dig a mass grave from Warsaw to Lodz? It was inconceivable.

"Think of Goethe, think of Beethoven!" Hermann concluded. "Those boys have to be lying. The Germans couldn't be shooting people into mass graves."

Still, the war wasn't going as he had expected. Incredibly, France seemed to be falling, and Hermann was thinking that maybe he'd underestimated Hitler. He had taken him for a buffoon, a monstrous child, but now he was parading up the Champs-Élysées, and seemed to have invented a new kind of warfare.

He called it *Blitzkrieg*, his "lightning war." He'd taken Poland practically overnight, before the Poles could even mobilize. And he was bombing England, firebombs falling from the sky every night. Hermann had seen the pictures posted on the walls, all over town. "London in flames!"

Horrible, and where were the Americans? There were words coming up in conversation that they hadn't heard before. Words like "transports" and "deportation"—what exactly did they mean? That is, he knew what they meant in the dictionary, and what they used to mean, but what did they mean now, especially when applied to people like them, law-abiding citizens in their own country, with proper papers?

Because citizens or not, papers in order, people were starting to disappear; there was no question about that. Sons were taken, supposedly for the army, but then when inquiries were made, the sons weren't listed anywhere. Or people set out for the market and never came back. The Germans hadn't sent many SS into that part of Czechoslovakia yet, but the Czechs didn't seem to need the Germans, they had their own Nazis, the Hitler *Jugend*, the Youth, former juvenile delinquents, the kind of boys who set cats' tails on fire and torture songbirds for fun.

Now they were given uniforms and encouraged to attack

anyone they caught in the street at night. This gradually progressed to killings, mostly of the hands-on variety, often with
clubs or stones. Afterwards, they'd hang the bodies from the
lampposts. You'd see them every morning now, two or three
at least.

"*By the end of 1939, we were petrified*," said Magda. "*We mostly
just stayed at home.*" Hitler had installed a Catholic priest, Jozef
Tiso, as his man in this part of Czechoslovakia, now called "the
Slovak State." Tiso was an ardent Nazi, and so enthusiastic
about Hitler's policy that he offered to pay the SS for every man,
woman, and child "transported" out of his country.

Hermann and his friends were still debating what that might
mean. Some argued "relocation," others "forced labor." It didn't
occur to anyone to go beyond that.

6

THE FIRST TRANSPORTS from Czechoslovakia started in 1941, and by then the word no longer needed quotation marks. They still weren't sure where they were going, but they knew by then how it started: people rounded up on the street, sometimes for a reason—they were refugees, immigrants—and sometimes not. Sometimes it was just because they were there, or their yellow star was too high or too low. One man was deported because the sewing was too "fancy," and another man because his star wasn't sewn on but simply pinned to his coat.

The Hitler boys kicked him with no compunction in front of the general populace, and then threw him onto a truck for "immediate deportation" to Germany, "to work," people were told. So not the worst fate, and the feeling was still that if you kept pretty much off the street, you should be all right.

But then late one night, there came a knock on Hermann's door. He and his wife sat bolt upright, clutching each other's hands—"My God!"

He cast around the room—the girls were sleeping, where to hide them? The first place they'd look would be the small closet, and then under the bed. He didn't think it would be like this, with no chance to think or take action—

Another knock—"Please, sir!"

He and his wife looked at each other. It wasn't the police. Hermann hadn't been "sir" to the police for almost a year now. He squeezed her hand and got to his feet. He opened the door just a crack. Goodmann was standing there, Goodmann the farmer, who'd once worked for him on what had been his farm.

Hermann was so astonished to see him that he almost couldn't place him. It wasn't that he'd forgotten about Goodmann. He'd known the man for twenty years, and it hadn't been more than a year since the two had traded places. But that was by the old calendar, and time moved differently under Hitler's "Thousand-Year Reich," which cared nothing for Hermann, but had made Goodmann's fortune. He was even wearing a German uniform that night.

Goodmann was now a ranking member of the Nazi Party, he said, which was why he'd gotten wind that there was going to be a deportation any day from the town. It would take all the young boys and girls, Goodmann told Hermann, and his daughters' names were on that list.

Hermann stood stunned. He'd done all they'd asked of him, and still they would take his children? And what now? Run? But how? There was a curfew, and the whole place was guarded by the thugs, the *Jugend*, whose sport was to pick off people who tried to move through the streets at night.

But Goodmann said he remembered Hermann's kindnesses over the years, and that he was willing to hide the girls. He named a very large sum of money.

Hermann accepted at once. He would have it for Goodmann the next day, he promised. He roused the three girls and kissed them, and then hustled them down the narrow stairs, still in their nightgowns, to Goodmann's wagon, which stood waiting out back, the horses stamping, horses they knew. Their horses.

And hidden under their own father's hay, the girls were taken out to the farm that night, and locked in a room with no window, and nothing on the walls except an oversized photograph of Hitler. Magda was eighteen, Gabi sixteen, and Vera just twelve. Goodmann's wife brought them bread and cheese, morning and evening, and sometimes Goodmann himself came at night, with a letter from their parents.

They weren't allowed out, even for a breath of air. ANYONE SEEN HELPING THEM WILL BE TREATED LIKE THEM—a man who'd made a joke, calling for "all bicyclists to wear yellow bicycles," had recently been arrested. Which meant that someone had reported him, someone who'd heard his little joke, so a friend maybe, or a neighbor. No one knew who was watching, who was listening, or even why. What good it could possibly do them.

But Goodmann's wife wasn't asking who or why as she turned the key in the lock twice a day, and a deaf ear to the girls' pleas for just a quick walk, even in the darkness. "You want me to be shot, too?" was all she'd say. It hadn't been her idea to have them there in the first place.

"So there we sat in that room," said Magda, *"staring all day at Hitler's picture."* His eyes, his nose, his infernal mustache—where was the mystery? she asked herself. Where did the hatred lie?

And why them? What crime, what offense had been so enormous as to bring old friends to hate them, and reduce them to incarceration in their father's former tenant's back room? Nice girls, all three—nice-looking, yes, but not too pretty, nothing to envy about them, and their parents were well-off, but not the richest in town.

So why? Why? Was it their violins? The trees in their garden? Their mother's nice coat, with the fur trim? But half the women in town wore coats with fur trim, all bought from nice Mr. Friedman, whose prices were considered fair, but whose shop was now closed and shuttered, after boys with swastikas on their arms had broken the windows and Mr. Friedman's leg.

And she'd heard that people had cheered at that, even people in Mr. Friedman's coats, but why? She couldn't make sense of the thing, no matter how hard she tried. Grown-ups, people she knew, her friends' mothers and fathers, were putting on armbands and turning on their neighbors. With a new look in their eyes, a new cruelty in their faces.

But was it fun, that cruelty? Was that what it was? Like picking on the slow child at school? But even if you teased him a bit, you didn't hit him, you didn't want blood to flow from his poor nose, you didn't cheer for that! She turned away from the picture, tried not to see it. Made it a game with her sisters—trying not to look at Hitler's picture.

"You looked!" "I didn't!" "There he is!" "I forgot!" The days in Goodmann's back room were long and tedious. They lived for their bread and cheese in the morning, the sweet notes from their parents at night. There was no calendar, and after a few days they lost track of time, and started arguing about how long they'd been there.

So they weren't sure how long it had been—a week, or even two—when Goodmann unlocked the door one night and told the girls to come out, "Quickly!" He was taking them back to their parents, he said. The horse and cart were waiting. He tucked them back under the hay and drove into town.

It was too risky for him to keep them any longer, he told Hermann. There were rumors going around, it had been noted that the girls were not on the transport.

"Noted by whom?" their mother cried. Certainly not the Germans in the town, who didn't know them, so who? Who wasn't satisfied? For whom wasn't it enough that two hundred other girls had been rounded up and shoved into boxcars and taken from their midst; girls they knew, girls whose mothers they knew, whose grandmothers even? Tall girls, short girls, some so young they were crying for their mamas, others proud and brave, heads high, but nonetheless deemed unfit to live among them.

And for whom hadn't that been enough? Whose rest had been disturbed by the niggling little question of where those last three girls might be, when the doors were slammed shut on the rest of them, locked and barred from the outside?

"Who? Who?" she cried to Goodmann, as Hermann tried to quiet her.

Goodmann shrugged; he didn't know. The rumors had started only after the train had left, he said. If the Germans had noticed someone missing, they would have held the whole thing up and searched right then.

So it was someone who knew them, someone who was watching as the rest of the girls were shoved into the boxcars— who? A teacher who'd taught them the tributaries of the Danube? A former maid who'd left their house with regular gifts of hams and cheese? A classmate? A friend? A neighbor? "Who?" cried their mother.

But the who of it didn't concern Goodmann. What concerned him now was that there might be a search for the girls, and he was washing his hands of them, though he was sorry. Still, what choice did he have?

"No choice," said Hermann quietly. What else was there to say? He showed the man to the door.

Goodmann said good-bye to him, definitively, Hermann noted, as if quite sure he'd never see him again. And then he went home in his Nazi clothes to his picture of Hitler. The farm was a good one, and his crops were growing, as they would for a thousand years now. Life for Goodmann, in a general way, had improved, Hermann had to admit.

But for Hermann, the general was now the personal, and whoever had missed his daughters on that transport might at any moment of the night or day take it up a notch and send someone looking. They had to get out, all of them, no question now, but first the girls, right away, no matter the risks. The real danger now was in staying where they were.

It was 1941 by then, though, and as Hermann pondered the map of Europe in his head, no matter which way he turned it, it didn't come out right. Germany to the north and west, Poland to the east, the golden door of America slammed shut just as they were fully realizing the worth of that offer. And now, even the places they'd never thought about, wild Australia, would no longer have them.

"We have no racial problem, and we don't want one," the Australian prime minister had stated the other day.

"Racial problem??" thundered Hermann. There were rumors that Roosevelt was proposing a haven in darkest Africa, or somewhere in South America—some time in the future.

But at the moment, the only places they could actually get to—on foot, or at best, by horse cart, hidden under hay at borders—were not far enough away anymore. Hitler held France, Romania, Bulgaria, Holland, Belgium. Europe was his.

But there was a chance that Hungary might still constitute something of a refuge. Hungary had its own fascist government, much like Mussolini's Italy or Franco's Spain, which made it a natural German ally, and the Nazis hadn't marched in. Hermann had heard that the Hungarians were not deporting people. He and his wife both had relatives there, and the girls could speak Hungarian. He managed to get a message—"*how, I don't know*," said Magda—to his wife's brother: he was sending his girls across the border the next night. Three local boys who knew their way through the woods had agreed to act as guides.

THE BOYS CAME right after dark that night to the back door of the apartment. Hermann took it as a good sign that the moon was new and had set early. That should give them a little extra time to make it. It was thirty kilometers, more or less, to the spot outside the village of Sátoraljaujhely, where Hermann's wife's brother would, with any luck, be waiting.

"Be with them, let them make it," he prayed over the girls' heads. He handed the boys a thick packet of money, kissed the girls, and went to bed. He couldn't watch them leave—there were guards to evade, though the boys seemed to think that would be all right. Maybe it would be. But if it wasn't, or if the boys themselves should hurt them—Hermann went to bed with his sobbing wife and listened in terror into the dawn for shots in the distance.

But there weren't any that night. The girls and their guides got safely down to the marshes around the Torysa River, and from there it was a straight slog across. "*We had to walk most of the night in the water,*" said Magda. She was a violinist, and her sisters both studied piano. They had planned, each of them, a life devoted to music. They were none of them athletic, not the sort of girls who went in for mountaineering. It is possible that the youngest one could barely swim.

But they didn't falter, just pushed on after the boys. They hardly knew each other, and they hardly spoke. The boys said they were thinking about joining the party. One of the Nazis had promised them "books on sex" that people like Hermann were said to keep in their houses.

But one of the boys said his brother had raided a house, and there hadn't been any such books, at least nothing with pictures.

Magda said she actually laughed then—"*Can you imagine laughing at a time like that?*" she said years later. "Does he mean Freud?" she whispered to Gabi at the time. But mostly they were silent. The boys were hunters, and knew how to walk without breaking any sticks. The girls' feet were unaccustomed and aching, and they had to summon everything they had to keep going; but finally, just before daybreak, the boys told them they had crossed the border into Hungary, and soon after that, right on the edge of the marshes, they met their uncle, who was waiting with another wad of bills.

The boys wished them well, and melted back into the swamp. They seemed nice, but there was still the chance of betrayal, and it was too risky for the girls to stay in the village. There were no yellow stars in Hungary yet, so their uncle put them on a train to Budapest, which seemed miraculous to Magda—to get on a train, like anyone else.

She sat looking around, almost in awe—no hateful looks, no faces turned quickly away. For the first time since it had started, a tear trickled down her cheek.

"What?" asked her sister.

"Nothing."

But it was hard, this vacation, this brief visit back to the land of normal living. It had been so good before, so beautiful, their lives, and why had it ended? Why?

She persuaded her sisters to walk once around the station in Budapest. They had very little money, but they bought a hot chocolate to share, and she drank her third very slowly. She wanted to run through the streets, pushing and shoving among the other people, one of them once more, no longer separated by a horrible strip of yellow. Just a girl—a shabby one no less. A poor girl—fine! She would take it. Even that would be beautiful, life as an indigent, a beggar, in a city filled with music and light.

But they had no papers, and every step outside was a risk, they'd been warned. If they were picked up for anything, or even nothing, they'd be shipped back, or off, and no one would know where. With one last look of longing at the streets, they went back into the station and waited, "*like mice*," as their uncle had instructed, for the next train to Debrecen, 160 kilometers to the east, where their mother's second cousin would be waiting to take them in.

WHETHER THIS COUSIN had room, whether anyone had room for such refugees, had by 1941 ceased to be a consideration. People took in whoever fled their way. Where or how any of them slept—a cot in the hall, a mat on the floor, no mat on the floor—no longer mattered. The alternative being a prison camp, or worse, if you could believe it.

Because now the stories coming from both east and west mentioned not just mass graves but poison gas.

"But who could believe them?" their cousin said. They were unbelievable, and once you started listening, there was no end to what people were saying. Mass shootings in Ukraine, tens of thousands into a pit, and giant death camps in Poland— impossible, even for the Nazis. If people were trying to scare them, said their cousin, real life, her own life, was already frightening enough, thank you.

As were theirs, lived mostly in a half-dark corner of their cousin's back room. They were, at least theoretically, still allowed in the streets here, not like at home, but they were still without papers, something they hadn't considered. The first morning at her cousin's, Magda had offered to go to the bakery, but her cousin said no, the baker knew everyone, and might inquire as to who the strange girl was.

And the same was true at the butcher's, and the dry-goods store. It was a small town, and hiding wasn't easy. Still, after a week or so, Magda began walking out in the evening, just to the corner and back.

Although one day she saw a police car pass slowly, with two people in the back, a man and a young girl, both tied up, with blood on their faces. There was blood running out of the girl's right eye. In the front sat two others—one driving, and the other looking calmly out the window. His gaze took her in, but that wasn't what scared her.

What scared her was the satisfied look on his face. She walked quickly home and had a nightmare that night—that same man, that same smile, coming in there, for them. She watched the door open slowly, watched the stark, sharp shadow move across the room.

She woke in a sweat before dawn, and didn't dare close her eyes again. It was odd, but when they were hidden at Goodmann's, she had been ready to die. Gloriously—she saw herself standing and fighting, or even facing a firing squad, "La Marseillaise," for some reason, on her lips.

But the more she ran and hid, the less she wanted to die. Later that day, as the light came into the room, she remembered the dream—the moving shadow, which reminded her of the work of an artist she'd seen once, on a trip to Venice.

De Chirico—did they know him? she asked her cousins.

"Italian, a fascist," her cousin's husband shrugged.

"No, he couldn't be, he's an artist—"

"If he lives in Italy, he's a fascist." End of discussion. No one here wanted to talk about art anymore. Her cousin's husband had lived in Paris and worked in the theater there, contemporary theater, but then Jean Cocteau had turned out to be a Nazi.

"Sympathizer," put in her cousin.

"Yes, but isn't that enough? Doesn't that mean that he wants me dead?"

"Not dead!"

"Just gone."

And so on. Even the safest subjects led to the same dark place. Magda's stomach started hurting badly—"nerves," said her cousin, and managed to get her some chamomile tea, which wasn't easy. "Just stay calm," her cousin said.

Though she didn't say how. On the one hand, time was standing still here, but meanwhile the leaves had fallen off the trees and the late-summer asters stood black in the frost. When Magda was a girl, she used to stand outside and watch the flocks of birds heading south, with longing in her own heart. But now what she longed for was not that schoolgirl's dream of "South," but the old places, wintry and bleak. Home. Her mother, her father. Life as a family, them.

But then one day a cousin brought great good news to the girls—their parents were on their way to Hungary. They would arrive by train, with false papers, the cousin said. The girls would live as citizens again.

Illegal citizens, granted, which would have been an unthinkable status for Hermann as little as a year ago, six months even. Illegal papers were for crooks, for fugitives, for

Russians maybe or even Poles, but not for Hermann the upright, Hermann the Czech, proud and free. He had never broken the law in his life, he told the man who forged their papers.

"The law?" the man had laughed, the laugh a bark. He himself had been born a Russian, then became, without moving, a Pole, then Czech for a short time, and was now Hungarian. Or would be, once he got the baptismal certificate he was working on, which would be even better than forged papers, but he didn't mention this to Hermann. It was a long shot anyway, and he could tell that Hermann didn't have that kind of money anymore.

"When was anything last legal?" the man asked.

Hadn't they seized Hermann's house, his farm, his business? Had that been legal, or the fact that they'd turned solid, patriotic citizens, people who'd never so much as raised their voices after dark lest they disturb their neighbors, into some strange new category of criminal just by virtue of their breathing in and breathing out?

Hermann had to agree. He was proud, even, of his new flexibility, this agility, proud that he'd managed to put aside, along with his love of his Czech homeland, his deep aversion to shady dealings. Prouder still that he was able to carry off a sketchy border crossing with his wife by train, and reunite with his three daughters in Debrecen, with false papers for them all.

REALLY BEAUTIFUL PAPERS, in their own names and with their pictures steamed in properly. That meant the girls could go out a bit, though still with caution, could show their faces now and then in the light of day, and once in a while feel the wind in their hair, the sun on their faces. They were almost ridiculously happy. Happy, too, to move together into a dank, tiny apartment of their own. Hug their own mother, and even laugh a bit, see their mother laugh again.

"If you'd shown this to us before!" they laughed, looking around at the poor furnished room, the sagging sofa propped up on bricks, the battered table, the mattresses on the floor.

But "before," their former life, was not to be dwelt on, said Hermann, not yet. The activity of the move had revived his spirits too. Hitler was proving himself the fool they always knew he was; he'd made Napoleon's mistake, and invaded Russia. Funny, the way these madmen couldn't resist it. It would prove fatal for him too in the end, Hermann was certain.

And then the Japanese bombed America—"Insane!" he said. "Thank God!" his wife added.

Yes, thank God. It was the end of 1941. America had come into the war at last. The whole thing would be over now shortly. All they had to do now was to keep their heads down and wait it out, and maybe by next summer surely, or at least by the fall, they would be back home, maybe even for the harvest. They would walk under their plum trees once more.

7

WITH HER PAPERS, Magda found work as a nursemaid. The people who hired her were pleased—a girl who couldn't hide her culture, but didn't mention it. Whom they didn't have to pay a *fillér* more than they'd give a simple farm girl, but who could speak French to the children. Who uttered no complaint when given an airless room under the stairs with no bath.

Hermann's wife and the other two girls took in knitting. This, together with Magda's meager earnings, was how the family ate. Hermann had had no source of income since they took his businesses toward the end of 1939.

And he'd been forced to pay out large sums of money just to get them to those small rooms in Debrecen—first to Goodmann the farmer to keep the girls off the transport, and then to the boys who'd led them through the marshes. Even more for the false papers, which took much of his life's savings. There was still, at least in theory, money in the bank, at least by the former rules, but who knew? He assumed that all that had, at least temporarily, gone the way of what had once been called his "real property," the house, the grain storages, the farm, all of which, instead of being real, had proved to be dust.

So the women were obliged to work for money, but while they sat and knitted scarves, lap robes, dainty mittens for their more fortunate Hungarian counterparts, what did Hermann do there in Debrecen? He was strong, and healthy, in his mid-forties, his prime. What did he do?

"*Not much*," Magda noted in her account, sadness creeping in. "*Not much*."

Meaning what? In the one picture that survived, Hermann looks strong, active, energetic. A man who would walk on the balls of his feet to get there faster, a man who would have played, in his enthusiasm, his joy for life, the clarinet or oboe, accompanying his daughters in little family concerts, after his work, work that felt productive, was productive, supporting not just his family but others in town, what with the plums and the grain they were exporting ever farther, into Ukraine even, he was just closing that deal when they shut him down—what would a man like that do in a room in Debrecen?

He still had the "affidavit" from America in his pocket, which apparently took some of his time and energy. There seemed to be some possibility of parlaying it into a ticket out to somewhere. But what this mostly entailed was chasing down the various rumors—refuge in the Swedish embassy in Budapest, or the Belgian Congo. He was hearing now of people going east, not west, into Russia, into Siberia, cold yes, but supposedly safe. Relatively. He spent a few days trying to find the man who was said to be willing to serve as a guide.

Which came to nothing, but at least it constituted action in that time and place. That and kicking himself for not having left when he could have, even with empty pockets and barely the clothes on his back. Their backs—and as 1941 turned to 1942, and the year wore on, with the Germans taking Sevastopol and

Rommel winning in Egypt, the English, incredibly, floundering in France, and the Americans bogged down in Guadalcanal, Hermann's initial optimism began to erode.

BECAUSE THE TRUTH was that Hitler seemed to be winning—could Hitler win? Would God allow it? Was there a God?

"How could I not have sold the house and left then?" he cried to his wife.

"But you couldn't have known!" she pleaded with him, tears in her eyes too.

He tried to agree, how could he have known? He asked himself that all day, every day, while he paced back and forth, back and forth, since he went out always less now. They were hearing about men like him being picked up, even with papers.

"*We didn't want to mingle with anyone*," explained Magda. "*We lived doubly petrified now, because of the false papers.*"

Since they were strangers there, and impoverished to boot. It would have been hard enough to wash up destitute on foreign shores even under normal circumstances; if, say, Hermann had gambled or drunk his farms away.

But now, as fugitives and outlaws both, hounded, despised, cast out, unpatriated, and all for nothing that had anything to do with anything they'd done or could control or change—it was becoming harder by the day for Hermann to keep the spring in his step. Harder even, increasingly, to say the normal daily prayers.

Which till then had constituted for him mainly a form of thanksgiving, to a good and just God who had blessed his hard work, his fruit trees, his daughters. He had prayed formerly, morning and evening, that this God's light may continue to shine upon them.

But now, in a small bleak room in Debrecen—had he offended? Sinned? So much? All of them? Everyone he knew, from Warsaw to Paris?

But not in America then, a much less godly place, surely?

What did it mean? What could it mean? The old words had no answers. They were coming almost to constitute betrayal to him.

He turned to the more obscure texts, prophecies, lamentations. "*He read the Book of Job over and over,*" said Magda.

You will look for me, but I will be there no more.

Who could be saying that, Hermann had always wondered, what kind of God? Now, with increasing horror, he began to understand. Job, too, had prayed to no avail, to an unfair God, a God who had allowed himself be tempted into a bet with the devil—at Job's expense. A different God from the magisterial All-Wise One Hermann used to thank. The one he thought he knew, both from life and from the rest of the scriptures.

But was Job's version who God really was and had been all along? Could it be as simple as that? A cruel and vain God, willing to destroy Hermann's family's lives as wantonly as He had destroyed Job's, just to beat the devil? To show that even as He threw them to the fire, they would die praising His name?

Was that possible? He looked around the room at his beloved wife, his two younger daughters—in the end, after Job's family were all killed, his reward was a new family. Hermann dropped the book.

The women, his wife and daughters, looked up from their knitting. They used to knit at home, of an evening, but not like this. Then it was for fun, or charity, or something nice for one of them to wear. But this knitting was fast and hard, and it made their fingers red, their faces white, and as soon as they finished one item, they started on the next. Often the items were identical, the same vests, the same sweaters, over and over, as if they were machines, his lovely wife and daughters.

And for whom were they knitting? Other women, Nazi women, or if not active haters, then at best silent women, like the ones living in their own house now.

He had to go see someone, he told them, and walked out the door.

"You won't be long?"

"No, no, it's just to check on a visa," but the truth was he needed a walk, he was used to walking, used to breathing God's fresh air under God's blue skies.

The Nazis', now—even the sky and the air. They'd wrested it from his God, he understood that now. As a boy he'd read the myths, about the days when the storm god, Wotan, had thundered through the land. A cruel and harsh god who rode a horse with eight legs, a god of the wild woods, of ravens and wolves—the opposite of Hermann's God, whose domain was the plum trees.

Who, along with his son, had banished Wotan, but they'd been merciful, or maybe weak, and they hadn't killed him, and now he was back, with his swastika rune, his one eye, and the shock of hair over his forehead—like Hitler's hair, it came to Hermann.

Which must be why he did it, why else? It was absurd, that hair, even ridiculous, except that it hit its mark. Hermann hadn't understood it till now—all those upturned faces, all those arms raised in triumph. Wotan was riding through the land again, and though Hermann had expected every day that people would come to their senses, he saw now that there was nothing to wake them.

Their church bells were too soft, and what had those bells done for them since the last war but offer consolation? And what was that to the call of Wotan's deep horns, summoning them from their cold gray towns to the darkest parts of the woods?

Which was where they went with Hitler, back to that place where they'd last been strong and brave, wild and free. Where they danced naked, even with their clothes on, around the ancient bonfire every time they marched with him, possessed, arms in the air like spears. "Heil Hitler!"

And Hermann, the man of the other god, was their enemy.

He sat down on a bench in a small park not far from the apartment. Forbidden to him, risky, but he had to sit down. It was true, he realized—the Nazis might be mad, but they were right, he was the enemy. He loved cultivation, he loved the sound of soft bells. True, his heart had leapt up too the first time he heard Wagner, but in the end it had repelled him, what he'd sensed lay beneath, the hatred.

So yes, he was the enemy, part of the civilization that had sent Wotan to the mountains. He read books, sang complicated songs, and prayed not for purification, fire and war, but for peace and comfort. He accepted imperfection. He chose aged wine over water from a babbling brook. He didn't like blond braids. He'd never worn lederhosen.

But how did a man like him, with a pen and a gardening spade at best, stand up to men like them, armed with iron spears forged in caves by demons? How did anyone, who wasn't seized with their madness? What defense was there? To whom did he even pray? Next to Wotan, the other gods paled. Christ was an innocent child, and God the Father a very old man.

A Hungarian policeman walked by. If he stopped, Hermann was dead. He'd spent long hours preparing answers should he someday be stopped and questioned, but he knew now that what they wanted from him weren't answers but blood.

Of course, this should have come as no surprise—it wasn't as if they'd been hiding it from anyone. Hitler's SS, with Wotan's runes on their collars, wore the skull and crossbones for anyone to see. And of course he had seen it, but instead of facing it straight—"Death's-head. They will kill us"—he'd approached it slant, through the lens of his own deep culture, and called it a child's game of pirates. "Ridiculous," he'd pronounced it, all the while handing in his bicycles, his radios, a yellow star blazing off his clothes.

And he was right in a way, it was ridiculous, but that didn't stop it from being deadly. That's what he, a humanist, hadn't understood. He had gone on about "the twentieth century," but maybe this was the real twentieth century, this combination of absurdity and bloodshed, and he was a man of the past. And maybe this was precisely where all his philosophy, all his democracy and his modern painting, his freedom and theater and science of the mind had always been leading him.

To a cold park bench, with false papers in his pocket, praying right then, with all the passion in his heart, to a God who couldn't help him, that a young policeman without a thought in his head would pass him by. That this plain and simple youth who held his fate in his hands would have something else to do that evening besides drag this remnant of the Age of Enlightenment into the local police station and beat him to death.

AND IN FACT, though the policeman glanced his way, he kept walking, so Hermann went home, and kissed his wife and daughters, as he always had, but that evening, as he tried to say grace over their hard bread, he started to cry.

"What is it? What's happened?"

"Nothing, nothing. Everything is fine, fine, nothing has happened," and so on. Still, the women were shaken. "*To see your father crying is a terrifying thing,"* as Magda would testify, years later.

On the whole, though, they were starting to breathe a little easier as the months rolled by. Magda liked the children she took care of, the people paid her and treated her decently, her mother and sisters were paid for their knitting, and with that, their father managed to buy enough food to keep them going. There was very little coal for heat, but there was some. Not like Poland, where they heard that the Nazis had taken it all, and that most of the old people and small children had frozen to death that first winter.

But Hungary was neither starving nor freezing, nor did they seem to be deporting people. And as the year wore on, the news from the front started getting better. The British and Americans seemed to be turning things around in North Africa, and Leningrad hadn't fallen after all. Spring was late that year, but when it came, the family's spirits couldn't help but rise a bit. Hermann saw a great blue heron flying toward the marshes, and told his wife that the war wouldn't last forever. It was 1943.

"BUT ONE NICE DAY, *soon after that,"* said Magda, *"the Hungarian police came to the house where I was working."* They already had her parents and sisters. Someone had informed on the man who'd made their forged papers, and the SS had arrested him. Under torture, he'd given hundreds of names, including theirs.

They were taken to the police station, along with scores of other people with false papers, a cross section of Hitler's Most Wanted from all over Central and Eastern Europe. The Poles among them had it the worst—the men, women, and children who'd managed to escape from the Krakow Ghetto, where people were eating stinging nettles, were shipped back, sobbing and pleading, that day. If Hermann's family were sent back to Czechoslovakia, they knew their fate would be deportation at best.

But their cousins managed to get them a lawyer, who convinced the local authorities that the place for these particular criminals was the town's prison. This took the last of Hermann's money.

But that was all right, the lawyer told Hermann, because the tide was finally turning against the Germans. The Allies were starting to bomb Berlin. Hitler was conscripting seventeen-year-old boys, "to die in Russia," said the lawyer. If he were Hitler, he would give up now.

Or if not now, next week—it was bound to happen, just a question of when. The lawyer's strategy was to keep them safe in a Hungarian prison, until it was over and they could raise their heads again.

"And so began our lives *as jailbirds*," said Magda. The girls shared a cell with their mother, with one blanket between them, and a mattress, and for a bathroom, there was a bucket. A German girl in the next cell, a Jehovah's Witness, told them the great luck for them was that it had a lid. She knew whereof she spoke, she said. Hermann's daughters managed to make this a subject for some merriment among them.

They were let out once a day, for exercise, which meant walking "*round and round, like prisoners in the movies. And once a week there were showers, and then we were locked up again.*" That, too, rather quickly became normal life, which, under the circumstances, wasn't so bad after all. The girls and their mother were together, their cousins were permitted to bring them food, and they had visiting privileges with Hermann. They were allowed to see him several times per week.

Which was a blessing, though they were seeing a certain fire in his eyes that hadn't been there before. There was a prophet in his cell, a mystic from Poland, who had explained what was happening, everything, from the scriptures, shown them where it had all been written, chapter and verse. They had been wrong, said Hermann, to leave the old ways behind. They were being punished now, but in the end would emerge stronger.

He urged his daughters to start praying—one day he gave them a little amulet, a small leather pouch with a holy word and magic number inside. This time wasn't wasted, he told the girls, just compressed. And afterwards, they would rebuild, not their old life but a better life, somewhere far from there, America, or even Paraguay, some people were saying. Anyway, in the New World, away from these medieval haters.

And as for now, Hermann told them, it was for them to see that their prayers proved acceptable in the sight of the Lord, their Rock and their Redeemer. They must pray to stay safe in this Hungarian prison, where the Lord had decided to show him His face.

HERMANN'S DAUGHTERS didn't know quite what to make of their father's jailhouse conversion, or what would come of it afterwards. But maybe he was right, maybe it was his new kind of fervent praying that had secured for them the luxury of actually wondering about "afterwards."

Because as the leaves fell from the lone tree in the prison courtyard, and 1943 turned finally to 1944, even Hitler had to know that his war wasn't going well. Surely he or one of his generals had studied their Napoleon, and could foresee what would happen as the Russian mud turned to Russian ice and snow, the same ice and snow that had finished off their predecessor's army.

But it had been easy for Hitler in Poland, easy, even, in France, so what was Napoleon to him? Napoleon had lingered in Russia, but the Nazis, with their planes, their tanks, their blitzkrieg, had planned to be in and out of Russia before that first winter, and all that land, all that grain, all that oil would be theirs.

"When the attack on Russia starts, the world will hold its breath," Hitler had predicted back in the summer of 1941. "We have only to kick in the front door and the whole rotten Russian edifice will come tumbling down." He had planned to host a reception at the Astoria Hotel in the heart of Leningrad on the ninth of August of the next year. He even had the invitations engraved.

And there was a celebration in Leningrad that very day, but it wasn't the one Hitler had envisioned. The city had been under siege for almost a year by then; more than a million had already died, and hundreds of thousands were starving. The German army surrounding the city expected surrender from one day to the next, and when they heard the music coming from the city, the officers assumed it presaged the town fathers filing out, heads bent, white flag flying. Hitler's reception would take place at the Hotel Astoria that night after all!

But rather than a plea for terms, what the Fourth Panzer Division got was the world premiere of Shostakovich's Seventh Symphony, written both to honor and to stiffen the city's defiance and endurance. Nor were those stirring notes the only warning to the German soldiers; the musicians were already playing in gloves that evening, though it was still August. The

Germans, for their part, had no gloves, or much else in the way of serious winter clothing, Hitler's plan being to have them home by autumn.

As in Poland, as in France, but Russia proved to be neither, and Hitler soon found himself fighting in the Russian cold, which, he was to learn, Napoleon-style, was unlike any cold he knew. Hitler's guns froze in the Russian cold, his planes' engines seized up, his fuel oil froze solid, so that his army had to chip off bits and heat it. Plus his trains were the wrong gauge for Russian tracks, and to compound that problem, Hitler had misunderstood the Russian roads. The Russian roads had looked good on the maps, looked just like the Polish and French roads his tanks had rolled down at lightning speed with relatively little cost to themselves, all told.

But few of the Russian roads were asphalt, or even graded dirt. The German tanks, with their narrow treads designed for speed, couldn't get traction in the frozen Russian mud. Nor were Hitler's horses any match for the native Siberian ponies, who could scratch up grass through the ice and snow with their tough little hooves, while their larger European counterparts, whose feed was stalled behind trains with guns and woolens, stood and starved, helpless, until they keeled over, brown and gray blocks of ice, 750,000 of them.

Still, since the Russians were fundamentally lesser beings whom the Germans had been born to rule, Hitler concluded that it was only a matter of standing tough here. He had already renamed the country "the East Reich," and once he'd depopulated the place, primarily through starvation, and moved in his own people, better people, Germans, he would get the roads in shape, put the factories on Berlin time, and then talk to the English. Or rather, the English would talk to him.

He refused to consider any significant shift of strategy;

refused even to adjust course in the face of facts. Men he should
have sent to finish off Leningrad were sent to Moscow instead,
to swallow all of Russia in one gulp, Nazi-fashion. That left him
with a line he couldn't supply, but "Stand or die!" Hitler commanded his armies.

Though stand *and* die was what they were doing in Russia, nor could the news from the Western Front have been any
more cheering. Bombs were now falling on Berlin with regular-
ity. It was rumored that Hitler had moved to a bomb shelter, and
wasn't getting out of bed till eleven-thirty in the morning.

All this was greeted in the Debrecen prison as proof of
the existence of God. The year was turning, it was now 1944,
another good sign—if you added it up, according to Hermann's
mystic cellmate. It came to eighteen, a lucky number according
to the Kabbalah. Eighteen meant luck, survival. Life.

8

HITLER COULD HAVE SHOT HIMSELF on New Year's Day 1944. If he had, much of Germany would have been spared destruction and despair. There would have been no firebombing of Dresden, and the Russians wouldn't have marched into Berlin, or Central Europe, for that matter. There would have been no Iron Curtain, and the death camps wouldn't have hit their stride. Millions of lives could have been saved. Tens of millions, if you count it up.

One bullet, but he wasn't the supreme leader of the madness for nothing; and there was still plenty of *Nacht und Nebel*, "Night and Fog," as he liked to quote Goethe, for him to dispense, and closer to home at that.

In March of that year, 1944, he invited the Hungarian prime minister, Miklós Horthy, to a conference in a castle near Salzburg, and when it was time to go home, Horthy found his door locked, from the outside. It was the nineteenth of March. That day, the Germans marched into Hungary.

Among the first administrators to arrive in Budapest was Adolf Eichmann. There was much still to do in Hungary, and Time's wingéd chariot, in the form of the Russian army, was drawing near. But when it came to separating out huge groups of people for deportation to death camps, Eichmann was the man. He was efficient, tireless, and a true believer. There were, according to his sources, 725,000 people there for the killing in Hungary, and he figured he had the summer to do it.

He had with him a special SS death squad, and they went to work at once, using the experience they'd garnered in Czechoslovakia, Greece, France, Holland, and Romania. The yellow stars were out in no time. Property was confiscated properly here, which meant straight into the hands of ranking SS men rather than to minor Hungarians. Collaborating community groups were impaneled and given the privilege of saving a few family and friends in exchange for facilitating the deportation and murder of hundreds of thousands. And the local Nazis, the Arrow Cross men, were given guns and encouraged to shoot any yellow stars they could find into the Danube River.

Which they did with such zeal that spring that their own waters went bad, but even that didn't stop them. Every day, there were more bodies, floating in the river, Magda's cousin told them in a letter. She no longer dared to venture out to the prison to see them. They had been forcibly moved into an apartment with a hundred other people, but they were trying to get some sort of protection from the Swedish embassy. There was no coal, and very little food. Every day someone jumped from one of the high windows, and people they knew had gone out looking for firewood or food and never come back.

Her husband's aunt was almost shot the other day, she wrote. Two Arrow Cross men had caught her outside the Swedish embassy and marched her at gunpoint, along with a small boy, picked up randomly, to a dock on the river.

"Turn around," they commanded, and her husband's aunt took the boy's hand and asked him, "desperately," if he could swim.

He'd whispered back yes, which made her "strangely happy," she said, but for some reason, the men didn't shoot, just laughed and walked away.

"So as you can see, you are safer in prison," their cousin concluded, though unfortunately, she no longer had any food to bring them.

WHICH WAS HARD, but not surprising. They'd been hungry since the Nazis had taken over. Rations had been cut and then cut again, the daily outing for exercise was decreased to twice a week, and worse, the girls were no longer permitted to talk to their father. All they could hope for was to catch sight of him now and then, parading with the others around the tree in the yard.

What was he thinking? That it would still be all right, in the end? Did he think they'd get out soon, and, if so, when? Their mother didn't look well. Someone had told her the Arrow Cross were going to come into the prison and shoot them, and she'd told them to be quiet, not to talk such nonsense, but her hair had turned white overnight then, just like that.

But what if they did come in to shoot them? Should they run, Magda wanted to ask her father, or try to hide? Try to argue with them, call for the Hungarian guards, who knew them at least? Would they help?

Hermann would know, he would tell them—she wanted to talk to him, even just to hear his voice, get a hug in his strong arms. Her mother had gotten thin and dry, like straw. But her father looked strong still. He would know what they should do.

And they did meet again, one day in the yard. The women were brought out early, before the men had been taken in, and Magda broke their lines and ran to her father—everyone did, pushing and crying, fathers and children, husbands and wives.

"Get back or we'll shoot!" shouted the guards.

"Shoot then!" people shouted. "Good!"

But the guards were Hungarians and didn't shoot, and she and her mother and sisters got over to Hermann before they were pushed apart, and he touched their hair and whispered a prayer, asked how they were, even kissed their cheeks, which was good, since they never saw him again.

BECAUSE A FEW DAYS LATER, out of nowhere and with no warning, an SS officer came through their wing of the prison with a list. Magda and her sisters' names were on it. This time there was no Goodmann to hide them, no midnight trip through the swamps to steal them away.

The cell door opened.

Her mother jumped to her feet—"No!"

But there was no "No!" with an SS man. He opened the cell door and motioned with his whip for the three girls to file out. "You should be happy, madame," he said to their mother. "The girls will be going to Tokay, to help with the grape harvest."

That was reassuring. Tokay was said to be beautiful. And how wonderful, to be outside again. Better than factory work.

"Quickly," he said, as they hugged their mother.

"Can't you take me too?" She turned to the SS man. "So we can stay together?"

"Don't worry, madame, you'll be together again shortly," he said, not impolitely, as he pushed the girls out the door.

"THE WITCH'S KITCHEN"

Faust, Part I, *Goethe*

9

IT WAS THE FIRST OF MAY, 1944, the day the fairies were said to dance around the sacred trees deep in the woods, on Brocken Mountain. All the girls and boys in the Debrecen prison were shipped out that day, "to Tokay," as if on a school outing, the SS made it sound. There was little panic, either among them or their parents. They filed as instructed into trucks that would take them to the station, to get their train.

Which they still expected to be a passenger train. Something meant for people, so it was worrisome when what pulled up was a boxcar, for freight. The platform was thronged—their group from the prison, and others, men and women, many with small children, who couldn't possibly help with "the harvest," or "work in factories," as they had been told.

Were they in the wrong place, then? Magda wanted to ask, but ask whom? The SS officer who'd brought them had been joined by others, many with dogs. She and her sisters clung together—Vera, the youngest, was almost fifteen now, and could barely remember their house or their garden. When someone in prison asked her if she played the piano, she'd turned to Magda. "Do I?" she'd asked.

"Yes." Magda hugged her. "You did. You will."

In the truck to the station, she'd asked the Hungarian guard when their mother was coming.

"Sunday," he'd answered, but had averted his eyes.

THE DOORS OF THE BOXCARS opened and then the SS, polite enough till then, started screaming. "In, *schnell! Schnell!* Quickly!" There were no steps up, and it was high—the girls scrambled up, *schnell*, but some of the older people had trouble. One of the guards hit an older woman on the back with his club. She fell, out of sight.

Magda stared in horror. But then she was pushed into the car, on top of people inside already, and then a guard shouted, "A hundred and twenty!" and the door was slammed shut. They could hear the bolt closing on the outside. A hundred and twenty of them in a car made for boxes. There was nowhere for the girls to sit—the hard floor was already covered with the old and the children. Nursing mothers, crying babies. All on their way to work in the fields, they said.

"For the harvest," they'd been told—but what do you harvest at this time of year? someone asked. It was May. You didn't harvest till August, he said.

Which was true. So maybe it was to plant the grapes, someone else said, or to work in factories. They were in boxcars, people were saying, because Hitler needed all the passenger trains for the troops. That's why he needs us to work, why we don't have to worry. We are needed. We'll be all right.

It was already stifling, and the train hadn't started to move. There were only two small windows at the top—not even enough for cattle, murmured someone. This car was only for freight. Cattle would have needed more air.

Nor was there a bathroom, they realized. Just a bucket, in a corner—was it possible? The girls looked at each other.

"Good thing Hungary is so small," one of the men said.

That was true. It wouldn't take more than a half day to get to Tokay.

When the train finally pulled out, there was some relief, but before long the latrine bucket was full, and the children had started crying for water. There were only two buckets of water for the whole car. Some people had brought food, and they gave the girls a bit of bread, but it was all they could spare. That was fine, though. "Half a day at most," the men were figuring.

But half a day passed and still they were going. "North," said someone, who'd climbed up to the small window to get a look at the sun. They should have turned west by now, to get to Tokay.

If they were going to Tokay.

Were they going to Tokay? Silence fell in the car.

Then, "Maybe it's hard to tell which way we're going from that little window."

The man at the window shrugged—"the sun is the sun," he said. But he didn't press it—why make it worse? The girls had thought maybe they'd be able to hold out, but finally had to go "to the bucket." Someone had rigged a blanket, and they held it for each other. Thank heavens, they whispered, their parents weren't here to be subjected to this.

Then they went back to their corner of the train and told stories to the children. "Soon we'll be there," they whispered. And finally, the train stopped—at last!

Which was a good thing, since the water they'd been given was gone, and the latrine bucket was overflowing. And the people who'd been trying to hold out badly needed a toilet of some sort, even the roughest kind, even a bush or railroad siding, and they all needed air. People were taking turns at the tiny windows, but it kept getting hotter, more airless. One woman had fainted and they couldn't revive her.

But at least they were there—wherever there was. They pushed to the door and waited, and waited, and waited. There was some shouting, then some shooting, some screams, and then a jolt. People looked at each other—were they attaching more cars? What did that mean?

People started pounding on the door, calling for them to give them at least some water. But the door wasn't opened and then, finally, the train started up again.

BY THE NEXT MORNING, the children had stopped crying. Some of them were dead. None of them could talk anymore. People had been told they could bring up to forty kilograms of baggage, but no one had thought to waste their precious allotment on water. Now it had become the only thing in the world. They'd brought food—but the food was like the dead bodies that were starting to pile up among them, nothing but torture. No one could eat any more without water.

The light turned to dark again, and then the dark to light, and the train stopped again. This time, no one moved. More shouting and shooting, and another jolt, one from the front this time. Another engine. And then one from the back—more cars. They had piled up the bodies, the old too, now, not just the babies. The train started up again.

A woman who'd managed to climb up to the window saw a sign—KRAKOW. "My God, we're in Poland!"

Silence fell on the train. No one knew what to make of it, but everyone felt it boded ill. Till then, they'd been telling each other that if it wasn't to Tokay, then they were going to Germany.

The Germans needed them, they said, in the fields, or the factories. Which meant they wouldn't let them all die on this train.

But Poland—what was in Poland?

"Poland has farms, too," one of the men finally said.

"And factories."

"Yes, of course," and so on. People talking not to make sense
but as a diversion. An act of kindness. Like any telling of tales,
all the way back to the cave, with dire wolves at the door.

Magda and her sisters had crawled into a corner. She had
thought till then that they would live through this, but now
realized they could die right there, in the boxcar, among strangers. It didn't matter so much anymore, though. She fell asleep
and dreamt she was lying in the deepest green grass, by the
little brook that ran into their pond in the springtime. She was
about to drink as much as she wanted, but then she was back
in her own house, their wonderful house, by some miracle, and
there was water in the tap in the bathroom, and she was about
to drink from that, too, when the train stopped.

It no longer mattered. They were all half-dead anyway.
When she opened her eyes, she realized she was lying on a
body. The stench was overwhelming. If she'd had anything in
her stomach, she would have been sick.

"What time is it?" someone asked.

A few of them still had their watches and could tell them the
hour, but no one knew what day it was anymore.

As they awaited another jolt, there came a different kind of
noise from outside, and they realized with a new kind of terror
that the doors were being unbolted.

A few of the men scrambled up to the window. "Where are
we?" people asked them.

They didn't answer.

"Can't you see?"

"Yes, but—"

"Well, which is it, farms or factories?"

"Not sure—"

"But you said you could see—"

"Look for yourself—" But then the doors slid open, and air rushed into the car. How good, how fresh! Did this mean water?

"Out! Out!" people were shouting at them, in all the languages of Europe, Hungarian, German, Czech, Polish. Hermann's daughters staggered to the door, gulping air. It was hard to walk, their legs were so cramped.

"*Schnell*, quickly!"

Magda tried to help someone with a pack—"Leave it!" a guard shouted. "All luggage stays in the train!"

Some people were pushing in—men, but very strange ones. More like skeletons in striped pajamas. They wouldn't look at people on the train, wouldn't speak—were they lunatics? Prisoners? Magda's first thought was that maybe they had come to work in a prison or lunatic asylum. Or had there been some dreadful mistake?

"Out, quick!"

There were no steps down to the platform. You had to jump.

"Fast!" Magda held Vera's hand and jumped, but Gabi hesitated, and was pushed from behind. This caused her to fall and hurt her leg.

"Get her up, fast!" hissed one of the skeletons as he pushed past, into the train. Magda pulled her up and out of the way, out onto a platform, but a platform where?

Where were the farms? Where were the factories? Or had they gotten the trains mixed up and brought them to a lunatic asylum? The suitcases from the train, full of the carefully selected valuables, were tossed out and heaved, willy-nilly, onto carts. People were pouring out of the endless line of boxcars, onto the platform by the thousands, young, old, blond, dark, rich, poor, doctors, philosophers, balloon women, men in fine summer suits, with ladies still in silk by their side—as wide a cross section as you could get, but all with the same look on their faces, confusion giving way to outright dread.

And together they made a sea of chaos, which surged and flowed into channels and finally was stopped dead, by a wall of green and black that stood against them, tall men with shiny red faces, well-fed men who weren't thirsty, in well-pressed clothes from another world. Shiny boots, snarling German shepherd dogs, and the skull and crossbones above the swastikas on their chests.

Magda clung to her sisters. If they got separated now, they might never find each other again. Already, all around them, people were crying out for lost ones. It was a scene of total confusion. It was daylight, maybe even morning, but morning where? Even the light seemed different, like the light in a bad dream.

"Out, fast!" the striped pajamas were shouting.

But people couldn't move fast. They stood dazed, looking around, searching the faces, trying to grasp where they were. They'd all been told they were being sent to work in factories and farms, but the train had stopped at a siding that seemed to be—nowhere. There was no station, no factories, and no fields anywhere in sight.

Though not far off there was a long row of low buildings, closed off by barbed wire, and then, beyond that, others, with two high chimneys, spewing columns of smoke and fire into the sky.

Could that be the factory? But what could they be making? There was a very bad smell, and the ground was covered with white ash, like snow. Everyone was pushing, shouting, calling for parents, reaching for children. Someone bumped into her—

there were thousands of people getting off the train, which stretched along the platform, as far as the eye could see.

"Line up, *schnell!*"

"What? What?" people were crying to each other.

"Five across!" someone was shouting into the confusion. But no one could see where to go or what to do. There were thousands of them—afterwards she thought they could have rushed the SS, despite the dogs, the whips and guns. Died fighting.

If they'd known—but no one knew yet. That was the amazing thing, the whole point. No one knew. Everyone still hoped. At least to save their families—that was the worst part. People were trying desperately to stay together, meanwhile dazed with thirst.

"Men to the right, women to the left!"

"But my husband!"

"My baby!"

"My mother!"

The officers had been standing off with their snarling dogs, laughing and joking among themselves, as if all this had nothing to do with them. But now one of them stepped forward.

"Silence!" The word went through the crowd.

As he waited for people to quiet, the clean and pressed superman from another planet pulled a silver cigarette case from his pocket and extracted a cigarette, which he lit with a silver lighter, and took a leisurely puff, which he blew out his nose, two long tendrils that floated up and away. Someone handed him a bullhorn, and he cleared his throat.

"Gentlemen and ladies," he said—Magda remembered for some reason that he'd said "gentlemen" first. Remembered wondering if that indicated anything. Something that she should know, that might save her and her sisters.

"We know that you are very tired, that you had a very long and exhausting journey. Neither food nor water was plentiful."

People had stopped, and were standing stock-still. The polite tone was almost the only thing they were not prepared for. Tears started rolling down the faces.

"We are sorry, but it was not our fault. And anyway, now it is behind you. Here we will put you in a camp, and those able to work will work. But all of you will live in normal conditions."

People were listening now with a new kind of attention. Listening to catch every word, so as to be able to comply well and speedily with this reasonable man's reasonable orders.

"I am sorry, but there is some bad news. It is three kilometers to camp, and there is not enough transportation. Thus, we are asking you now: All mothers with children no older than fourteen, and all sick or disabled, please come this way to get a ride in the trucks."

How kind of him, how understanding. "We heard you were going to kill us," said one of the women.

The officer looked shocked. "Do you think that we Germans are barbarians, madame?" he asked her.

He looked around the crowd. "Who is sick? Who cannot work? Step this way for a ride in the truck if you'd rather not work."

The women and babies and all the small children, the old and the sick started off.

"Don't worry about saying good-bye," he told them. "You'll all be together very soon."

Magda was worried about Gabi's hurt leg. "Maybe you should take a ride on the truck," she whispered to her, "and then you won't have to work so hard at first." But the sisters had never been separated before, and Gabi told Magda she'd rather walk and stay with her.

"Now if all able men would step to the left, and all women able to walk and thus able to work step to the right."

The masses started shifting. It had been bad, very bad, that train, but it was over now, and they had survived that. They were here to work—good, they would work. Work hard and well and survive that too, in this camp with their families. "Yes, yes, you'll be with the women and children shortly," said the officer, to those who took courage from his kindness to ask.

"Five across please"—it was extraordinary how quickly things went now, thanks to that kindness and understanding. No longer terrified, people were happy to do what they were asked, to show how they would cooperate in exchange for their lives and the lives of their families. In less than half an hour, the groups were separated—and the women and children, the old and the young, waved as their trucks rolled away.

Taking them to some sort of "family camp"—they were glad for the ride. Meanwhile, their menfolk had fallen into ranks, five abreast to the left, and their sisters and older daughters to the right, all of them with reasonable hope in their hearts. The trucks with the women and children were followed by some smaller trucks, painted white, with red crosses on them.

Everyone found this reassuring. "The Red Cross," people comforted each other.

But these "Red Cross trucks" weren't Red Cross trucks at all—they were the opposite of Red Cross trucks, carrying not nice rolled bandages but cans of Zyklon B poison gas.

This little side game, which after all had taken some preparation and forethought, could have been seen as another manifestation of the SS humor that had welcomed them to this "family camp," but no one coming off this transport got that yet. "This way, please, ladies," said the Nazi gentleman in his polite tones. Behind him, the men in striped pajamas were in the process of throwing the dead bodies out of the boxcars. These they piled onto carts, which they pushed away.

To be buried? wondered Magda.

"Yes, yes, keep going," the officer waved them on. She was sorry he wasn't accompanying them. To explain, should there be any misunderstanding, that they were workers, to be treated well. They started down the dusty road to the camp—only it wasn't dust, it was some kind of ash, from those chimneys.

Vera was managing to keep up, but Gabi was limping and falling behind; Magda turned back to see if she was all right. There was a very small child not far behind them, a little girl with soft curls, clearly lost, separated somehow from her mother. The child was wandering around in circles, not part of the line.

"Why isn't she in the truck?" asked the polite Nazi officer, and then, with the same nonchalance with which he'd lit his cigarette, he kicked the child to the ground, drew his pistol and shot her, twice. One of the striped pajamas quickly hauled off the body.

Magda turned back quickly, fighting panic. Her sisters hadn't seen. Which was good, they were right: You don't look back. She remembered the stories from her childhood—Orpheus looking back and losing Eurydice. Lot's wife turning into a pillar of salt. Though now that she thought about that, maybe that wasn't the worst fate, being turned to salt. Compared to being kicked to the ground and shot twice in the head.

She tried to make sense of what she'd just seen. It didn't square with what she'd just heard. Maybe the child was—what? A threat to the Nazi officer, so she had to be shot? Had the plague and he had a trained eye, he could see it, so had to shoot her to save them? Or maybe he hadn't really shot her. Maybe it was some kind of joke. There hadn't been any noise, and no one else seemed to have noticed.

But then why had the striped pajama carted her away? Another wave of panic surged up, and she felt that shooting pain in her stomach, but didn't dare stop walking.

Finally, they were ordered to halt, near a straggly birch tree —the only tree around, but it must have given the place its name. The gates said AUSCHWITZ-BIRKENAU, a "grove of birches," in a village presumably called Auschwitz. There was a table just outside the gates, where another handsome Nazi gentleman was standing, this one even more elegant, with his soft leather riding boots and jodhpurs, and fine suede gloves, even though it was a warm day in May.

They were instructed to form a single line, to pass before him.

"How handsome he is," Gabi whispered to Magda.

An officer approached him and clicked his heels—"Dr. Mengele."

So, he was a doctor. That was good, Magda told herself.

"How strong you all look, how healthy!" he said to them in pleasant tones—those same pleasant tones the officer had used. Before he shot the girl.

The doctor called for a photographer to take some pictures of them.

"See how we treat our guests?" he was saying. "Are they underfed? Are they in striped clothing? Let the world see."

The girls and women were passing in front of him. "Who is sick?" he asked, with concern in his voice. "Who cannot walk? Step to this side please if you'd rather not work."

He said it so kindly that Magda turned again to Gabi. She had been protecting her younger sister since kindergarten. "Maybe you should go over there, so you won't have to work so hard," she suggested again, but Gabi looked at the exhausted women moving to that side and decided to stay with her sisters. She was afraid that she might be assigned to a bunkhouse with those strangers. She was still imagining a sort of cottage, since the officer had said "camp."

"Are there any twins?" asked the doctor. "Twins to the side, please." He seemed quite pleased when several sets of twins stepped out of the line. "Perfect, wonderful, you'll come with me," he told them, and it seemed a special privilege. The rest of the women were told to file past. He looked them over.

"You to the right, please, and you to the left, thank you. How old are you?" He stopped one woman.

"Thirty-five," she answered.

"To the left, please. Thank you." He was whistling as he looked them over. In his gloved hand was a riding crop, with which he beat time.

Hermann's daughters filed past. "To the right," he pointed with his crop.

Which meant harder work, Magda figured, since the girls on their side were the strong ones, no question. The older women, and anyone who looked a bit tired or sick, were being sent to the left. Likely they'd get the easier factory jobs, or maybe not have to work at all. They were lucky.

Her group, though, looked like it had been chosen for heavy labor. Several of the girls ventured to ask the smiling doctor if they could join the other group.

"Of course, my dears." He couldn't have been more agreeable. "By all means, join them if you like."

Magda considered. Gabi was limping, her own stomach hurt badly, and how would the little one, Vera, fare with hard work? Maybe they should join the other group as well, she was thinking.

And what stopped her? she wondered afterwards. The answer couldn't be God, since there was no God in Birkenau.

10

THE GIRLS AND WOMEN passed through an iron gate and then continued down a mud road, through the ashes. They still hadn't eaten or drunk, and one of the girls was saying that the strange smell in the air must be bread—what else could it be? "They're making us bread," the girl insisted.

But she must never have smelled bread baking, Magda said to Gabi, how else could she think that this stench had anything to do with bread? Smoke and ash were pouring out of two tall chimneys, and the girls were moving closer to them with each step. That must be the factory where they were to work. Not baking bread, obviously, but making something.

Whatever it was they made here, and where were the other workers? There didn't seem to be anyone normal around. All you saw were either the guards or the madmen—where was everyone else, and what was this place in the middle of nowhere? It couldn't be a village—there was no sign of life, no houses, no shops, but there seemed to be hundreds of low buildings, half-finished, surrounded by rows and rows of barbed wire with towers in each corner, where she could now make out figures with big guns.

Was this where they were going to live? But the farther in

they went, the less it looked like a camp where families could live "normally," as the officer had promised. On the contrary—especially since everyone they saw seemed to be divided into those two strange teams of crazy opposites: either human skeletons in striped pajamas or red-faced giants with whips and boots.

So had the officer been lying? Bold-faced like that? But for what? Magda wondered. It made no sense to her. The sign had said BIRKENAU, which meant birches, but there weren't any birches here, no trees at all, so the name was a lie, too? The place seemed to be a sort of wasteland. There was no sign of any activity, no one working at all—what did people do here?

"Forward, faster!" The women were approaching a sort of yard, enclosed by more barbed wire, triple barbed wire. On the other side was a similar yard, and as they passed, some of the striped skeletons, the crazy people, came running to the barbed wire, crying "Bread! Bread!"

They were clearly desperate, starving, but when a girl near Magda threw them a tin of sardines, one of the guards took out his gun and shot her.

The whole group froze then, and Magda found her own eyes fastened on her shoes. They were called "oxblood," a sort of beautiful, deep maroon, and she'd worn them in Hungary, and in Czechoslovakia, and long before that, in Vienna. They had a low heel, and an elegant but sensible shape. A lovely fringe that covered the laces. Her mother had spent the money on good shoes for her, since Magda's feet had stopped growing. She'd wear them for years, her mother had told her father.

She remembered the box they'd come in, a deep gray with cream script lettering. Remembered the lovely smell. Her sisters were clinging to her—she could feel them both shaking.

"Be still!" she whispered to them harshly.

The guard had shot that girl without a word, with no warning. Casually, very, very casually, just like the officer back at the platform, lighting his cigarette with that same nonchalance. Unspeakable acts with untroubled brow—was that how the so-called master race did it here?

"*Schnell, schnell!*"—new voices, female now. "Move around her, quickly!" they were shouting. Big strapping blondes with starched uniforms and black boots of their own. And dogs, who were snarling and snapping at the girls as they walked by.

One of the girls, closest to them, was bitten. She cried out.

"Silence!" The woman guard struck her with her whip, right across the face. The girl staggered. Everyone turned and stared in horror—expecting, almost, an explanation. There was no trace of anger on the blond guard's smooth, apple-cheeked face, no sign that she'd just struck a defenseless person a vicious blow for no reason. From the looks of her, she was German or Polish, just off the farm, a nice enough girl if you passed her in the street.

"In here, all of you, quickly, *schnell, schnell*!" she was shouting at them.

They had come to a big room, not far from the chimneys. Everyone looked around uneasily—the ashes were snowing down on them now.

"In, *schnell!*" The sound of the whip, snapping. They filed into a big bare room with empty shelves along the edges.

"Clothes off, *schnell!* Fold them neatly!"

If you didn't speak German, you were dead here, Magda could see that. When someone didn't understand, the guards would scream louder and then resort to the dogs and whip. Luckily, most of these people were Hungarian, and had been taught German along with their French in school, but two girls, maybe from Greece, were beaten badly, right there in that room,

for not understanding that they were to tie their shoes together
and put them here, not there.

"Clothes off, faster!"

Everyone was hesitating. They had stripped to their underwear, which was bad enough. Some of them were country-
women, who'd come in in their long skirts and shawls. They had
never gone out without covering their heads. Now they cowered
in their underwear, even in front of the other girls and women,
likewise half-naked.

"All off!" A crack of the whip, a cry. Someone who didn't
speak German, didn't understand. Magda had already learned
not to look, not to see.

"Quick, fold them neatly!"

They folded.

"Put them where you can find them later."

"Later"—they all looked up as one. So there was to be a
later!

"Quick, to the showers!"

"What about our baggage?" someone risked asking.

"Later," said the guard, and started shoving them through
an interior door, into the next room.

And there they stopped short as they came face-to-face
with a group of men—the guards, extravagantly clothed, barely
deigning to look at the naked women. Just standing there,
laughing and joking and picking their teeth.

"*We tried to hang back*," said Magda, but there was no hanging back in Birkenau. Those who wouldn't go fast enough were
beaten into the room, cringing and covering themselves the
best they could, with their hands.

Where had she seen this? Magda wondered, almost wildly—
she'd seen this before, but where? Then she remembered a
painting, in Vienna, by Hieronymus Bosch, of dead souls enter-

ing hell. The same chaos, the same nakedness, only there the devils had cloven hoofs, not shiny black boots.

"Quick, to the disinfection," a guard was shouting. So at least this particular circle of hell had some purpose—that was reassuring. "It's so we don't get bugs," Magda whispered to her sisters.

They were formed into several lines, single file—they couldn't see at first what was happening until they moved forward, around a corner where there were more men, this time the striped pajamas, waiting with razors in hand.

Every single girl and woman in there gasped in turn when she rounded that corner and saw what was about to happen to her. They reached their hands to their hair—Magda's was black and thick, long, luxuriant. She wore it wound round her head. Gabi's wasn't so dark or so long, but was, anyway, her hair; and the youngest's, Vera's, was honey blonde, and still in the braids their mother had done for her the morning they were taken.

Back then, before they had any idea of what was coming. That day when they'd awoken as on any other day, and eaten bread with their own mother and drunk tea by her side, and chatted as she braided the little one's hair. A hundred years ago, Magda was thinking, a thousand. Hitler had been screaming about his "Thousand-Year Reich," and for them, he was right. They had lived it already, on that train.

"No, please," she could hear some of the girls ahead of her pleading, trying to hold onto their hair, to no avail. Off it came, along with all the other hair in there that day. Blond hair, raven hair, long most of it, beautiful hair. Piles and piles of it on the floor.

Nor was it the great commodity it had been even a year before, when it was swept up diligently and carted off to dry in specially designed lofts in the crematoria, before being neatly packaged into twenty-kilo sacks. These the merchants of Auschwitz had sold for the equivalent of twenty dollars a sack, all over the Reich. To the nearby Schaeffler factory, where it was processed into felt for warm blankets and socks for submarine crews; to the distinguished firms of Paul Reinmann or Färberei, where it was made into excellent rope and cord; even to the most fashionable Berlin tailors, who found it made excellent linings for their bespoke suits.

But by May of 1944, what with a quarter of Berlin already in ruins from Allied bombing, there wasn't the same call for custom suits lined with human hair. Nor were the Nazi submarine crews, the once-dreaded "wolfpacks," requisitioning the quantities of rope or socks as during the "happy days" of the early war. In fact, the majority of them were sleeping with the fishes by then, and the truth was that by the time Magda and her sisters arrived in the camp, there was already a glut of lovely girls' hair on the German market.

In fact, it had become rather a problem in the death camps— one more thing to burn. And yet, though it was no longer cost-effective or, for that matter, even practical, still the Nazis continued to shave the girls' heads, because the process was fundamental per se, a timely and efficient introduction to life in the death camps.

Since most of these girls were still not fully apprised of their situation. Some of them still thought they were going to sleep with their mamas and papas in a nice workers' cottage that night and then head out to pick grapes in the morning. But one quick shave of the head, and all that was behind them. There were no further expectations, no tedious questions along those lines, once you cut off their hair.

Magda's young sister Vera was starting to cry. She was still fourteen. They were naked. There were men there. The girls were clinging to each other.

"Loosen your braids," Magda whispered to her, "and when they see how beautiful your hair is, maybe they won't cut it."

Afterwards, she would scoff at that. That she'd thought the Nazis would even look. But at the time, she still thought maybe, somehow—and actually starting praying then, not for their lives, but for their hair.

But her prayer went the way of all the rest of them in Birkenau; and had heavenly attention been directed their way that day, surely she'd have understood if her own prayer had been triaged to the back of the line.

Would have even urged any Answerer of Prayers looking down upon them to rush first to the girls and women, the men and children whom Magda herself had seen and even talked to earlier that day on the platform, the same ones who had climbed politely into the waiting trucks and were at that very moment being shoved naked into a concrete room that they no longer believed was a "family camp" where they would live "normally" or even at all.

But since those prayers went unheeded that day in the air-tight chamber, where the doors just then were being shut and locked tight on the maximum number of men, women and children who could be crammed into that space, along with the minimal amount of Zyklon B gas required to kill them all—not in the most timely fashion, granted, since what mattered to the Nazis was not how long the screaming lasted, but how much they had to pay to IG Farben's Degesch for the cans of poison pellets on a monthly basis; since even those prayers changed nothing and reached no one, Magda too could have saved her breath.

But that she didn't know, not yet, and she prayed, hard and strong, for her hair, her sisters' hair, as she progressed steadily in line toward the men with razors and was ordered to step up onto a stool.

Her poor barber didn't even look at her face, just shaved off the long dark hair she'd spent her life growing. Three quick swipes, one, two, three, and then a strange and terrible chill upon her head.

"Raise your arms."

The razor was old and it pulled, but he'd had practice. One swipe each and the hair was gone from her underarms.

"Stand straight."

Another swipe, rough and painful, and her pubic hair was gone.

"Next."

She half stumbled off, then turned to wait for her sisters.

"Move along, *schnell!*" from one of the blond beasts. But they were quick, those barbers, and her sisters were done, too, and they "moved along" together, eyes on the ground, unable to risk a look at each other right then.

They were still naked, more naked now, and more ashamed. And the chill to the head—why did they do this? she wondered. Cleanliness? But everywhere she looked was filth. Some of the girls still had excrement on their bodies from the train ride. And the barbers' striped clothes were filthy, their razors were filthy, the floor—even the guards, in their blatant spotlessness, seemed in some way part of the dirt. Just the other side of it.

She would escape from here, somehow, get them all out, all three of them. There had to be a way and she would find it, she was already telling herself, when she was stopped by a very strange sight: a girl who looked familiar, but with a bowling ball for a head, and two ears sticking out.

She touched her head—so did the horrible girl. And then she realized, with dawning horror, that the Nazis had hung a mirror right there, to catch them as they came out, right in the face. Lest anyone still doubt. Nor were there any "Get moving's," or "*Schnell*'s," as they stood there, one by one, frozen by a dreadful image—themselves.

Their new selves. "*Wilkommen* to Birkenau," a nearby guard stood, repeating.

Magda turned—was he joking? For one wild moment, the whole thing—the *politesse* on the platform, the elegant doctor, and now this pleasant welcome—slipped into a sort of wild joke, a giant farce being played out here, with a cast of thousands. But why? And what was her role?

She looked at her sisters—her former sisters, weird freaks now, dirty and bald. Were they supposed to be funny? Or was it the guard who was the clown?

She looked at his face for a moment, but his eyes glittered hard at her, and she saw in them what she looked like, no longer a girl, but what? That was still the question—what? A bald, naked *something* on the edge of somewhere—what came next? A giant pit? A black river? Had she sinned and gone to hell? What had she done? She couldn't understand, she didn't understand, not that it mattered anymore. Because whatever *it* was, it was done, definitive. They'd taken her in, stripped her bare, shaved her hair—even if she ran away, who would recognize her now as the girl she was? Not even her own father.

She followed, stumbling half-blind, into what was called "the sauna." Which in this part of Birkenau meant a huge crush of people, a small trickle of cold water, and no soap. They pushed desperately toward the water, but there wasn't enough. "Please, we are filthy," but they were all filthy. That was part of the point at Birkenau.

But this group didn't know that yet, and they were still trying to wash themselves, somehow, when they were herded out again, shivering—no towels for the likes of them—to another room, where they were doused with petroleum, "disinfectant," and then moved on to the next room, where they were given clothes.

Not their own clothes, so nicely folded as they entered this place, but striped uniforms, and that's when it came to Magda that those skeletons in stripes must have once looked like she had this morning. But how long ago? That was the only question left: How long did it take to transform a perfectly normal person into a half-crazed inmate in this lunatic place?

As the girls filed past, each was handed a garment, randomly. Some were given nothing but long shirts, but Magda and her sisters were lucky and got dresses, though coarse and scratchy, oversized, and with no undergarments at all. Likewise big rough boots that wouldn't fit anyone outside the Norse myths. And then they were complete, the bald heads, stripes. Girls coming off the trains tomorrow would look at them in disgust.

They walked in silence out into the May afternoon, evening now. It was warm, but somehow dank. One of the girls stumbled out of her oversized boots in the mud. A woman guard came by and hit her with a whip. The girl lay in the mud. Someone stopped to pick her up and was beaten as well.

Beside them, the ditches were on fire. Behind them the chimneys were spewing fire and ash. "They're burning garbage," the girls tried to reassure each other. Fighting the growing sense that something here was truly wrong.

Finally, one of the girls asked a guard, "What is that smoke from the chimneys?"

The woman laughed. "That smoke is your parents, your children, your friends."

"She's joking," Magda whispered to her sisters, but—what was coming out of those chimneys? And what was that smell?

It was like nothing she had ever smelled before, just as the place itself was like no place on earth. It had been May when they were taken from prison, but did they have May here? There was no way of knowing, since there were no trees and not a blade of grass to be seen. No green at all, just mud and ash, making what the old nursery rhymes called "a mire," worse than mud, mud that grabbed your horrible boots, held you, and beyond that, barbed wire, rows and rows of it, strung on the ugliest posts she'd ever seen. Concrete posts that bent in, wanting to catch you, too, with their claws, to hurt you if they could.

All making part of a whole, as if the universe had conspired. When had they done all this, the Nazis? How long had it been since they'd taken control over everything, turned God's blue sky murky, and the earth beneath their feet to mud?

And them too—who could even begin to believe now that these bald-headed, filthy creatures in stripes slogging through the mud had once been nice, clean, pretty girls living at home with their parents, in a brick house on a friendly street? Czech girls who'd loved art and music, with grandparents and cousins—and where were all of them, now? Her old aunt would have fallen getting off that train. Would that gentleman officer have shot her? Had he shot her? A tear started down Magda's cheek.

They clumped on, through the mire that was part of it too, trying to catch their boots, trip them, and get them a beating. The only way was to shuffle—as she'd seen the striped pajamas doing when they first arrived. She'd thought it had something to do with them, their characters, thought they were shufflers. Now she was a shuffler, too.

But what did it matter if a bald-headed girl comported herself with dignity or shuffled? They continued past what seemed to be half-built sheds on either side. What were they? Did people work here? Sleep? It was getting darker now, and the smoke from the chimneys glowed red as the sky turned black. They could see fire shooting out into the night. One of the girls behind her started crying. She wanted to cry herself, just lie down and cry. There was a shot. This time she didn't turn around.

They were ordered to halt in front of one of the buildings and given, finally, something to eat. Food—she'd forgotten there was such a thing. Still they were hungry, famished in fact, and they ate the hard bread with no salt that tasted of dust, and drank the dark liquid that must have been something, but wasn't coffee. As they stood eating in silence, a group of girls came out of what seemed to be a barracks—girls in filthy clothes like theirs, though a few had belts around their baggy dresses, and scarves on their heads. A great improvement.

"Anyone from Poland?" "Who's from Czechoslovakia?" Magda and her sisters looked up—were you allowed to answer? Was it a trick? Would they be beaten? Shot?

"Lodz!" called someone beside Magda. Some of the girls with scarves ran over to her.

Magda looked uneasily at the guards, but they were chatting together, and didn't turn around. Her sisters clung to her side.

"Trebišov!" she said low.

"Trebišov?" A girl came toward her and looked at her closely. But Magda recognized her first, thanks to the scarf.

"Aranka?"

She was taller than when she'd last seen her—it had been three or four years at least—and very thin, but not dying-thin. And her hair had grown out a bit. She hadn't been exactly a friend, but her family had been part of their lives at home.

They were poor back there, and Hermann had supported the father with odd jobs and food from his farms, even money now and again.

Aranka studied her closely, and then the two sisters. "Magda?" she said.

And that's when Magda started to cry.

11

But don't cry, Aranka told her. Not here, she said. She kissed them all, and hugged them close. "*Try,*" she said to Magda, "*try, and maybe you can survive.*"

She would help them all she could, she told them. She'd been there for a while and had a position. The first thing would be to get them on a work detail, right away. Otherwise they'd just be gassed like all the others.

"Gassed?" What was Aranka saying?

But she didn't answer, just took their arms. "Did you get your tattoos?"

"No, thank God!" They'd been spared that desecration at least.

"Well, that's the first thing we have to organize," said Aranka. She explained that if they didn't bother to tattoo you, they weren't planning to keep you.

"Don't worry, I can help you. Come inside"—Aranka took them into the shed, which was their bunkhouse. It had been built to stable fifty-two horses, but now held a hundred and eighty girls. The brick floor was uneven, since it had been built right on the marsh, with no foundation, and the whole place smelled like a cellar, damp and chill.

It was lined with bunks built into the walls, from floor to ceiling. Not so small, about the size of a twin bed at home, except, as Aranka explained, almost apologetically, each one had to hold eight girls. Nor were there mattresses on the bunks, or even straw. The top bunks were best, "since nothing falls on your head," but they were all taken, so Aranka got Magda and her sisters a middle bunk at least. They'd been given only one threadbare blanket for the three, but Aranka would try to "organize" them another.

"And scarves"—she looked at them ruefully, but you had to take things practically here, she said. The fact that they'd bothered with the haircutting was actually a good sign. It meant they weren't going to kill you right away.

"But they're not going to kill us!" said Magda. "We're here to work!"

"To pick grapes?" said Aranka. "But where are the grapes here? Where are the factories?"

"But the chimneys—" said Magda.

"The chimneys!" A strange little laugh. Birkenau wasn't a work camp, explained Aranka. The other Auschwitz subcamps, a few kilometers away, sent slave labor to the factories that had sprung up around them, but Birkenau had no factories.

Still, there was work to be done, even here, which was why Aranka was still alive, and meanwhile scarves would help, they'd help a lot, though they were hard to come by and sometimes you had to trade a whole day's food. But it's worth it, said Aranka. It helps you to care. And they pay attention to such details at selection, she told them.

"Selection?"

Again Aranka didn't answer, instead looked down at their feet, and shook her head at the oversized boots, already caked with mud.

"Still, you're lucky," she told them. When she first came, the prisoners were given wooden clogs, "like from the Middle Ages," which fit no one and bruised their feet terribly. And "death here," she told them, "can start with the shoes." One small cut gets infected and then turns red, then black, and if they see it, or you can't walk, that's the end.

But now they were gassing so many people that they couldn't ship out all their shoes, "so they give us the worst ones, which are better than what we used to have." She'd try to find them something smaller, and even socks and underwear, eventually. "It's not like there's not plenty around."

Magda could only stare at her, trying to fathom. Had Aranka gone crazy? Talking about gassing like that? But she didn't seem remotely crazy—so was the place crazy, then? Was what looked worst actually the best for you? If they stripped you naked like a beast, paraded you before men, and shaved off your long hair, it meant that you were lucky? If they defiled your arm, permanently and forever, with a brand like an animal, you might live?

If, on the other hand, they took you nicely in your own clothes in a perfectly good truck, they meant to kill you? Gas you somehow? Right then, with your hair still on your head?

"But—why?" was all Magda could say then.

"Oh, there's no why in Birkenau," said Aranka.

She told them her story. Her family hadn't had any money to get out of the country or pay someone to hide them, so they'd been taken in the first transports, and she'd managed to stay alive here almost two years, some sort of record. She knew the ropes now, but had almost died at the beginning. She'd come down with a bad case of typhoid fever—"It's rampant here, because of the lice"—and was so weak that they sent her to the infirmary, which is only a waiting room for the gas, a nurse warned her. So she'd tried to get up out of bed but staggered and fell, and one of the Nazi doctors saw her, and since they were getting rid of all the children there that day, she was sent out with them.

What do you mean, "getting rid of all the children"? Magda knew that a nice normal person would have asked. But she knew, too, that as of that day in that place, she was no longer a nice normal person. Nor did she ask again about the smell, or what was burning in the ditches. The whole thing had become fully comprehensible to her, all at once, the way a nightmare sometimes does.

Aranka said that the doctors told the children they were taking them to a better place to sleep, "near their mothers," but even the small children knew the truth, and were running back and forth in the outer room, where they take your clothes, holding their little heads, and crying pitifully.

But there's no pity either in Birkenau, and they were all shoved into a concrete room with some shower heads but no signs of water, her too, and when she heard the door locked behind them, Aranka knew she was going to die.

And she would have, except that an older girl who was on a cleaning crew was still inside there, cleaning up the excrement from the last round, and noticed her, towering above the children.

"How old are you?" she whispered to Aranka.

"Fifteen," said Aranka.

"You're eighteen now," said the girl. She threw Aranka her own head scarf. "Quick, put it on."

Then she gave her a bucket of human excrement.

"Pick it up, quick."

Aranka picked it up.

"Come on, hurry!"

Aranka followed the girl to the door.

The girl pounded. "Cleaning *Kommando!*" she shouted. The door opened a crack. The SS man looked suspicious.

"Two?" he said. "I thought there was just one."

The girl held up the stinking bucket toward him. "I needed help."

He stepped back in disgust. Such filthy people. "Get out," he said, and the two girls slipped past with their buckets of shit.

So instead of dying that day with the children, Aranka had lived, but her hands still hadn't stopped shaking. "See?" She held them up—it was true, they trembled like an old woman's with the palsy.

"Funny, no?" said Aranka.

Funny or no? Magda had no idea. In fact, she couldn't speak. Vera, the little one, didn't seem to understand. She asked Aranka about her family. There'd been a little sister, her age. The two of them used to play under the plum trees. "Is Anna here?"

Aranka looked at her for a moment, then said, "She was your friend, wasn't she?"

That was all, though, and after that, there were no more questions. Magda learned that too, the first night. No questions in Birkenau. If someone had something to say, they'd say it. Otherwise, it was better not to ask.

THAT NIGHT, IT WAS routine by ordeal. The Nazis hadn't let them dig a proper latrine—just put a long line of holes in a concrete box, which filled up in no time, but was cleaned out only sometimes, and they beat you if you didn't sit down, so that it was impossible there not to smell of it.

And then came the meals which would kill you if nothing else did—300 grams of bread that wasn't really bread so much as sawdust held together with only the flour it took for that, shared among five girls. The etiquette was five bites and pass it. Same with the dark drink, a half-liter of the non-coffee, non-tea. You got the cup, took three sips, passed it to the next one. No one cheated, Magda saw.

But if there was a little bread left, or if you "organized" an extra piece, you had to sleep with it under your head at night. Otherwise it would be gone in the morning. Your boots too.

Aranka had gotten them a bunk with just four other girls, but that still meant seven girls in a bunk for one. And all the boots under the heads, the laces tied together—crucial, Aranka told them. If someone's boots were stolen, she would have to steal yours. Because if you showed up in the morning without boots, you went straight to the gas.

"Straight to the gas"—there was still a chance, Magda was thinking, that Aranka was crazy, or a liar, with her horrifying talk of gas and children and buckets of shit. *It's not really true, is it?* Magda wanted to ask her. Beg her: *It's a bad joke, no?*

But then there was a whistle, and everyone went clambering into their bunks, tying their shoes together, putting them under their heads, as Aranka had said. The other girls in their bunk put the three sisters down at the foot end—they slept head to foot—and explained that when someone wanted to turn over, they all had to turn. And then silence fell, only it wasn't really silent. Soon people started breathing fitfully, and then moaning in their sleep, murmuring, some even laughing. Which must constitute escape around here, even for just a few hours at night, but Magda pitied those girls. To wake up from a good dream here must make it worse.

She herself couldn't sleep. She tried to swat the bugs she could feel crawling up her legs, praying these particular ones weren't carrying spotted fever. Tried even to say her old prayers, blessing the individual members of her family, naming each name, even of far-flung cousins, but she kept stopping in the middle and having to start again. From outside, in the distance, there came an occasional scream in the midst of what seemed to be a low-level, ongoing wail.

Was it praying, that wail? But then what about the screaming? Or was it all a dream? But she wasn't asleep, or at least that's what she thought until she was shocked awake by a terrible gong ringing, and then Aranka, at their bunk, shaking them, "Hurry, get up, quick!"

It was still dark, half past four in the morning. "Get up, right away," Aranka urged them, speaking fast and intensely. "Hurry, they beat the last ones out."

The three girls half fell out of the bunk and stumbled outside after Aranka, boots on, dresses never off. She showed them how to line up, five across—the Nazis loved five—for what they also loved: their roll call. During which the prisoners were required to stand stiff and straight, for as long as it took, hours and hours, sometimes half a day, sometimes all day into the night, with no food or water or even latrine, while the SS men strolled through the lines and counted them at their leisure.

If there was a miscount, they'd start again. Under the blazing sun of high summer, the wind, the rain, the sleet, hail, snow in winter. When people dropped of exhaustion, and some always did, during the long ones, it was absolutely forbidden to pick them up. They had to be left to be shot, Aranka warned.

And roll call was tricky in other ways too, she said. It was here that most of the routine beatings took place. "If they beat you, try to stand it." But best was to get a place in the middle. If you're on one of the edges, sometimes they tease the dogs at you, for no reason. For fun, said Aranka. Then, if you flinch, they beat you. Or sometimes if you don't.

And keep your eyes down if they come your way.

But no one came their way that day, nor was this roll call one of the long ones, and all the girls there lived to sip their ersatz coffee and gnaw off their bites of so-called bread.

Aranka was in a hurry to get them their tattoos. There wasn't much work in Birkenau, and what there was went to the girls with the numbers on their arms. The others—

"Fuel," another girl piped in. Especially the new girls, she added, who weren't starving yet and still had fat on their bodies.

Magda turned to her.

It's true, the girl shrugged. New girls were sometimes "selected" just to help burn the other bodies, since skin and bone didn't burn so easily without some fat. "Breasts," she said. "And this"—she patted Magda's behind.

Magda wondered if this girl too had gone crazy. She'd been here almost a year, long enough to lose her mind, and she smelled—they all did. These girls all had mud on their legs, and shit too. They were filthy. She hated them all, suddenly. They made her sick, with their dirt and their shit, like crazy women.

But she was dirty now, too, and there was no water for washing.

But why not, since there was water everywhere here? The ground was mud, the bunkhouse was dripping. Why couldn't they just wash? Then maybe they wouldn't have to be burned.

Magda started to cry without a sound, started to shake. "Try!" Aranka whispered to her. She pointed out a few of the girls who were stumbling around with glazed eyes and blank looks on their faces, some holding crusts of bread they weren't even bothering to eat. "Musselmen," Aranka said they were called here, for some reason, or no reason, maybe a play on words. Auschwitz slang for people in the last stages of starvation. Walking skeletons, no longer answering to their own names.

She went over to one of them and took her bread. No reaction. "She's already gone," said Aranka. She offered some of the bread to Magda, who just shook her head.

"Eat it," said Aranka, "you have to try. Do you want them to burn you too? Turn you to ashes?"

Magda shrugged.

"Ah, that's when they win," said Aranka. Of course, the main goal is to kill us, she said, but part of the game for them is to turn us into that—she pointed at the walking ghost. The living dead, indifferent even to the gas.

Aranka sympathized with the girl, she said, had even come to respect that form of escape. But as for her, she was determined to live to "tell the tale," and to that end, had developed certain strategies. For one, she said, she called the shit dried on their legs "Nazi stockings."

"Because it's them, not us, the filth, you have to understand that. It's all them, their foul bread that makes us sick to begin with, and their fevers that give us the dysentery they won't let us wash off our legs. Their filthy clothes, their bugs, their latrines, their smell"—she pointed to Magda's head—"their haircuts! You saw the mirror?"

Magda nodded, though barely.

"They wanted you to think it's you, but it's them you were looking at." All of them, too, not just the ones in here. All those clean, long-haired girls in their starched, pressed dirndls, said Aranka, and the good-looking boys with their hats and horns. Every mother and father on their way to church on Sundays, and all their writers and philosophers and music lovers and beer drinkers with their steins and their sausage, who were, in one way or another, through commission or omission, the reason for the shit on the legs of the filthy, bald-headed girls in here today. And that's who's really staring back out of that mirror, said Aranka, and she for one was going to live to hold the mirror back at them someday.

"Or die trying," said Aranka, "and you have to try, too. You and your sisters. For your parents. Think what a victory it will be for them if you all three make it."

Magda nodded—tried to. She hadn't considered, till then, that they might not all three make it. Had never once imagined going home to her parents without all three.

But Aranka was right. They had to live, all three of them. Her parents would die of grief if one of them was killed here.

"Here's how you do it," said Aranka. "When you see someone suffering, you have to tell yourself that they're not really suffering, they're somewhere else, way beyond all this, because you can't help them, and it just hurts you."

It just hurts you.

The next day the new girls were told to line up for tattoos. Which was good news, said Aranka, since they weren't doing it so much, not like they used to, they didn't need so many workers, and more to the point, didn't want to keep such close track anymore.

Which means they know they're going to get caught someday, she said, so they're trying to hide it, starting at the low numbers again, not that they'll ever be able to hide any of it in the end. For one thing, the men who carried the bodies from the gas chambers to the ovens had been strewing the teeth on the ground along the way, so that afterwards, people could tally the millions. And the truth those men themselves wouldn't live to tell—they were killed off systematically, every three months, so they wouldn't live to testify—would be told by the teeth.

The girls were lined up by last name, and then slowly moved up toward the tables, where two prisoners, older women, sat. One had a book in which she wrote their names, and the other had what looked like a fountain pen with blue ink and an injection needle at the end. Magda had to fight off the urge to bolt. Tattoos were barbaric, hateful to her. Her hair could grow again someday, but they were marking her arm forever. She didn't look as they took her arm and started pricking. Told herself that this pain and desecration, here in this place of dark reversals, meant that she might live instead of die.

"Don't cry!" she said to her sisters. "It's nothing," but she couldn't bring herself to look for a while. And afterwards, when her sisters added up their numbers and found good luck in the sums, Magda just shook her head.

"Try, and maybe you can survive," Aranka had said. Not "Try and you can," but "Try and maybe." That was the best you could do here.

Magda was hit with dysentery that night, seized with stomach cramps at the start of the evening roll call, but she knew that they weren't permitted latrine till it was over. She knew, too, there was no such thing as asking for that privilege, to use the so-called bathroom even just this once, as if she were a human being. But the thought of soiling herself—no, she would hold out, hold it all in somehow. She breathed in, breathed out, looked up, and thought about the stars that must still be in the skies, somewhere. Here you couldn't see them through the smoke.

She tried to remember the names of the constellations. If the guards let them go soon, she could still make it. If that was even permitted. Because they'd had one latrine—was there another one at night? She tried to remember. There were some buckets, though, in the barracks. If she could get there—but the counting was never-ending, and finally, she felt the warm, stinking trickle start down her legs.

"*Nazi stockings*"—but even so, could she live like this? With her own shit on her legs?

"But that's part of it," Aranka told her. "They're good at this." Not only do they want to kill you, but they want to make you wonder if they might be right. If a girl with her own shit on her legs should be walking the earth anyway.

"But if you let them make you feel that way, then they've won."

WHEN MAGDA FINALLY GOT TO the latrine that night, there was some shouting and crying, a sort of scuffle going on. A woman had collapsed, eyes open but barely conscious, into the filth, and a sobbing girl was trying to pull her up. She'd been her teacher, the girl was saying, in Budapest, at school. She'd taught them *Faust*, and Shakespeare's sonnets—

"Leave her!" the girl's friends were crying.

"In English! The poems were so beautiful!"

Her friends dragged her off. "Do you want to die, too?"

But Magda, too, was pulled up short at the sight of the woman's face, clear and bright somehow, in the filth and the shit. She too had learned some of Shakespeare's sonnets, from Fräulein Steiner, a teacher like this one. Passionate and clean. *Look in thy glass and tell the face thou viewest—*

"*Schnell!*" A smack from the guard caught her, across her back. Magda staggered.

"Quick, sit down," hissed Aranka. "Sit and then out, hurry!"

Magda stepped around the beautiful teacher and sat on the

stone hole in the filth, and let whatever was still in her stomach run out. They'd been given soup that night, or what they called soup. Ditchwater boiled with some rotten turnips. Magda's cup actually had a dirty button floating in it.

Full many a glorious morning have I seen—

A guard walked over and kicked the woman, the teacher. Magda could see that she was still breathing. Had Fräulein Steiner been kicked to death in a latrine as well? What would her beloved Shakespeare say to that?

But he knew nothing of this—none of them did. Not Goethe, or Schiller, or Schopenhauer even, with all his dark complaints! Fakers and fools—what did they know, with all their words? Nothing! Even when they had cried, they cried at nothing. "The human condition." Death in bed.

Which was what, compared to this?

"Come on." Aranka grabbed her arm. They were hauling the woman out. Her body, Magda told herself. Even if she's breathing, she's far away. *Farewell! thou art too dear for my possessing.*

She walked slowly back through the mud to the barracks. "Go to sleep," Aranka told her. "Try to dream about food." She herself planned to have her grandmother's mushroom barley soup that night in her dreams, followed by roast chicken with some of the plum sauce Hermann used to give them after the harvest every fall.

12

THE IMPORTANT THING was to work, said Aranka, and she got them on a detail sorting clothing—but don't be tempted to take anything, not yet, she warned them. Not that you couldn't steal; you could, almost anything you wanted, including food, but you had to do it right, which meant knowing the ropes. Who was on duty, who you were working with, what they didn't mind letting slip that day, and so on.

"But don't try anything yet," she cautioned. "Soon enough there'll be scarves and belts for you, even underwear."

Of which there was plenty—scarves, belts, and underwear. Their job was to fold and sort clothes taken from the incoming prisoners—shoes in one big cart, men's suits in another, dresses here, children's clothes there, and so on. Once sorted, the clothes were taken to "Canada," as the giant warehouses were bizarrely called, more Auschwitz slang. Something to do with plenitude, vastness. This one was behind Crematoria III and IV.

And from there they were sent on to Germany, particularly the good things, particularly the baby clothes. All the little suits, the tiny shoes—Aranka held up a cotton sailor suit, still with signs of pressing, though there was a dark stain in the pants. "From the train ride," she shrugged. Her strategic shrug. Magda couldn't speak, just shook her head.

"The Germans love these," said Aranka.

But even this steady supply line of dead babies' clothes to nice German families was breaking down. The girls had heard the guards talking—their trains couldn't take clothes into Germany anymore, and "Canada" was out of control now, overflowing, clothes piled up everywhere, and thousands upon thousands of shoes scattered around in the mud.

But still, the Nazis kept the girls sorting, because the clothes kept coming in, better clothes now, the best clothes ever seen in Birkenau, from the Hungarian transports. The latest arrivals, the ones who'd supposed themselves lucky when they weren't deported earlier. Who'd lifted a cautious glass, "to life," in the winter of 1944, and thought that since the war was nearly over, they were safe.

But it was these very people, the Hungarians, who were coming in now, nonstop, by the trainloads. They weren't even being "selected" as they got off the train, just sent straight to the gas. It was true that the war was nearly over, the Russians were coming from the east, and the English and Americans from the west, but against all that, the gas chambers were at their absolute peak of efficiency. The Nazis had finally honed the whole process to perfection and didn't want to waste it now.

Which was ironic, since by then it was clear even to the SS that their dream was no longer attainable. They would not, in fact, manage to rid the world of all undesirables.

Still, the romantics among them were determined to carry on to the end. By June of 1944, they had four gas chambers running around the clock in Birkenau, two below ground, and two above. Each chamber could handle from fifteen hundred to two thousand people at a time. The process itself took from ten to twenty minutes, depending on how much poison gas was put into the slots, and who was in front of the vents—with children, of course, it was quicker. And then came the ventilation, and the clearing of the bodies, which also took a certain allotment of time. But on a good day, the Nazis could still gas up to twelve thousand people. Eight thousand of whom could be cremated to fairly good ash, the rest burned in open pits, and all of them, ashes now, dumped into the nearby rivers, which were, by then, pretty much clogged. But there weren't any fish left in the Vistula or the Sola anyway.

To further facilitate the process, and skip the bit with the trucks, the SS in Auschwitz had a spur of the railway extended, practically to death's door. From there it would be an easy walk through the woods to the gas for the 700,000 Hungarians they hoped to kill that summer.

Magda and her sisters could see them going by, in the distance. The long lines of men and women in their summer clothes, walking in formation from the platform along two paths into the small woods that hid the gas chambers. A beautiful, colored band they made, the Hungarians, always so stylish. And now they walked in their lovely silks and linens into the woods.

A little later, there'd be a flash of red, and then thick white smoke from the chimneys behind. And then another train at the station, forty cars, fifty even. Sometimes a few new girls would show up at their barracks, still thinking they would see their mothers "on Sunday"; but mostly no one new came in anymore. Even the young and strong were walking into the woods now. The chimneys, all five of them, were smoking all the time.

The girls watched those lines moving by in the distance,

mercifully too far away to recognize any faces. They could make out, though, the women pushing baby carriages, and the men with their arms around their sons.

"A shower," the girls knew they'd been told, "to refresh yourselves, and then you will be put to work."

"Fine, then, we will work," they knew the fathers were telling their sons as they walked, and it made sense. "There's no doubt that Hitler needs us," these people were reasoning. And they were right, only the universe was wrong.

And when they got to those showers, they would be told to take off their clothes. Told to fold them nicely, tie the shoes together, and remember where they left them. They would be comforted by that last bit. By the signs that read CLEANLINESS BRINGS FREEDOM, and 1 LOUSE CAN KILL YOU! Both of which they would take as boding well. The former with its hint of freedom, the latter with its show of concern.

And there were shower heads in there, in the gas chambers, the girls knew. A clever touch that, all part of the game. But once the women and children were shoved in with the naked men, to everyone's shock, there would have to come that moment when the little game was over. And then the shouting would start and then the screaming, then the clawing, but in the end, always silence. The Degesch exterminator on duty that day, overseeing it all through a peephole, would then give the SS a thumbs-up. Time to ventilate, and then send in the prisoners whose job it was to haul the bodies out and shove them into the ovens, and after them, the girls with their buckets, to clean up the blood and the shit.

And then, they'd be ready for the next batch. The Third Reich might be collapsing around them, but the death camps chugged along in tiptop order that June. One day, in the distance, Magda thought she saw her mother moving by in the line.

If not her mother, then her aunt for certain. No one else walked quite that way.

Tears rolled down her face but no one asked her why, because they all knew why. There wasn't a girl in the barracks who still had a mother. A few days later, they were all terrified by a command to return to their barracks. That meant the Nazis were going to kill an entire block of prisoners, with no selection, for one of their reasons—either disease or because they wanted the room.

The girls lay there through that night in the darkness, terrified, listening, but the dump trucks they used to transport prisoners didn't stop at their door. They rolled past, and then, from another part of the camp, they heard some activity. "The Gypsies?" someone whispered. They had been kept with their families, about a kilometer or so away, on the far edge of the camp, and had a slightly favored status, were allowed to live together, almost normally, for Birkenau. The doctor, Mengele, visited them often, and brought the children chocolate. "Uncle Pepi," they called him.

But the next morning, when the girls walked by their camp on the way to work, they saw it was deserted, the barracks doors gaping open. There were some clothes strewn around, and a few fiddles lying in the mud. The Gypsies had a little orchestra and gave performances, which Mengele often attended.

Later they heard that it was he himself who'd gotten them all out of there so smoothly, with no resistance, by bringing them first extra rations of decent bread and even salami, to "strengthen them," since they'd be going to "a new camp, a better camp," he promised. And they fell for it—ate the bread and salami, and followed Uncle Pepi to the showers, and were gassed, all three thousand of them, in one night.

Dead, all of them, just like that—but hadn't the Nazis liked their music, liked their children? And yes, Mengele had been clever to trick them into going with no fuss, but how much of a victory was it, since the guards were there to beat them into the dump trucks anyway, if they hadn't walked in themselves? The story went round that Mengele had even driven some of the children, his favorites, to the gas in his shiny car, but surely he left before the game was up? Surely even he didn't have the stomach?

Because there always came that moment of realization, no matter how elaborate the ruse. And then, could even Mengele have whistled in the faces of the people he'd befriended—his version of befriending? The people he'd set up for the worst mass death ever devised? Could even Uncle Pepi have waved to the small children as they were shoved, screaming with horror, into the gas?

Magda met a young woman, a Pole, who, like Aranka, had been inside and made it out. She'd been sick with spotted fever, typhus, but was recovering and had started working in the infirmary for a woman doctor, a prisoner herself, who'd taken a liking to her and had been able to protect her. But when the doctor was out one day, all the girls in the infirmary were loaded into a dump truck, and told they were being taken to the showers.

But the truck backed down a ramp, and they were dumped down a chute, like sacks of flour. Those who were hurt and couldn't get up were shot where they lay, but the others were herded into the so-called showers. The room was dark, the young woman said—the only windows were small ones, high up, near the roof. There were shower heads, and even towels and soap, but as soon as the doors were closed behind them, she felt her eyes begin to water, she started coughing and felt a terrible pain in her chest and throat. There was some screaming, and people closer to the windows were falling down, coughing, foaming at the mouth, and biting their own hands.

But then, the doors were opened and an SS man wearing a respirator came in, calling her name, and pulled her out, then quickly shut the door again. The infirmary doctor had come back in time to make a plea for her life, and she'd been lucky. A minute later and she'd have died with the other girls in there that day.

Though afterwards, she said, she couldn't eat anything for days without vomiting, and she'd had a heart attack too, though she was only twenty-eight. They told her her heart would never be right again.

"But that's only if I live." She laughed, one of those short laughs that Magda would always associate with Auschwitz.

"You'll live," someone said to her, but would she? Would any of them? And if they did, how they would live? As what? That day, as they were walking back from the sorting, they'd had to pass by children's bodies burning in a pit. It was said that children slowed down the ovens, since they had so little fat. But up against that was the fact that you could stuff more of them inside. So it was a toss-up.

Something for the Nazis to debate. But as for Magda, she had been there two months and learned not to dream at night. She slept among what she called *"the octopus of legs"* without moving, like a mummy, or one of the living dead.

The next day was Sunday, which was sometimes good, sometimes bad. Sometimes they didn't have to work so much, and sometimes they had to work twice as hard for no reason. And sometimes on the Sundays when they weren't working, the guards in the towers took potshots at them. A girl sitting next to Aranka had been shot a few weeks back, and the noise was so loud and so close that she told them she thought she'd been hit herself.

But she hadn't for some reason, or maybe none. That Sunday as they waited, hoping for a bit of rest, they were called out to work as usual. But as they were filing out of the gate, fifty of them, including Magda and her sisters, were counted off and told to turn left instead of right. They all stopped for a heartbeat, terrified — Crematorium II was over there. The gas chamber too, and the woods where they'd watched so many disappear.

Was this it for them, then? On a Sunday morning like this one, with no warning?

"Get moving, quickly!"

They started out. "I will at least die fighting," they'd all told themselves as they watched others being taken, but how could they? They were surrounded by guards, and dogs, and in her case, her sisters. And maybe even more to the point, the over-riding fact that for as long as they were walking, breathing in and out, looking toward the sun, they were still alive, even if just for one more minute, and there was still a chance, small but conceivable, that they'd live.

It was a sunny day, the end of June — around the twenty-fifth, she figured, though they had no calendar. Magda noticed then that both of her sisters had fuzz growing on their heads. She must have as well — it was nice of their hair to be growing in, brave of it, she thought. They had underwear too now, and head scarves, and boots that fit, relatively speaking.

Should we run? she was wondering. *Let them shoot us?* But sometimes they didn't shoot, sometimes they hung you, and not just regular hanging, but Nazi hanging. Strung you up, and when you were almost dead, brought you down so they could do it again. She'd heard that's what had happened with several of the French Resistance women who'd tried to escape.

But would that be worse than the gas? She didn't want to go in there with her sisters—couldn't bear to watch them foam at the mouth and bite their own hands, then turn blue. Alone she could at least just die, but to have to watch her sisters—

"Pray," she told them. She hadn't been praying lately, but what had she gained from that? Punished God? What good had that done her?

"Pray hard!" she whispered to her sisters as they were sent through a grove of birch trees she hadn't seen before. So Birkenau had its birches after all.

Birch trees with their lovely light green leaves just out, dancing in the sun, the way they did anywhere else. Her first trees in a long time, and maybe her last, because behind them was a crematorium.

"Halt." They did. If they were told to strip now for the showers, maybe she would run. She didn't want to see her sisters die.

But instead, they were marched into a high-ceilinged room behind the crematorium, echoing, empty except for a large number of baby carriages.

The girls stopped in their tracks, horrified, all of them. It wasn't as if they weren't used to the trappings of wholesale murder—they stood sorting the clothes from it, all day, every day. But the sight of these ghost-carriages brought it all home to them again, the very worst of it, even though it probably meant they weren't going to the gas that day.

"Get moving, *schnell!*" There was apparently a shortage of baby carriages in Berlin. A special train was being requisitioned. The prisoners were ordered to each take one and push it "with great care" to the railway platform.

They held back, awestruck, as if from the sacred.

"Quick!"

The crack of a whip, and they took a collective breath and moved forward, each one, to her carriage. They were good ones, beautiful ones, Budapest's finest, some even from London, with English names. Each one had come in with a baby, maybe just yesterday.

"*Schnell!*"

They set out, single file, in absolute silence. It was true that they were saved, they hadn't gone to the gas, but the horror didn't fade from their faces. It was about three kilometers from the crematorium to the loading platform for the trains out, and the girls wound up the path, like a dance of death from those paintings from the Middle Ages, it occurred to Magda, with the guards as the Grim Reapers, whips instead of scythes. Among the younger girls, horror had turned to fury, and they were pushing fast and hard, but the older ones, some of them mothers themselves in a former life, handled the carriages with great delicacy, as if a child were still smiling out from the lace pillows inside. The small beloved who just yesterday, at the break of dawn or the fall of dusk, was locked in a room with its screaming mother and made to breathe gas till the blood ran from its little eyes.

Who even then was wafting as smoke from the chimneys or burning in the ditches they were walking by, and where had God been then? What a fool she'd been to pray! She looked over at the barbed wire—electrified, but only at night. People waited till dark and then "went to the wire," as they said here.

Though the Nazis considered even that a minor loss for their team in the game of Auschwitz, the fact that prisoners would still dare think of their lives as theirs to take. When someone killed himself, the guards would pick ten others randomly and shoot them or hang them. Whatever suited. If Magda "went to the wire," they would surely come for her sisters.

If, though, she got them out of here alive, then she would win. It was that simple. Her game was that. There was no further point in thinking about God and the meaning of life, or any whys, for that matter. Since there was no why, just a simple win or lose here.

A simple "*Try, and maybe you can survive.*"

13

THE NEXT WEEK, there was another lockdown in the barracks before dawn, and this time it did mean a selection. The sickest and weakest would be sent to the gas. A few others too, randomly, if they happened to be in a row with the sick and the weak ones. It was easier to send the whole row of five, so it all came out even.

"Clothes off!" the guards were shouting. That made it harder to hide a small cut or a bite that would get you "selected." Because a spot might mean typhus, and even the smallest bruise in the filth of the camps could turn to gangrene, so why take chances when you could just as easily rid yourself of the girl then and there?

"Pinch your cheeks just before you go by," Aranka instructed Magda, "and stand straight, walk fast, and run if they tell you to." She said it in German—*laufen*. If they say that, or anything like it, she said, run fast, for your life, no matter how cramped and stiff you feel.

It was hard to walk outside naked, harder still because they were all so dirty, just like the Nazis said they were. FILTHY, VERMIN, COCKROACHES—she remembered those posters on the walls, when they were still at home, clean and clothed. She had never,

never once in her life, gone to bed dirty at home, let alone filthy, but they hadn't been given a shower since they'd gotten here. Just a few seconds to splash on some ice water at a trough, with no soap—

"Attention!"

There they were, all of them, five across, a thousand girls and young women, standing naked, at attention, waiting to live or die. An hour passed, another. The sun rose and the shivers turned to sweat. It was hot now, but still they were kept standing. With no possible reason, except to make them as miserable as possible. To kill them once before they killed them twice.

Finally, "He's coming" went through the crowd. They didn't have to say who. The doctor, Mengele, walked up to the front of the group. It was true that he was handsome, like an angel, "the Angel of Death," they called him.

But Magda had once seen him beat a girl's face to pulp, a beautiful girl with bright blue eyes and a thin straight nose, right there in the line, just start beating her head out of the blue, for no reason except maybe that she was lovely, and he didn't stop until her head was gone, and in its place was something red, nothing like a face or head.

And then he'd called for some perfumed soap and a basin and, humming his little tune, had washed his hands, right there in front of them, and then strolled off, still humming, his uniform splattered with blood.

And another time, he'd asked for girls who played the piano to step out, and, with a smile, sent them to clean the latrines till they died. His little joke, part of an ongoing routine, thematically unified if somewhat predictable once you'd caught the thread: the standard Nazi fare of "Us (armed) vs. You (naked)," with some slapstick variations thrown in on the side, as with Mengele's "Our Acts (unspeakable) vs. Our Soap (perfumed)."

Which made him less the Angel than one more player in the Death Camp Follies, it came to Magda, as the selection finally began. There were all the women standing naked, five across, as against Mengele, at the front, in his sharply pressed jodhpurs and crisp white shirt. Barely deigning to move his finger as he pointed, to the left, to the right, as each one walked past him. Death for this one, life for that, or was it the other way around? No one knew yet. Just knew that if a girl didn't go the way he pointed, the SS were standing by to attack her. Mengele himself paid no further attention once he'd indicated her fate. Just waited pleasantly for the next one—"Yes, yes, very good, to the right please, to the left."

Magda had heard about a woman, an Italian, who'd been a singer before the war. As they were taking her to the gas, one of the SS thought it would be amusing to force her to sing naked atop a pile of dead bodies. This she did, with such a charming smile that he too was soon smiling, and then she leapt at him, grabbed his gun, and shot him dead.

But Mengele's gun was under his jacket, and the only way to kill him would be to live this thing out. Since even now, even here, time was passing.

"Pinch your cheeks," she whispered to her sisters as they moved closer. They were starving, everyone there was starving. But Magda and her sisters hadn't been there long enough to become skeletal. Too thin, yes, but still they could walk, even run, if they had to. If he said, "*Laufen*."

But he didn't, though he looked at them closely. Even moved Magda's arm away from her side, gently, with a doctor's hand, to see if she was hiding any spots. But she wasn't, and his finger moved to the right, for all three, and Aranka too. They still weren't sure if that was the live or die side, but the girls around them looked stronger, and the weak ones seemed to be to the left.

And sure enough, their group were ordered back to their barracks, and the dump trucks came around for the other girls. The selected girls started crying then, wailing—they weren't newcomers off the train, to be beguiled by tales of showers. They were too weak to fight the Nazi soldiers, too sick, too thin, but they could cry and the SS had to hear it. No charades with this group. Just the darkness, face-to-face.

Two girls in Magda's own bunk bed were sent to the gas that day. One was from a village near theirs. She'd been a kindergarten teacher. The other was only seventeen. They were nice girls, kind, smart girls, dead girls now. Magda and her sisters said a prayer for them that night, more for their own sakes.

But there was also the arithmetic of Auschwitz, which meant that there was now more room in the bunk for them.

ALTHOUGH BY ANOTHER VARIATION of that same arithmetic, this one graphing the 1,300 calories they were fed per day, a few more months here and they'd be among the walking skeletons, the ones selected by the moving finger for the gas. There was no help for this, beyond an occasional extra crust or scrap of cheese found in the clothing of the dead, but a week later the word went around that there would be another selection, this time for girls to go to a factory to work.

No one knew where—just that it wasn't here. Which made it automatically preferable, and "*by some miracle*" Magda and her sisters were all chosen, and Aranka too. They would be leaving right away. "This way, fast, march!"

They were taken to a dressing room, and given their first shower since they'd gotten to Birkenau, four months earlier. They were also sprayed again, this time with a disinfectant powder, and given better clothes—underwear, a dress, and even a coat, though it was late August and still hot. This was a very good sign, said Aranka. It meant both that they actually—probably— were going to work somewhere, and that they were expected to live till winter.

Then they were marched back along the road they'd come in on, to the platform where a line of boxcars was waiting. A few months earlier, they'd been shocked at the sight of a similar train, but now it looked like redemption on wheels. It was tak- ing them out of there—four hundred of them. The SS counted them, once, twice, again—kept them at attention. There was the train, but still they were kept there, standing outside.

Another death camp charade? A little joke on girls on their way to the gas? Like the salami with the Gypsies? It was pos- sible. There seemed to be an argument going on among the SS. Not to mention another group of girls shouting and crying nearby, locked in the cellar of what looked like a farmhouse, but with bars on the windows. It was one of the holding cham- bers, where they locked people waiting for the gas. There was no hope for those girls, Magda knew.

But for them? Finally, they were ordered into the boxcars, and the doors locked behind them. But still the train didn't move, and now they could overhear the arguing outside. The SS officer in charge of the gas chambers had space right then for a few hundred more women. The girls on the train were exactly the number he needed to fill his slots.

But the officers who'd gotten them out to the train had gone to a certain amount of trouble over these girls, what with the selections, the showers, the clothes, all part of their obligation to provide a precise number of prisoners for the munitions fac- tory nearby. The girls sat listening—live or die? Not that work in a munitions factory guaranteed life in the long term. But if the train pulled out, they would live that afternoon.

An hour passed, and then another. If the doors opened, they knew they'd be taken straight to the Little White Farmhouse to accompany the girls already locked inside to the gas that day. None of them were speaking—they all sat, attentive and still. People called the gas chamber "the mouth of the dragon." Others said "wolf," but dragon had seemed more fitting, since it implied mystery alongside the death. That's what Magda had started telling herself—that maybe there was some mystery there. Not just horror. Not only death.

Some glimpse of something just before—or after, she was praying for the girls she'd gotten a glimpse of through the bars of that cellar, girls who looked beautiful to her, girls who were alive and were about to be murdered. *Grant them some mystery as they stare in the face of the dragon,* she was praying, *and us too*—she had given up other prayers, prayers for safety or deliverance. She had concluded that God was old and weak. He couldn't do it.

But something at the end, some flash of joy, even enlightenment, for them and for us, some overview, some tiny jot of meaning, she was praying, there in the boxcar, sitting stock-still with her sisters, when suddenly there was a jolt. The girls looked at each other with wild hope—another jolt, and then a whistle, and the train started off. One of the girls had overheard the officers saying that if they didn't provide the labor, they might suffer some consequences, might even be called to answer, and that must have clinched it.

"The cowards!" she'd laughed.

They all laughed at that, too much. Laughed almost like crazy women, but then the laughter turned to crying, and they fell sobbing into each other's arms, all four hundred girls, as the train took them away from Birkenau late that August afternoon.

14

THEY DIDN'T GO FAR—but it felt like the right direction. North and then west, toward home, what used to be home. Czechoslovakia, anyway. Would they cross the border? A sort of hope took hold in the hearts of these girls, most of them Czech, just to be going west and not east. At least that part of it was better, had to be better.

It was hard to keep track of how far they'd gone, since the train stopped and started, stopped and started, and there was no light, no window, and, of course, no food or water, nor did they expect any by then. Even as newcomers to the death camps, they'd arrived fully apprised of the logistics of Nazi train travel.

And given that introductory journey, this one seemed almost civilized. No one died. No one became unhinged by thirst. No one started crying and then begging for bread. The latrine buckets did not overflow. There were no children on board to triple the pain.

The train finally stopped and the doors were opened even before the cramps in the girls' legs became serious, threatening their ability to jump like well-fed gymnasts from the boxcar and run past whoever was pointing to the gas or not, wherever it was they were going.

But the great thing, the almost incredible thing, was that there didn't seem to be those death camp smokestacks in the place where they landed, which was called Gleiwitz. Nor did this seem to be a camp where they wanted you to die. What they wanted here was for you to work hard, and they seemed to acknowledge that this required a certain amount of food and even some limited comfort.

The girls were marched to a barracks, where they were assigned only four to a bunk, and shown to a real latrine, one that had been dug out properly. No overflowing—"*a five-star hotel to us,*" said Magda. That night they were given potato soup and a slice of bread each. And then the girls on the night shift were marched off to work.

Magda and her sisters were lucky. They got the day shift that first round. It started at five in the morning—each shift was five to five. As they were heading out that first morning, though, Vera, the young one, was stopped. She would be sent to work in the fields instead, one of the guards told them.

Magda and Gabi turned, terrified. "No, please, she's with us—" Magda started, but one of the other prisoners, a girl from Holland who'd been there for a few months already, told them that it was all right, that it wasn't a trick. Vera actually would be sent to work in the fields. It would be better for her, the girl said. Outdoors.

The sisters were still scared, but "*Who wasn't scared then, all the time, anyway?*" and what could they do? Nothing, ever, no one could ever do anything except follow along and hope for one more day, or in this case, half a day, as life was divided in this Nazi slave labor camp. Which, despite being, like everywhere else on earth, better than Auschwitz, was not without its own torments.

First, there was the work itself, which in Magda's case

meant making gunpowder. This entailed either mixing the sul-
fur, charcoal, and potassium nitrate, or running the machines
that put it into the cartridges. Both left her covered with black
powder, and both required standing for the entire eleven-and-
a-half-hour shift.

Her ankles swelled the first day and never unswelled after
that, not even at night, which proved extremely painful. But on
the positive side, the Nazis gave them soap to wash off the black
powder, and showers, every day. Even oil to clean their eyes—
they couldn't make bullets for the Reich if they were blinded.
And then—"*I don't remember how it happened,*" Magda said—it
was discovered that Gabi had beautiful handwriting, and she
was taken into an office and set to recording. Long lines of
lovely numbers, the kind the Nazis liked. She was even permitted to sit by a window to work.

But the really good news was that Vera came back every
night. It was true, it hadn't been a trick—she had been put to
work in the fields, and given extra bread and soup with real
potatoes. Her hands were raw with blisters, but it was worth it
for the food. And the other girls told her that in a week or so the
bleeding would stop.

At that, Magda looked up. A week or so—that sounded
almost dangerous, almost like hubris. She hadn't thought long
term like that—a week—in a very long time. How long she didn't
know, wasn't even sure what month it was—still warm, but the
days getting shorter, so probably early September. Not that it
mattered. What mattered was that the girls slept together every
night and none of them were starving to death. Magda's lot was
the hardest, but she was the strongest, the oldest. It would have
been worse for her, much worse, had the roles been reversed.

They were still hungry—conversation among the prisoners centered almost exclusively on food. What they used to eat,

what they would eat when—if—they got out, how they would cook it, or better, much better, how their mothers would cook it. Some still had hope of that. Others like Aranka had seen their own mothers' smoke.

But Magda didn't talk about "after," tried not to even think about it. She was twenty-two—six years had slipped away since that day in Vienna, when the boys in uniform walked her to the station and sent their regards to the Sudetenland. She could still see them, still remembered the two *S*'s on their collar, but not normal *S*'s. They looked like lightning bolts—runes, someone told her. She'd liked the idea at first, the ancient echo.

They'd still smiled at each other that day—they were still boys and girls. She'd put on her traveling suit to go to the station, a very grown-up affair, tweed, from Herr Dratch's ladies' shop. Not the children's section of the shop anymore—she'd been thrilled about that. And now, here she stood, six years later, her feet a bad red, her ankles stiff and thick like their old cleaning woman's. And when any of the girls spoke of the future—marriage, boyfriends, study, jobs—it was all she could do to keep from crying, "Marry who? Study what?"

Because what was left of the future now, now that the best had been taken? Supposing they did live—and maybe they would. They were fed enough to live on, and there was no chimney in the background now. So maybe they would walk out of here one day—but to what? She had seen babies burning in Birkenau—actually seen them, seen men, fellow humans, throwing small children from a truck into a pit of fire. Live children. She had seen that with her own two eyes.

Every girl in here had seen that. The other night one of them came running in with the news that Hitler's generals had tried to kill him. The Russians were closing in. Soon the war would be over.

But over for whom? For her? She knew there was some chance that her parents were alive, since anything was possible. But she'd seen those lines of Hungarians walking by, sorted their clothes afterwards, the slim skirts, the close-fitting jackets, clothes of young women, slim women, younger and slimmer than her mother. If they'd been sent to the gas, then how not her mother? How?

Don't think, she told herself. Her new prayer. *Don't think, don't think, don't think, think, think*. She said it in French, in German, in Czech. Hungarian. Learned from the Dutch girl how to say it in Dutch. From the Greek girl how to say it in both Greek and a dialect from the islands. She had never "known winter," the Greek girl told them, till the Nazis took her, in her thin pajamas, in the night. The trip had taken ten days, maybe more. Most of her family had died on the train.

And her older sister, a beautiful girl who'd had dark hair down to her waist before Auschwitz, was caught taking a can of sardines over the wire from one of their brothers and beaten to death, right there, in front of them. But the boys were both boxers and strong, and she'd heard they were still alive when she left the camp.

"So you have to try," said someone. "There's a reason."

Finally, Magda could stand no more. "Why is there a reason? What is the reason?"

No answer.

"Is that what the lice in the bed say? When I crunch one with my finger, he says, 'There's a reason'?"

More silence. Then, "Maybe it's a her. Not a him."

Laughter. "A she-louse, is there such a thing?" "There has to be," and so on. That's right, Magda figured. What's gone is gone, and what's left are the she-lice.

Don't think. Ne pensez pas. It got colder. The fall holidays passed. No one knew the date, but they saw a crescent moon rising that seemed to speak to them, call back the old times. Day shift, night shift—day shift was better because you got fed before work. But night shift had its advantages, since more of the guards fell asleep then.

Every few weeks they were given clean underwear. People fell sick, but there wasn't wholesale typhus here, like at Auschwitz. Magda's sisters were both surviving. Winter set in. They worked separately, but slept together every night. There was a chance that they'd make it through till spring.

ONE NIGHT ONE OF THE GIRLS came rushing in from the night shift. She'd overheard a BBC broadcast in one of the guards' offices.

"The Russians have liberated Auschwitz!" she told them. She even knew the date—January 27th, 1945.

So it was happening, finally. Russia was proving fatal for Hitler. Just as her father had said, years ago, when it still would have mattered to them. When they were still a family, still normal people—uprooted people, true, dispossessed people whose worldly possessions had been taken from them, complete and entire. But still people, with mothers and fathers, cousins and aunts in the world, people who could still crowd around a rickety table somewhere, anywhere, even in a cellar if it came to that, and break bread with each other and find a reason to smile.

But where was that place now, if there was no one to sit with? The grandest palace on earth, with gold plate and no one?

Although maybe, if they were still alive, Hermann and her mother, or even—for she had to face this possibility—Hermann or her mother. Even if one of them was still alive, then maybe. If she could rest her head on one of their breasts and cry for a while. See the joy in her own mother's lovely eyes, upturned a bit, or her father's smile, the spring back in his step, when he caught sight of his three girls, walking toward him again one day.

Auschwitz liberated! And what were the Nazis now, the SS beasts, without their Auschwitz? Wasn't it, as much as their conquests, who they were? What their conquests were about, in the end? And if they no longer had Auschwitz? She knew there were other camps where they gassed people, but Auschwitz could gas twelve thousand a day. It was the height of their achievement, the jewel in their crown.

And without Auschwitz? The Nazis blew up some of the crematoria, the girls heard, before the Russians got there, to try to hide their crime—which meant they knew it was a crime? Magda actually lost her breath at that.

And the whole thing changed color for her then, in that one moment, slipped from the black of nightmare into the white glare of noon. Till then, Auschwitz had been another universe, governed by a new set of laws that had nothing to do with what used to be called human.

But if they were trying to hide what they'd done, if they too knew it was a crime, a shameful crime and not a whole new subset of the rules of nature—then it was over. Not a new world after all, but just history. Just something people would read about in Hitler's "thousand years," like the Mongol hordes, or Attila.

A week passed, a month, two months. There was still snow outside, but the days were starting to get longer. They could hear the planes all the time now, and the sounds of something in the distance. REINFORCEMENTS ARE ON THEIR WAY, WE WILL NEVER SURRENDER! said the German newspapers that were pasted up on the walls where the girls were working.

Which had scared them at first, but then one of them pointed out that if you take away the "never," what's left is "surrender."

Which was true. There'd never been talk of surrender, even "never surrender," before. Always of movement forward, more and more, for a thousand years.

One night about a week later, an alarm rang in their barracks and the guards swarmed in, hitting the bunks with their sticks.

"Everyone up! Out!"

It seemed too early. They had just gone to sleep. They stumbled to their feet, started to file out, as usual.

"No, this way."

"But—"

"Out, *schnell!*"

"But our shift—"

"No more shifts. Out the door, line up, five across."

Raw fear rose anew in every throat, Auschwitz fear—*Are they going to kill me, right now, today, after all this? My sisters? My friends? All of us?* There was no gas here, but there were armed men with guns pointing at them, outside in the snow. Were they to die here, before dawn, that morning?

It was still freezing outside, everything was still covered with snow. Some of them had grabbed coats, but most had little more than their stripes. Magda couldn't bear to think about the girl from Greece. She had told them once about the breezes in the islands, soft breezes, warm, zephyrs. "Like in the Greek myths," she'd said, and then started talking about the food. The pastries with pistachio nuts and honey.

"More Greek myths," they teased her.

But all the food they described to each other, in minute detail, seemed like myth to them here. French myth, Hungarian myth—her own mother's wild mushroom sauce, Hermann's plums. Aranka's grandmother's goulash, with carrots and beets. Peeled potatoes.

"*Eins, zwei—*" the guards were counting, but too fast, carelessly. Nothing had ever been careless with them before. Word was whispered through the ranks—the Russians were a day away. The Nazis were running.

"Quick, march, fast!" There was no soup that morning. The gates around the factory were opened, and the girls were ordered out. Someone fell in the snow. A guard shot her.

"*And we were back to square one,*" said Magda.

THE PINK
TULIP

15

No one knew to call it a death march. No one knew anything, not even the men with the guns. When someone fell in the snow, they shot them—that much, at least, was standard Nazi procedure. But where were they going? This not even the guards seemed to know.

Magda's group was marched first north, and then west, through the snow. Somehow, the girls got hold of burlap bags, which they tied around their shoulders as blankets. There was a little bit of bread the first night, and melted snow for soup. Nothing else. The next day more of them dropped and were shot. Sometimes the other girls were allowed to cover the bodies with snow. Mostly they were forced to keep marching, right over them, not even permitted to push them to the side.

But Magda and her sisters managed to keep walking, and Aranka too, and the Greek girl. The lovely Dutch girl dropped then, already dead even before they shot her, a smile on her face. And there she lay, her miserable striped shirt up above her waist, half-naked in the snow, smiling. *She's beautiful*, Magda realized then. It was the first time she'd ever seen her smile.

Don't think, she told herself. In Dutch, for the girl. *Niet denken*.

When they stopped in the woods by the side of the road
to get their crust of bread, they could hear the sound of guns,
and the rumble of tanks in the distance. The planes came overhead in waves. One of the planes dropped packets, from the Red
Cross. The girls were starving. They ran to get them.

"Stop! *Verboten!*" shouted the guards. Forbidden. They shot
the girls who picked them up.

So the guards were still Nazis, though without quite the
same gleam of perfect faith in their eyes. Still willing to shoot
starving girls who tried to pick up food dropped by their friends
from the sky; but knowing, even as they shot them, that it was
those girls who had friends in the sky, not them. In their own
sky, by the way. What used to be their own sky, these Nazis.

AFTER A FEW DAYS OF MARCHING, they saw a sign on the road—
BRANDENBURG. So Germany. The northeast, not too far from
Potsdam, or even Berlin. Magda had learned the German states
in her geography classes. She used to think the name Brandenburg was beautiful. Bach's Brandenburg Concertos, the Brandenburg Gates.

Now nothing German would ever be beautiful again. They
walked along the road—maybe toward Berlin? They hadn't had
anything to eat in two days. There were thousands of them,
thronging the road, the guards on the sides, but no longer
shooting the girls who fell. Just leaving them to die in the snow.

They came to a fence, barbed wire. "My God, a camp," the
girls whispered through the lines. RAVENSBRÜCK, said the sign.
There were the horrible chimneys, but they were cold—no black
smoke, no red fire.

It was a women's camp, someone said, women and children.
They didn't have gas here, that wasn't how they killed people.

They starved them to death—you could see some of the striped skeletons, moving in that slowed-down way across the barbed wire. Or else worked them till they dropped, in the Siemens factory, right next door.

But that was over here as well. The SS commander who met them at the gates told their commander that he was evacuating the camp. The Russians were coming, and quickly, he'd heard. His orders had been to kill all the witnesses, but he didn't have enough fuel to burn the bodies in pits. He'd thought of just shooting them, but if he left them lying there, that too would tell its own tale, hence his dilemma. He was troubled, confounded, not exactly sure what to do next. Maybe kill them along the way? But wouldn't that too leave a trail for the Russians to follow, like Hansel and Gretel's, through the woods?

Although he was thinking to march west, into Mecklenburg. Maybe the Russians wouldn't get that far.

MAYBE. MAGDA'S GROUP was ordered into the camp, to help with "packing up the place," as she put it. A day or so later, the women still able to walk, about twenty thousand all told, were marched out of Ravensbrück. The four thousand women and children unable to walk were left behind. Seven thousand, mostly French, had been turned over to the Swedish Red Cross the week before.

Which news was another reordering of the universe. The Swedish Red Cross—actually there, inside one of the Nazis' sacred places, hitherto sealed shut from the outside world, taking girls out—incredible. They'd marked the back of their jackets with big white *X*'s, the girls who'd been selected. Or not selected, if you were using the Nazis' lingo.

But maybe the Nazis' lingo didn't apply anymore. "*We weren't sure of exact dates,*" said Magda. "*We still knew absolutely nothing of the outside world.*" But it had to be March, or even April. The snows were melting, which made water harder to find. But there were the first shoots of grass, and the girls ate that, as they were given no more bread. They could hear the sounds of war, coming closer. Bombs were falling, sometimes around them— bombs that could kill them too, but their bombs nonetheless.

They would jump into ditches, or take cover in the woods. Some of the girls started slipping away then. "Shoot them!" the commanders shouted, and the guards did at first, but then the girls noticed that the guards seemed to be melting away as well. "Should we run?" everyone was asking each other, but the real question was where?

They were in Germany, bald girls in stripes. It wasn't as if residents would take them for errant milkmaids. But how much did the *Volk* here hate them? Would a farmer or goatherd shoot them on sight? Go for them with his plowshare or pruning hook?

Still, the girls who stayed on the march were dropping dead all around them, and if they did run, they might be able to make their way to the Russians, who might feed them. The next day, the commander counted off a hundred girls closest to him and ordered them to come back to his wagon. He was going to dis- tribute bread, he told them.

No one could remember the last bread. But as soon as those girls filed back to the wagon, the commander ordered the guards to open fire.

They all stood, horrified. But instead of the thunder of gun- fire, there was a great silence, and some of the girls broke then and ran for the woods.

"Shoot them!" the commander shouted.

More silence.

The rest of the girls started to run.

"Shoot," the commander shouted to the guards, "or I'll kill you!" He fired a few rounds from his pistol and hit one of the fleeing girls.

But still nothing from the guards. They were starting to look around, with strange, almost startled looks on their faces, like men waking up from a long dream. They stood staring at the girls, as if they weren't sure who they were.

"Shoot!" the commander was screaming now.

The guards turned to him, as if not comprehending. Then one of them raised his gun and fired into the air.

The commander pointed his gun at him but didn't shoot. Magda and her sisters watched, not even breathing. One after another, the guards raised their rifles and shot into the air, then started running, in twos and threes, toward the woods, ripping off their SS badges and flinging them behind them as they went.

"Let's go," whispered Aranka to Magda. She and her two sisters, along with Aranka and the Greek girl and a few others, turned and fled into the woods.

No one knows how many people died on these marches. The usual statistic is one in four, but this doesn't count the large number of people killed in great haste—shot and left in piles— in the camps before the marches started, or whole groups finished off once there was nowhere else for the Nazis to run. There was one group from Auschwitz, six thousand or so, who survived a march all the way to Danzig and were then forced into the Baltic Sea and shot.

Which could have happened to Magda and her sisters, but didn't. That first day, after they'd fled the march, they hid in an outdoor "*washroom*," the first building they stumbled upon. The German countryside was populated, filled with farmsteads. That night, they found a barn, and slipped in and hid in the hay. There were pigs there, and, miracle of miracles, slops. Spoiled milk and moldy bread, potato peels, the best food they'd had since they'd left Gleiwitz. And the best sleep too, despite the mice. The next day, they lay low—they could hear the sounds of war coming closer, planes and tanks in the distance, but they weren't sure whose.

But then they started seeing the hammers and sickles on the tanks rumbling down the road, followed by soldiers with red flags on their jackets, who swarmed over the farms and into the farmhouses. They heard shots and screams, but German screams now.

"Should we turn ourselves over to them?" the girls wondered.

But better to stay hidden, they decided. One of them slipped down and milked the cow. They drank that, and as soon as night fell, moved on.

They traveled on the smallest of roads, under cover of a darkness darker than anything they'd ever seen before. The electricity was out here, and once the moon set, the only light they saw was an occasional candle in a farmhouse window. They somehow managed to make their way, though, following roads too narrow for tanks, too rough for SS motorcycles, lest there still be checkpoints. They slipped into root cellars and barns, stole food, and "*used the outdoor washrooms.*"

Before dawn, they would choose a barn and sneak in, eat whatever the pigs were eating, and then hide in the hay to sleep.

Every day there were more Russians, running over the land. "*But we were hiding from them too,*" said Magda. "*They were like wild animals unloosed—it was unbelievable, how primitive, how wild.*"

And crazy for jewelry, with ten, twelve watches on each arm." Liberators, theoretically, but the girls were almost as frightened of them as of the Germans.

Not quite, though. They weren't sure exactly where to go, but home was east, and they headed that way. They sneaked through the countryside, coming out of the forest only at dark, darting from tree to tree. There was nothing yet coming up in the gardens, but there were root cellars with preserves and rotting potatoes. These they ate raw, "*a banquet,*" said Magda.

They didn't know where they were, or even what day it was. The countryside seemed to be getting richer. One evening, just at dusk, they caught sight of a girl going into a farmhouse. She had long blond braids and was wearing a wool sweater, pleated skirt, and kneesocks. The girls watched, stunned at the sight of her. Shocked that such a creature could still exist.

Magda and Aranka followed her to the house and knocked on the door. She opened it, and they were faced with each other.

Magda and Aranka were probably about the same age as the German there in the doorway, but weighing about forty kilos, and with their stubble of hair and filthy stripes, they must have looked less like girls than the kind of trolls who lurked under bridges, waiting to eat nice German girls in snowflake sweaters, should they be caught out after dark.

Magda felt the anger rising. She looked inside. The kitchen behind the girl was beautiful and clean. There was a pink tulip, she told Gabi afterwards, in a vase on the table.

Magda wanted to hit her, kick her, plump and pink with kneesocks and tulips, but instead half whispered, "I had a sweater like that."

"What?" said the German girl.

Magda took a breath. "Please give us some food."

"We don't have any," the girl said, and moved to close the door.

Aranka put her foot in the door. There was a bowl on the floor with some scraps.

"Will you give us that?"

"The dog's food?" asked the girl, incredulous. She shrugged—these two trolls were beneath contempt.

And Magda and Aranka ate the girl's dog food. They were too hungry not to eat it, Magda told Gabi.

But afterwards, she didn't look down. "Give our regards to our friends the Russians when they get here," she said as they were leaving.

THAT NIGHT, MAGDA GOT VERY SICK. They'd found a barn and eaten more raw potatoes and the few weeds they could find in the yard. Magda couldn't travel the next morning, from the pain in her right side—"Afterwards, I found out it was a gallstone attack." When the farmer came in that morning, he heard her moans.

He climbed up in the hayloft, looked at the girls, then went away, and came back with a pot of soup for them.

They hesitated—"Don't be afraid, I won't poison you," he said. The war there was over, he told them. His two sons had been killed in the east. The young one had been only seventeen. There had been that moment, the farmer admitted, when he'd thought about joining the party, because it was so bad after the other war, the last one, and he was thinking of Germany's destiny, but now—"Over. Lost"—he looked around, gestured with his hand. "Everything."

He said he himself had never hated anyone.

They asked him where they were.

Outside of the town of Prenzlau, in eastern Germany, about fifty-five kilometers from Ravensbrück, as the crow flew. But how far they'd wandered between the two, who knew?

No one spoke for a while. Then, finally, someone thought to ask him the date.

"The first of May," he told them.

A YEAR TO THE DAY since Magda and her sisters had been taken. But only a year? Magda felt the pain in her side subsiding. The soup was good. Potato soup, with real potatoes, each bowl had pieces of good potatoes, cooked, and some milk, some bread. Good bread. Butter and gooseberry jam.

The first of May 1945. The farmer's wife came out with some cheese and gasped when she saw them. Tears started down her cheeks.

Yes, cry now, Magda was thinking, but didn't she know? She knew! Where did she think all those shoes were coming from, year after year? All those baby carriages?

Still, she'd lost her sons—unless the man was lying. Who knew? Who cared? Were these people saints because they didn't pick up their hoes and beat to death these girls whom their country had turned into fair game for them for the last ten years?

It was "over," said the farmer, but over for whom? wondered Magda. Were her parents still alive?

She suddenly felt much better and realized she had to get home. If they were alive, that's where they'd be. Her mother! Her father! Maybe they were still alive.

"Are the trains running to Czechoslovakia?" she asked the farmer.

Not from there, he said, but maybe from Berlin. It was about 120 kilometers to the southwest.

———

THEY SLEPT THAT DAY, and started out the next night. They took shelter in another barn the next dawn, where they found an SS uniform, buried deep in the hay. There were two horses in the barn as well, and a cart. As soon as it got dark enough, the girls managed to hitch the horses to the cart, and set off along the road to Berlin.

It seemed like a dream to them afterwards. What Magda remembered best was feeling almost giddy with amazement—first that they'd gotten away with the horses, and then at the enormity of the theft. Two horses and cart—what would their father say to that? His well-brought-up daughters—horse thieves!

They started laughing a bit at that, laughing and then stopping. A laugh and then an abrupt stop. They couldn't know then that that's how it would be, for the rest of their lives. But that morning, it wasn't that, it was just the first time they'd felt close to free, or close to safe, in six long years. Seven girls alone on a road filled with refugees, desperados, and foreign soldiers, riding in a stolen cart pulled by stolen horses—and still safer than at any time since the Nazis had marched into their lives.

Which was not to say safe. They had discovered, though, that their stripes and shaved heads had, as part of the overall miracle that seemed to be taking place around them, turned into a sort of safe conduct for them through the Russians. Those wild men had been let loose on the general population, and every one of them was there with not only a national but a personal grudge to avenge. But when they saw the girls' stripes, they wrote out passes, certifying them as "victims of National Socialism," worthy of "special consideration." When they saw the numbers on their arms, they cried and gave them bread.

Fresh bread, with salt, and vodka, which the girls drank, one and all, even little Vera. Not so little anymore, though—she'd turned sixteen in Gleiwitz. Still, she was so thin she looked like a ten-year-old. They all did—sick ten-year-olds, with their boyish heads, their great big eyes in thin little faces. They hadn't had their periods the whole time they'd been in the camps.

Which was just as well, considering. No underwear, no supplies—but *don't think*. Just get to Berlin, and then home.

Not that it would be home—unless her parents were there. But there was a chance. The whole thing was over. Not just the war. Everything, as the farmer had said. Her parents were strong and smart. Her mother was beautiful. Maybe she'd been put to work in an office. Her father could have been out in the fields, or even sorting clothes.

Something. Even the Nazis wouldn't have wasted his talents. Even they would have seen how strong he was, how capable. How noble and good, both of them.

They couldn't have just killed them, not even the Nazis. The closer they got to Berlin, the better a chance it seemed. Her parents had to be alive. They were probably traveling along a road right now, like this one, somewhere. Who knew but that they might even come upon them in Berlin?

"Imagine that!" Magda said to Gabi. Imagine us driving around a corner, and there they are.

They laughed, then stopped. They had seen the Hungarian transports. Watched from across the camp as the long lines trailed into the woods. Her mother was forty-two, her father forty-eight. Old to be selected for work.

But it could have happened. They could have come on a day when they needed workers. There were a few days like that. They could have gotten through.

Though when she thought of the SS on the ramp, with their

dogs and their whips, their cruel little games—"So sorry about the conditions on the train"—her heart froze. But "Either in Berlin or back home," she told her sisters. The news was all good now, and better every day. Germany had surrendered. Hitler had shot himself in the head.

16

THE OUTSKIRTS OF BERLIN were wrecked and deserted when they drove through. They passed houses with their fronts sheared off by the bombs, and the back halves still standing with their furnishings, like the dollhouse Hermann had brought them years ago from Prague.

They stopped to try to find food at a big house that stood relatively intact but deserted, the front door open wide. They walked in—the Russians had been there. The grand piano was turned over and the silver strewn all across the floor. There was a small silver tray, like one they'd had at home. This Magda took for their mother.

They drove on, into the city, under the Russian banners hanging on the gates: LONG LIVE THE SOVIET ARMIES THAT PLANTED THEIR VICTORY STANDARDS IN BERLIN! They made their way in silence through the rubble-filled streets, past the bombed-out apartments and overturned tanks with SS license plates. The streets were deserted except for the very old and very young, out scavenging for firewood or standing in long lines at the pumps for water. The Russians seemed to be camped in whatever apartments were still standing, with makeshift stables and little farmyards in the squares.

Whatever reserves of strength and even ecstasy that had gotten the girls that far gave out on those streets. Magda couldn't quite remember what came next—if they slept in one of the deserted houses, or just lay in the cart. It started to rain— she realized how lucky they'd been with the weather till then. Anyway, soon after they arrived, someone, maybe the Russians, took them to the Belgians, *"who saved our lives."*

There were four thousand Belgian soldiers in Berlin, *"the first truly decent people we met,"* said Magda. When they saw the girls, they rushed them straight to a hospital they'd set up in one of the big houses still standing, *"and there they cooked for us and fed us like starving children. And slowly, they brought us back to health."*

MAGDA DOESN'T GIVE DATES. It's hard to know how long they stayed there. She mentions the Belgians leaving—*"We were so sad when they left, we were all waving."* Which is another thing the Belgians did for these girls from the death camps—got them to wave. No small feat, considering.

By then the girls were well enough to travel. The trains had started running again, jammed with refugees trying to get home. There was no fare system in place yet, and *"people were climbing in through the windows,"* said Magda, but somehow she and her sisters managed to get onto a train.

It was about 900 kilometers from Berlin to their home-town of Trebišov. Magda doesn't mention their route—probably south to Prague and then east to Budapest, down to Bratislava, and then east again to the town of Košice, where the train still stops, about fifty kilometers from Trebišov. How they got the rest of the way, who knows? Bus, cart, taxi—she doesn't mention money, either. Never says how or even if they paid for food along the way.

Still, there came that moment, sometime in the late summer, or maybe the fall of 1945, when the three girls found themselves back in the place they had once called home, walking down the street where they used to live, their hearts pounding. There was a small chance, had to be, just one in a million, or in this case, 450,000, but that was all they needed—just that one chance that when they got to the house where they knew every brick, the door would be opened by someone they loved.

THOUGH THEY PROBABLY would have known right away, before they knocked, as soon as they saw the house. Something would have told them—the wrong windows open or shut tight; curtains drawn on the sunroom. Bricks out of place on the front walk. And in truth, they probably would have heard something by then, either among the displaced persons in Berlin or even on the train. Would have met someone who'd given them their own version of "the worst of all news."

Because that's how it mostly happened, people say. Not always the worst news, though; sometimes it was the best. Those who made it through mostly found each other by word of mouth. Someone on a train had seen someone else, who could tell them that their brother was living with a cousin in Debrecen, or their aunt was back at her house in Munkács. One girl on the train with Magda met an acquaintance who told her that her mother was waiting for her in the next village.

"Her mother!" Everyone on the train started to cry.

So the girls must have known that if Hermann or their mother had come home, they probably would have heard something by then. Still, there was the chance that no one had seen them yet, or even that one of them was on the way back, right then, and that they'd meet on the street. At the station. In the house.

But when they held their breaths and knocked, the door was opened not by one of their parents, but by the man who'd been given the house by the Nazis. One of the bystanders, for whom 1942 had been a very good year.

He had in his hand what passed for a newspaper those days, a Russian broadsheet that combined a version of the news with the latest requirements of martial law—information on where to register for ration cards, obligatory work, and so on. He opened the door a crack.

Behind him the girls could see their parents' paintings still on the wall, and their Persian rugs on the floor, where they'd left them.

They couldn't speak.

He stared at them a moment and then turned white. "How come you're still alive?" he blurted. "We heard you were all dead!"

Of course he was right in the aggregate. They were all dead, statistically. But the exceptions who proved the rule now had the law on their side.

Which meant that the house belonged to the girls again. Magda left and came back with two Russian soldiers to inform the man of that. They would stand by, the soldiers said, while he and his wife packed, quickly. After which, their bags would be inspected. If they tried to steal anything from the house, they would be sent to Siberia.

And, that accomplished, the Russians drove the three girls out to pay a visit to Goodmann.

When Goodmann's wife opened the door and saw them, she fainted.

The girls stepped around her—into Goodmann's version of their parents' dining room, "*set up exactly like it had been.*" Their table, their chairs, the needlepoints of fruit and pheasants made by their mother in her own fine hand. Even the chest with their linens, and the sideboard with their crystal and china—the soldiers loaded it all onto the truck, "right then, before they could hide it."

Magda walked back into the closed dark room where their nightmare had first taken form. The giant picture of Hitler was gone. Goodmann now had a small red Russian flag flying, cut from one of his old Nazi banners. You could still see that bit of the white on the edge, from where the swastika had been.

Goodmann himself came running. "See how we kept everything for you! Just like you left it—we've been taking care of it for you. We never lost hope!" And so on.

Only this time, the desperate worry was in his eyes, not theirs. The Russians immediately stripped Goodmann's watch from his arm, he being an ethnic German, part of the *Volks-* whatever it was they'd called themselves. The ones who'd run to inherit the earth with the Nazis, and now had the Russian army in their living rooms.

"Where's your Nazi pin?" Magda asked him, but in Czech, so as not to have to watch the Russians beat him right there.

A FEW DAYS LATER, Goodmann came by to see her, hat in hand. He begged her to testify in his defense. He had been denounced as a Nazi and threatened with expulsion—would she tell the court how he'd hidden them? How he'd tried to help?

Which was true—he had helped. For an extortionate amount of money from her father, but still, he'd taken a risk, he and his wife, just the same. Which is what she said in court—though she refused to go further, to make a plea for him. When she looked across the courtroom at him that morning, she could still picture him in his Nazi uniform, "strutting like a peacock." And the surviving members of the community told her that Goodmann had been a key player in the transports, naming names, checking lists—fine. Let him be expelled, let his beloved Germany take him back, along with the rest of those turncoats, who were being pushed, destitute, out of Central Europe now.

Which was fair enough, Magda figured. They were "German, not Czech," they'd all shouted when Hitler marched into what they called the Sudetenland. Now let them be Germans.

For they have sown the wind, and they shall reap the whirl-wind. People used to quote that at Birkenau. Fine. Let Goodmann reap.

LET THEM ALL REAP. But what about her? What about her father and her mother? Had they sown the wind? She took a taxi out one day with her sisters to Hermann's plum trees, outside of town. It was fall. There were a few stragglers out there, picking the plums, but no real harvest. Half the trees had fallen, anyway, or been chopped down. Much of the fruit lay rotting on the ground.

She picked up one of her father's plums but couldn't eat it. Her parents weren't coming back. She knew it now, had even heard the details. They'd been taken with the transport from the border town of Sátoraljaújhely, not far from home. She remembered the town—a nice place before the war, famous for its friendliness, its good schools. But all that had changed as the

Nazi winds had blown through the place, even in the early forties, and by the time her parents had fled there, from the Hungarian prison, in 1944, everyone they knew had been pushed
into a few blocks, and were starving and filthy. "Doctors and
lawyers, teachers and farmers, patrons of the arts, Hungarian
patriots," a young man told them.

The girls knew that. Knew who was there—that is, everyone.
It didn't matter that they'd given their sons in the last war and
left their whole fortunes to found schools for the local children.
Had family roots there going back to the 1500s, and Hungarian
names, Hungarian faces. They were still shoved into the boxcars that left on the night of the twenty-eighth of May, 1944, and
that was the end of them in that town. Two trainloads, and they
were gone forever.

The trains had stopped in Birkenau the next day, the young
man went on, and there was no selection, no workers saved.
The transport from Sátoraljaújhely with Hermann and his
wife, like all the others coming in from Hungary that summer,
was marched straight from the train tracks to the gas that day.
The girls probably saw them in the distance, disappearing into
the woods.

The three sisters moved back into their house, "theirs" again
officially, though to no avail. Without their parents, it was a
dark, dim place. They wandered through the silent rooms, "trying." They put their mother's sheets back on their beds, they sat
for dinner around the dining room table. They ate, they drank,
they kept the holidays, a cold exercise. God might still be God,
they neither knew nor cared anymore, but as for this world,
"*There was no warmth, no one left.*"

One day, before the snows, Magda and her sisters took shovels out to the plum trees and dug up the places where they'd helped Hermann bury the last of the gold, in glass jars. Magda thought she remembered the spots, remembered pacing it all off with Hermann, him showing her just how to find everything again, "when we come back." But despite digging all day, in the right spots and nearby, allowing for some shifting what with the frost and the rain, the sun, the roots of the nearby trees, they never found anything, or even a trace of anything, not a shard of glass, or even a cast-off lid.

Someone must have gotten there first—maybe several people, maybe everyone in town. *People would have guessed that those leaving would be burying things*," said Magda. Maybe they'd come digging before the family had even left town.

17

IT WAS VERY COLD, that winter of 1946. The Russians had fought for every inch of this part of Europe, and they weren't leaving. Hermann's dream of a Czech democracy had gone up in the same smoke as his friends and family, along with his quest for real citizenship, for true belonging in the land that he'd loved. The Russians incorporated the eastern part of the country, the state of Ruthenia, directly into the USSR, and a few years later put the rest of Czechoslovakia under Communist rule. In her recording, Magda didn't mention whether they got the farm back. Even if they had, this was the eve of the era of collectivization. Private ownership would soon be a thing of the past. There was no further talk of her father's grain business.

Nor does she say how she and her sisters lived that first winter. *"It took a big courage to come back to life,"* was how she put it. A young woman she knew who'd made it back tried to hang herself, but someone had caught her in time.

"Thank God!" Magda hugged her.

The woman shrugged. "Maybe, but it seems to me that I'm not alive anyway." She lit a cigarette butt, hand trembling. "Can you come out of there alive?" she asked.

Magda didn't know. "You have to try."

Yes, she tried, said the woman, but she couldn't stop thinking about "back there." The day she tried to hang herself, she'd woken from a dream that was more a memory, about one morning when they were woken for roll call—"Nazi morning, still pitch black"—and she scrambled down from her bunk and realized that her sister wasn't moving. "I called her name, but I knew she wouldn't answer. Even without touching her, I knew that she was dead.

"And I fought to live, to come back, so that all those deaths wouldn't have been in vain, but it seems to me now that they were in vain anyway.

"What did they die for? So that I, you, a few others might return?" Another butt from the overflowing ashtray.

Magda looked out the window. When she was recovering in Berlin, she'd heard that workmen were being paid with bags of old butts. It was all they had.

Her friend went on. "We came back with that hard kernel that we all forged, at the core of our hearts, to prevent our destruction, preserve our identities, keep our former beings—"

Magda nodded.

"—but all that, that superhuman will, only worked there, in the camps." Here, she said, it just "melted, dissolved, and we're left with nothing."

The butts had all been smoked, once, twice, already. Still she sifted till she found one she could relight.

"They were braver than I was, smarter than I was, stronger even."

Magda nodded. She knew. Survival was less a matter of heroic triumph than of simple chance. It occurred to her that that somehow made it harder, for some reason.

"I do what one does in life," her friend continued, "I eat,

sleep, walk around, but I know very well that this isn't life, because I know the difference between before and after."

Yes, that was true, they all knew the difference. Magda looked down at the shoes on her feet—real shoes, nothing like Auschwitz, but nothing like the ones her mother had bought her in Vienna, either. She'd never have shoes like those again.

"I know I should keep going, in memory of her, of all of them." The young woman got to her feet. She was done talking. "But the truth is I died in Auschwitz, too, only no one knows it."

"TRY," SAID MAGDA, but she didn't bother with reasons, because all the reasons were just variations on the same lie, and the truth was that she didn't know why, and no one else did either. Why should they keep living? Out of spite? Vengeance? To affirm the ultimate beauty and light of the universe, the goodness of God?

Another woman she met who'd just had a baby confessed that even at the birth, she'd felt no joy. Right then, when her child was born, and they were all celebrating and congratulating her, a scene had flashed before her eyes, from the infirmary at Auschwitz where she'd been forced to work. A baby was born there, to one of the prisoners, and an SS man grabbed it and held it under a running faucet and drowned it.

"Here you go, little Moses, down the river," he'd laughed.

"I know I should be happy now," the woman told Magda, "but I'm like stone inside."

"TRY," REPEATED MAGDA, and she herself did try, she and her sisters. They heard of a cousin who'd made it back to a village nearby. "Before the war, we barely knew her, but now she became a close relative." The girls went to visit her often that first fall, and even married men she found for them. Two young men who had fought in the Resistance, one with the Czechs, the other with the Poles. They were both strong, healthy, and unmarried. Neither of them had been in the camps.

Perfect, the cousin told the girls, even before she'd met them. The point now was to marry; it almost didn't matter who. The cousin told them that she'd been at one wedding, in a displaced persons camp after Auschwitz, where just before the ceremony a boy had smiled across the room at a girl and asked her if she'd like to "take advantage" of the ceremony and get married too?

He had no one left in his whole family, and neither did she. She was twenty. He was nineteen. They were both tall and nice looking.

"Yes?" he asked her.

"Why not?" she'd answered.

And for some reason, said the cousin, that had made everybody happy. People started clapping and singing, people she'd never seen smile till then. "It was as if, suddenly, we saw a way that we could live."

And when it came to the vows, everyone laughed again since it turned out they didn't even know each other's names.

But they liked them—"Beautiful!" they'd each cried as the other spoke them.

"What were their names?" asked Vera, the young one. Seventeen, but with the mind of a child, Magda was coming to see. As if she'd been stopped right where they'd taken her.

But how could it have been any different? Given that absolutely toxic mixture of what she'd seen, what she'd lived through?

"What does it matter?" Magda said to her shortly.

But the cousin had smiled and said their names were Margot and Peter.

"Beautiful!" Vera agreed.

Yes, and the two young men for Magda and Gabi had beautiful names too, she said. "Eugene and Alex." One could marry one, and one the other. The girls could sort that part out themselves.

WHICH THEY MUST HAVE, since Magda married Eugene that January 1946. "*There was a terrible blizzard,*" she laughs on the tape, "*but I wanted to be married outside.*" She doesn't say why. Someone loaned her a white fur coat, and two children who'd been born in hiding served as flower girls.

And then Gabi married Alex, and the two couples lingered a while longer in the town. The last people were still straggling back from the east. The girls accepted the fact that their parents had been killed, they'd heard it from several sources, but between themselves and in whispers, they agreed it wasn't entirely definitive, it couldn't be. Since the people who told them hadn't been there, not right there, not in the gas.

Or else how would they have lived to tell the tale? And even if they'd been on the same transport and thought they knew, they didn't know, not entirely, not beyond a shadow of doubt. They hadn't walked into those fatal woods with Hermann and their mother, weren't shoved into that concrete chamber, weren't inside when the door was bolted shut and the screaming started, and the people began climbing over each other to get to the last of the air.

The Nazis.

But the point was that no one who'd lived to talk about it

afterwards had actually seen her parents go through that door, Magda repeated to Gabi.

Maybe they'd been marched to the east somehow, and then taken ill. Maybe one of them was still lying in some far Polish hospital, too weak to walk, but alive. Amnesiac even. There was a chance, and a chance, too, that they'd still come home—who could say there wasn't?

Though on the twenty-eighth of May that first year, the day the transports from Sátoraljaújhely had left for Auschwitz, the girls lit candles. That didn't mean their parents were necessarily dead, they told each other. Just that their daughters were remembering.

And the same thing the next year as well.

But the year after that, Gabi's husband Alex and his brothers bought a farm in Canada. Both she and Magda had babies by then. Even Vera had gotten married. It was time to move on.

They began a new life in the New World, far from the death camps, but far from everything else as well. The rich, cultured parents who had loved them, the smiling aunts and uncles with their lively children, reduced to a few crumpled old photos that had fallen behind a bookcase, and that they'd been lucky to find in their house before they left. The girls in pleated skirts and hats with streamers, the boys in sailor suits—Magda kept them out at first, but they were hard to make sense of in a cramped Toronto apartment, and one day she put them in a drawer.

"IT TOOK A BIG COURAGE *to come back to life*"—when Magda said that to the camera, she was an old woman with nine grandchildren. Her son had become a doctor. He lived in a big house on Long Island, outside of New York.

He'd made his own way back to a life his grandfather would

have recognized. His children grew up as Magda had, nice girls, rich girls, studying music and art.

Magda herself, however, had said good-bye to all that. Not that she and her husband hadn't done well, considering. Their life in America, though, had gone very much as Hermann had foreseen when he'd hesitated so fatally on that brink. She and her husband had arrived penniless, to a land where plum trees meant little, and music studies in Vienna even less. English had proved a demonic language. The *v*'s and *w*'s never did come out right.

"He would have suffered here," Magda once blurted out, in the middle of dinner. She didn't say who, but her husband had turned the cold eye she'd come to know by then.

"So it was better there? In the gas?"

No, no, she said quickly. It wasn't better in the gas.

She made friends in Canada, most of them outsiders like herself, faces still turned east to a place that would, on the other hand, never be far enough away. Some of them took pills, or shot themselves in despair. One friend took a train to New York and jumped from a tall building. A woman whose husband had done well, and just bought her a big house outside the city.

But "I keep dreaming—" the woman wrote, and then her note broke off. Any one of them could have finished it for her.

But Magda didn't have time to dream. She and her husband both had to work hard to get started, first in factories, and then Magda learned hairdressing, and Eugene did something in "wholesale jewelry," and they ended up owning a dry cleaning plant. By the end, they had a nice apartment in Toronto, and went to Florida in the winter. It had, one might say, all worked out.

"*Thank you, Magda,*" the interviewer was saying, and then the screen went blank.

CONSIE GOT TO HER FEET, went over, fiddled, played it back. Had the disc skipped the end, cut off early? Wasn't there a bit more, when Magda would mention that even though the settled story was that her father had been sent to the gas on May 28th or 29th, with a specific Hungarian transport, there was a chance, a rumor, that he had escaped? Wouldn't she just want to float that, as a sort of antidote, up against all the rest of it? As something that might actually matter to her, some true consolation, as opposed to, say, the Florida winters?

Consie listened again—nothing. No word of Hermann, nothing about any escape. And then it struck her so hard it took her breath away, one more tragedy to add to the heap. Magda—of course, of course!—had never read Consie's uncle's letter. Never heard mention of her father's escape.

"FOR NOTHING IS RESOLVED, NOTHING IS SETTLED . . ."

Jean Améry

18

"DEAR"—HAD CONSIE PUT "DR." OR "MR."? She didn't remember. There had been no title listed before his name in the directory. But surely doctor? To the curator of an archive, even in Southern California, no?

Whatever she wrote got a quick and courteous reply. "Wed.?" she'd asked, abbreviating, lest he be impatient with email, and "Wed." it was, along with the directions that were taking her east on the 10 that morning, away from the money of Malibu, Santa Monica, Beverly Hills, past the delis to the north on Fairfax, the crumbling clapboards on Crenshaw, all the little houses, a few still with sheep and chickens, on all the old streets north and south of Vermont, of Western, of Normandie, which someone out here thought to spell in Olde French, and then off at Hoover.

Named for the president, she trusted, not the vacuum, unless the vacuum people had donated some giant sports center on the street? Who knew? And, thinking twice, why not a street for the man who'd invented such a blessed machine, rather than the one who'd stood in spats as the stock market crashed around him?

The traffic was stopped long before any of that anyway,

around the San Diego Freeway, a virtual parking lot, the worst
in town. Lucky for her she hadn't joined the flight to those
northern suburbs where the lower middle, once happy in rent-
als in West LA, had taken the bait for "home ownership" in the
last ten years. They'd bought all the spec houses the developers
had thrown up out there near Magic Mountain (an amusement
park, not a book in this neck of the woods), and now spent two
hours on a good day commuting back in to a job that no longer
paid the mortgage.

Poor them. Anyway, the point was her lane was moving.
And there was another point too—because since the thing had
been left, in a way, with her, she had decided to take it a bit further. Rather than let go of that one fleeting glimpse of a man in
stripes on the run through the Nazis' woods.

Because it had been with a growing sense of joy that, as she
checked all the sources of the dead, she'd found that Hermann's
name didn't come up anywhere. Not in the Auschwitz ledgers,
not in Washington, not in Jerusalem, though the list-makers
stressed the incompleteness of it all. Many names apparently
weren't entered in the camp records, particularly those from
the Hungarian transports, who were sent straight to the gas
toward the end, when the Nazis had stopped counting.

Which would have been Hermann if, instead of escaping, he
had been killed that May, upon arrival.

But against the logic of all that, the near-perfect percentages in the math of extermination that spring, there, holding it
all off, stood one line in an old letter.

"He was at Auswetz Concentration Camp with them," according
to those two mythic girls, "Klara and Alice," who'd come into
their lives once, on paper, and never been heard from again.
Had disappeared themselves into the mystery of Communist
Europe.

But before that, they were two girls in blue who claimed to have seen Hermann in Auschwitz. Girls who knew him—he was their mother's brother. Girls who went on to state categorically that "*They do know that he escaped.*"

"Know," they'd said. Not heard. Know. A beautiful word, given the context, glittering like a jewel in all that ash. Academic, granted, since Hermann never came back. But still, a picture she was reluctant to turn away from. One man, smart and brave, pausing to gauge the sun or listening for footsteps. Sleeping under leaves, or whispering abstract thanks beside some half-choked stream. Scared to death, or maybe less scared than he'd been in the death camp. Maybe no longer afraid at all, beyond fear. Defying it all without a gun in his hand. Defeating the Third Reich with every step he took, even if he didn't take many.

Hard to let slip back away with the rest of it, especially when, after having done a bit of preliminary research, she found that it might be true. "*Escape was extremely rare at Auschwitz,*" she'd discovered, "*but not unknown.*" It turned out that there were six hundred cases of escape from Auschwitz, of whom almost four hundred were recaptured.

"*When an escape was detected, all prisoners in the camp stood at attention for hours on end, while the fugitive was hunted outside the camp; once captured, the escapee was tortured, then paraded around the camp with a sign saying 'Hurrah, I'm back,' and then was hanged in front of the rest of the camp.*"

Standard Nazi operating procedure, with even that touch of what passed among them as humor, but that still left two hundred escapees at large—so why not Hermann among them? A month after Hermann got to the camp, if he did get there, that May of 1944, there was an escape that galvanized the whole Auschwitz community, that of Mala Zimetbaum and her Polish lover, Edek Galinski.

"She was a Läuferin, or runner, in the camp, able to move about on errands and carrying messages. Both had been members of anti-Nazi undergrounds, he in Poland, she in Belgium. He obtained an SS uniform, she 'organized' a pass, and they left the camp together in the guise of an SS man transporting a prisoner.

"Many Auschwitz survivors remember them, for they inspired everyone with tremendous hope."

For two weeks, until they were caught by a German border patrol in the Beskid Zywiecki mountains, not far from the Czech border.

"Back in Auschwitz, both were tortured and then led to the gallows for public execution. Mala slashed her wrist with a razor blade she had concealed, was beaten to the ground and loaded onto the crematorium truck without ever being hanged. Across the camp, Edek leaped into the noose and kicked away the bench before the death sentence was read; the SS rescued and re-hanged him."

An Auschwitz ending, but you can't hang a good idea. A month later, in July of 1944, a Pole named Jerzy Bielecki repeated the same process, but with better contacts on the outside. Dressed as an SS, he went to the laundry where his girlfriend, Cyla Cybulska, was working, asked for her by number, and informed the SS woman guard brusquely that he'd come to take her for an interrogation. He marched her through the camp, and at the checkpoint showed a forged pass authorizing one guard to escort one woman prisoner to a work camp outside the gates. The guards opened the gate for them—"Heil Hitler!"

"Heil Hitler!" Bielecki barked back as he left.

Out of sight of the guards, he and Cyla embraced and then started running, for ten nights, west into what the Nazis called the General Government, part of Poland. There Cyla was hidden by a Polish family, and Jerzy joined his brother in a Home Army partisan unit. Both survived the war.

But—Auschwitz—afterwards, each was told that the other had died, and they went their separate ways, Cyla to America, Jerzy back in Poland. Only by chance, in June of 1983, did Cyla hear of a man on Polish television, telling her story. Nearly forty years had passed, but Cyla was on a plane to Krakow the next day.

Jerzy met her with thirty-nine roses, one for each of the years they'd been apart. They met fifteen times after that, until she died. Each had married, lived other lives, thirty-nine years of marriage and jobs and children, and some success, or how could he have paid for the roses, and she the fifteen trips? So, much success, and the attendant satisfactions, large and small, ranging from community approbation down to dinner at nice restaurants, and all of it nothing to their ten days on the run in the mountains.

Ten days in two long lives, but compounded of all that was the most essential—the clear light, the bright shining stars overhead, the heat, the cold, the desperation, and mostly, the crazy love. Because it would have been crazy, with the whole Third Reich on high alert for them. Thousands of men on their trail, and the two of them lying together in some leafy grove or hidden cave, wondering which it would be that day, live or die? If it was die, they might as well make love. If it was live, all the better.

And then one of them would burst out laughing—the "Heil Hitler!" as they had walked out the gate. Then they'd fall silent. They had poison, but the SS had revived others who'd taken poison so they could hang them. Hang them badly, painfully, the way they'd engineered it, so that it took longer than normal hanging. Both Cyla and Jerzy had witnessed it. They didn't want to hang. They fell into each other's arms again.

Consie had seen a picture of them on the internet—two old

people, smiling. Nice, but not as nice as if they'd met again in 1945. She looked up—the sign said WESTERN, her exit. How had that happened? She screeched across four lanes, but made it somehow. No one even honked—funny, that was the one thing people out here seemed to forgive on these roads.

She groped for the emailed directions but it turned out to be easy, the way it is in proper SoCal. Right for a few straight-forward blocks, then a clear left, a clear right, all marked with big green signs, and then a nice big turn into the USC campus with its ample easy parking, as long as you've got eight bucks—but who doesn't have eight bucks out here?

It was a beautiful day, California winter, hard to beat. Big sun, blue skies, even when it rains, or so it seems. She parked amid the Ranges and the Audis, and followed the blond student body past the roses in bloom to the Doheny Memorial Library.

A nice place, a lovely old building, tall brass doors, marble floors. Who was Doheny anyway? One of the thugs who killed public transportation out here? There are mansions and librar-ies all over this town called Doheny, and even a street in West Hollywood, a big street. The movie so-called royalty were small fry to this.

She'd shaken a resale suit out of her closet to present herself in that day, but the assistant who greeted her turned out to have long hair and jeans. He had her list ready—"Escape References, Auschwitz." Three pages—she'd had no idea.

"All these people escaped?" she asked him.

"Or else it's referenced for some reason in their testimony."

"I see," she said, almost giddily, half expecting him to retort, *Said the blind man.*

But he said nothing, just unlocked a door, led her into a very grand room, the Feuchtwanger Collection, donated to the university by the wife of the best-selling German writer who'd escaped the Gestapo dressed as a washerwoman and then bought a villa in Los Angeles where he hosted his fellow refugees—Brecht, Thomas Mann, Schoenberg.

Lovely, she thought, appropriate even. A perfect place to research her subject in comfort and light.

But they continued on through, glancing neither left nor right, to a sunless, grimy little cubicle, with a down-at-the-heels computer with headphones and an elaborate series of passwords to boot. Followed by one of those "If it stops in the middle, just click this, and then do that."

She would need him, she could tell. To her nervous "Where will you be?" he gave a "Down the hall, unless I'm out."

She didn't want him to leave, at least not till she got the thing started. He sounded like a Midwesterner. "Do you like California?" she threw out.

Of course he liked it; all the Midwesterners out here like it, starting with the weather.

Nothing to talk about there, but her job now was to be nice enough to this guy to get him to help her with this shockingly drab, ancient computer—hadn't Steven Spielberg funded this project? What had they done with all the money?

"I'm from near Cleveland," she tried, but no dice. Best she could get was, "I'll be here for an hour anyway," as he slipped out.

WHICH WAS GOOD, because she called him three times in that hour. The first time was because when he'd taken her to lock her bag in a locker, she'd forgotten to pull out her glasses, and then the key didn't work, till he came and it worked with one quick try. Next came the fact that the tape didn't seem to want to play; and then it skipped. And then the thing went back to the beginning instead of playing through—How do you contact

Spielberg? she was wondering by then. To tell him that his work here had been in vain?

But then, one of the clicks went right, and a man was speaking. He was old, and he looked mean at first, a crosspatch glaring at the camera. His name was Chaim Feig, and he was from Romania, he said, and then came the childhood, the aunts and the uncles, all the cousins. Nice hot tea and a piece of cake in the morning. Fish in the river. She pushed fast-forward. It didn't work, and then it wouldn't stop. By the time she stopped it again, the crosspatch was in tears.

He had been part of the *Sonderkommando*, the "Special Command," the SK—the prisoners who were forced to move people in and out of the gas chamber, and then to the oven. *"Pieces,"* he said the Nazis called them when they were dead. His own particular assignment had been the children, *"nice little boys and girls, holding their little hands, five in a row—"*

She pressed fast-forward again.

". . . all day and all night, into the gas. We'd hear them crying for their mothers—"

Where was the part about escape? This man had arrived in Auschwitz just a little bit before Hermann. If he'd escaped, since he'd escaped, maybe Hermann had left with him.

"And all their little bodies, so beautiful, so clean, so perfect, in contrast to the filthy rags they were wearing—"

She pushed the button—what was wrong with this thing? Even her computer at home was better.

"We put them five at a time into the oven. But they were so thin that sometimes we needed a woman's body, with some fat, to help it burn—"

She hit the thing. It went back to the beginning.

She called the assistant—"But feel free to leave a message."

She got up, walked out to her locker, opened it successfully this time, and got a pill. Drank some water from a fountain, walked back, and put on the headphones again.

"After six weeks, I made up my mind to get out, somehow, some way."

At last.

But it turned out his escape was more sideways than out. On the spur of the moment, he hid under a load of clothes from the dead children he'd been loading into a truck. The SS searched, as always, with their bayonets, stabbing through the piles, but they missed him by an inch, and the truck pulled away.

"Now what?" he said he thought to himself. The SS almost immediately noticed he was missing and were searching, *"each one with fifty eyes. It was very, very important to them that no one get out of the SK."* The truck would have been searched again if it had gone out the gates, but instead it pulled up outside a deserted barracks in another part of Auschwitz. Once night fell, he crept out cautiously and into some barracks, where he found a chimney that didn't have a metal grate. This he took as a sign that he might live. He crawled inside and fell sound asleep.

He heard the dogs barking, but for some reason they didn't smell him there. The second night, he sneaked out and stole some bread—he didn't say where—and filled a bottle with water. This became his life in those days. During the days, he slept in the chimney, and at night he'd steal his bread and water. He counted ten days, he thought, but was no longer sure. He was alive, true, but beginning to feel confused.

But then he overheard some prisoners talking about a transfer out, to a work camp, the next day. *"This is it,"* he told himself. He waited till the men assembled for the predawn roll call, and then melted into the throng.

The trucks to take those selected for work were waiting, but the roll call wasn't coming out right, there was one too many. One among the fifteen thousand—"*me*," he smiled now at the camera.

The SS started screaming, "*Schwein!* Pig! Get out!" but despite counts and recounts, there was no way they could identify the one bald, half-starved man in stripes, standing at attention with all the others, who was there out of order.

Making a mockery, in fact—"Step out, pig, filth!" Chaim Feig looked neither to the left nor to the right. These men were not his buddies, but no one turned him in. Finally, an officer shouted, "Load the trucks anyway." This was a first for the SS, this concession. But it was mid-1944, and by then the Nazis' need for labor trumped their passion to spend the time it would take—starting with the random killing of men on the outside lines till they got to someone who would squeal—to flush out the one defiant prisoner who was laughing up his ragged sleeve at them that day.

AND THUS IT WAS that an "*ecstatic*" Chaim Feig clambered into the trucks with the rest of them and was driven out through the gates of Auschwitz and away.

Which in fact constituted the end of his escape, since he was now part of a detail of prisoners again. But though most of his colleagues were beaten or starved to death over the next few months, Chaim Feig was still alive in April of 1945, when the British marched in.

He was turned over to the Swedes, "*who were really human, and really tried to help us*," treating him with great kindness. But his whole universe was gone, there was no one he knew still alive, no family, no friends or teachers or even enemies, and the worst part was that he knew how they'd all died. Knew exactly how his mother, his sister, his little nieces, his father, had walked into the *"High Gothic room,"* as he put it, quoting Goethe, still with some hope in their hearts. Knew how they'd folded their clothes and noted where they'd put them, as instructed. Knew what relief they'd taken at that.

And Chaim Feig unfortunately knew, too, the signs of the sinking feeling as the charade played itself out, and the pushing started. Knew how some started praying, some screaming, some still took hope from the false shower heads on the ceiling. A few brave Czechs once sang the national anthem, and some French women sang "La Marseillaise."

Until the gas, of course, when the singing turned to screaming, and then the screaming turned to choking, and then the chokes to gasps—but it wasn't quick, that transformation. It took twenty minutes at least, of screams, chokes, gasps, blood from the mouth, blood from the ears—the Nazis had really done it. Found the worst death since the beginning of time. You died faster if you were burned at the stake, a French priest had told him. A prisoner there, too, who was obsessed with Joan of Arc.

And though suicide was a mortal sin for a Catholic, the priest told Chaim Feig that he couldn't face the gas. And he was no longer sure that there was anyone to punish him anyway. Was there a God? The priest was thinking maybe not, and a few days later he *"ran to the wire,"* and electrocuted himself. The best you could do at Auschwitz.

As for himself, said Chaim Feig, afterwards, when he was turned out of the displaced persons camp in 1946, *"the only thing I could think to do was to go to Palestine and kill the whole world. I wasn't just shooting Arabs there, I was shooting everyone—"*

She clicked again, and there he was, back in the present tense, living outside LA, and being interviewed in what looked like a nice room, with photos of grandchildren in the background.

"*. . . But every night, when I close my eyes, I see them still, all those children, good little girls and boys, holding hands so nicely, five across, walking into the gas—*"

"*And how do you feel?*" the California interviewer asked him.

"*How do I feel??*" His voice was rising as she clicked it off.

FINE. SHE WANTED TO KISS HIM, wanted to look him up on the internet and send him flowers. She was glad he'd gotten out of there—glad for his marriage, his children, his comfortable life in the San Fernando Valley.

But now she could see them too, all those little children—and for what? She was coming to think there was no meaning to any of this—that Auschwitz was either a "one-off," a bizarre detour from the progressive path of life with no message beyond its particular horror, or else a true unmasking of the real face of Man. Maybe "holocaust" is the natural state, and it takes every Washington, Jefferson, and Lincoln, Susan B. Anthony and Martin Luther King, Angela Davis, Noam Chomsky, and all the Kennedys in the universe just to keep it at bay.

But be that as it may, Chaim Feig's escape was a fluke, and had nothing to do with Hermann, and she should have clicked out right away and gone on to the next one.

Which she did now—a woman who'd been a young girl in the camps, twelve at the time, when she was selected for her beautiful skin to be made into gloves by Ilse Koch, the wife of the camp commander at Buchenwald.

Wrong camp, then. The thing was obviously mismarked on her list. It was supposed to be "Escape from Auschwitz."

She should click out—but *gloves*??

"*Who was Ilse Koch?*" an interviewer was asking in soothing tones.

"*A maniac.*" The woman, Irene Zisblatt, looked away. The wife of the director of the camp. She would ride through on her horse, seeking beautiful skin or an interesting tattoo. She would then have those girls killed at once, and their skins sent to her.

Her house wasn't far from the barracks, and one day Irene and five other unblemished young girls were marched over there by two SS, as a sort of offering to their boss's wife. But Ilse Koch wasn't home, so they were marched back to camp and lived that day instead of being turned into gloves.

From there, though, Irene Zisblatt was sent to Auschwitz, to Dr. Mengele, who was experimenting at that point on various ways and means of removing the numbers from the prisoners' arms. It seemed that most of the SS had gotten tattoos as well, their signature death's-head, and now that the Russians were coming, there was increasing interest in wholesale removal. To this end, Irene Zisblatt had her arm injected, cut, scraped, Auschwitz-style, with no anesthesia, but the numbers didn't come off, and the whole thing got infected. Mengele shrugged and told a nurse to give her a lethal injection of phenol to the heart and send her to the crematorium.

But the nurse was a member of the underground, and instead of phenol, gave her a sleeping drug, wrapped her in a blanket, and threw her into a load of clothes that was being tossed into a train, which stopped at a work camp, where she woke up, crawled out, and sneaked into a barracks. And there, by a continuation of the same extravagant luck that had already saved her twice, she found her last surviving cousin, and the two of them worked together in a factory till the end, and then escaped from the death march and hid in the woods till they were found by General Patton's army.

A good ending, except that Irene Zisblatt, old now, somewhere in Florida, had started to cry.

She and her cousin had been wandering in the woods for weeks by then, she said, with nothing to eat. But they found a little stream and drank some water. Then they went to sleep under some leaves, *"for a day, five days, we didn't know,"* just drifting, until they were brought back to life by something poking them.

It was a rifle. The cousin, Sapka, covered her head. *"They're going to kill us now,"* she said, *"but at least they didn't make us into ashes."*

That had been her mantra at Auschwitz—*"Don't let them turn us into ashes!"* She closed her eyes tight, but Irene peeked out at the boots. They were brown, not black. The legs were khaki.

"It's not an SS," she whispered to her cousin.

She looked up. A man—*"so tall!"*—was staring down at her, openmouthed.

"Are you alive?" he whispered, in a sort of German. He was an American, he made them understand. He put them both on his back and carried them back to his camp. When General Patton saw them, he yelled for the medics and swore revenge. They were taken to a hospital in Pilsen and given scrambled eggs, Sapka's dream in the camps.

But she died that night anyway, of typhoid fever. *"I buried her in the woods and left a marker,"* said Irene, though when she tried to find it later, it was gone.

Or maybe she was looking in the wrong part of the woods— *"but,"* sobbed Irene Zisblatt, *"at least Sapka wasn't ashes."* True. She herself was taken to a DP camp near Salzburg, where she met *"kids from all over, alone, looking for a home."* Most of them figured that it would have to be Palestine. But Palestine was closed to them too then, at least legally; and while they were waiting to hear about an illegal boat from Spain or Italy, an uncle in the Bronx saw her name on a list and managed to have her brought to New York. Her father had owned a resort in Czechoslovakia, but when her uncle called, long distance, thinking maybe to get it back for her, they told him that "no one's home."

Another fine. Consie clicked out again—she'd seen the triumphant pictures in the BG, as the scriptwriters call it, the children, grandchildren. So a marriage, and the usual measure of success despite it all, beyond expectations. Certainly beyond anything that the Native Americans or even Black Americans had been able to muster from their own tragedies, which was strange, now that she thought about it. Even a half-dead European is better prepared for life here than anyone else.

She glanced at her watch. It was now two thirty, time to go. Much past three and you could sit for hours in that inching mass that makes up the daily fare on the freeway, the countless thousands of cars heading back now, one by one, into the sun. Both ways they get it in the eyes, east in the morning, west at night. Maybe they were used to it, maybe they didn't know any better, had never been on a subway, a trolley, a train that could be whisking them all the way, together, in speed and comfort, reading the paper as they went.

But not in LA. Not even the dream of it in LA. With luck now, it would take her a good forty minutes. And she was hungry.

BUT NOT HUNGRY LIKE AUSCHWITZ, said the little voice that had been whispering in her ear for some time now, and next on the list was a Czech, who'd arrived at Auschwitz in 1944, just when Hermann had. It might take a bit longer to get back, but better maybe than driving down again, plus the parking. She might as well get her money's worth. She'd give the guy half an hour and then hop into her car.

She typed in her name, password. It jumped right up, even before she finished typing. So the machine was getting to know her, good. Clicked here, then there, and could even go to the chapters, the different topics laid out: Biographical Profile, National Identity, Awareness of Political or Military Events, which you could skip, which was precisely what she planned to do with this one. With all due respect.

"*Mr. Martin Slyomovits,*" a different sort of interviewer was saying. They were in Australia. Good. Surely less of the "*How do you feel?*" there.

Which wouldn't have worked with this man, anyway, she could see even before the sound caught up. He was tall, distinguished, with a small mustache, sitting ramrod straight in a chair, all business. Nice clothes, better than the others she'd seen. A well-cut jacket, tailored shirt.

He was born in Czechoslovakia, he was saying, in a village in the Carpathian Mountains, the region that was taken by Hungary in 1939, just at the time that—

She knew that part. The relentless march of the Nazis and their clients. The cruel betrayal of poor Czechoslovakia. She clicked. The screen went black, just for an instant, but when it flashed back on, everything had changed. The Czech with the military bearing was now slouched in his chair, crying, telling the interviewer that he didn't think he could go on.

"*Stop the camera,*" he was saying.

But the camera didn't flinch. "*Please continue.*" The Australian was relentless. "*This is for history.*"

The Czech took a breath. He was talking, in fact, about an escape, but not his own. That of two fellow Czechs, Rudi Vrba and Alfréd Wetzler, who had managed to get out of Auschwitz in April of 1944, with a specific mission—to warn those about to be deported to resist.

Both boys, Vrba and Wetzler, had been in Auschwitz long enough to have seen the whole picture, seen transport after transport come in, from all over Europe, filled with people still thinking they had come to work. They'd seen them pushed, half-mad with thirst, from the trains with their families, still uncomprehending. Seen them separated with no chance to say good-bye. Seen them walk to the gas chambers thinking they were going into bathhouses, and by the time they understood, they were trapped.

Trapped, in fact, from the minute they got onto the trains. And still they boarded, not knowing, still thinking that if they followed orders, they could save their families and maybe themselves. "You're going to work," they were told. Some variation of "to pick grapes in Tokay." Which sounded all right, better, certainly, than starving where they were, they were still thinking, fatally unaware of the terrible secret that the Nazis had somehow managed, for the most part, to keep.

The Czech, Martin Slyomovits, knew the whole story. After the war he'd met Vrba, who told him that what had tipped him off first was hearing the guards' talk of "Hungarian salami," famous throughout Europe. Every transport had brought its own food, which constituted key perks for the guards—wine and olives from the Greeks, cheese from the Dutch, sardines from the French. Now, they were talking about the salami, and the camp prisoners understood who was coming next.

THERE HAD BEEN NO Hungarian transports till then. People from all over the region had taken refuge there, thought they were safe. But it was as if the Reich had been saving them till last, when everything was at peak capacity, and they could kill them all seamlessly. There had been feverish preparations all that spring—more ovens, expanded "undressing rooms." The train tracks had been extended almost to the gas. That meant the Nazis could skip the truck routine, the "who would like a ride" bit. Now even the feeble, even the small children, could walk to the gas themselves.

Vrba was determined to get out with a warning. *"Because,"* Martin Slyomovits on the tape was saying, *"we still didn't know. They told us we were being resettled. No one thought that they would kill us. It didn't even occur to us."*

But if they were warned, Vrba, the man in the camps, figured, they could resist. And if they died, they'd die fighting, *"like soldiers, not sheep.*

"And we could have run then and hidden in the forest," Slyomovits continued. *"Our village was only three kilometers away from the deep woods. We were all woodsmen, all hunters. We would have had a chance."*

The Polish underground had found its footing in Auschwitz by that point, and they helped Vrba and his partner set up an escape. Two of them who worked outside the camp's barbed-wire inner perimeter hollowed out a hiding place for them in a woodpile. Others got them work passes for that detail. A Russian POW who'd escaped but been caught *"filled in my Manual of What Every Escaper Should Know,"* as Vrba wrote after the war.

"Lesson one: trust nobody. Don't even tell me your plans. Because as soon as you're reported missing, they'll come and torture me.

"Lesson two: don't be afraid of the Germans. They try to convince you that they're superman, but they can die just as quickly as anybody else.

"Lesson three: don't trust your legs because a bullet can run faster. Be invisible. Never move by day.

"Lesson four: carry no money. If you're starving, you'll be tempted to buy food, but you've got to keep away from people. Steal and live off the land.

"Lesson five: travel light. You'll need a knife for hunting or defending yourself, and a razor blade in case you're about to be captured. Don't let them take you alive."

He told them to take matches and salt, because *"with salt and cooked potatoes, you can last for months."* He taught them how to use a compass, and instructed them to steal a watch and consult it, so as to never be caught out in the daylight.

He gave them some strong black Russian tobacco, which, soaked in gasoline, would put off the tracker dogs. *"But only Russian tobacco, Machorka. It's the only kind that works!"*

On the afternoon of the third of April 1944, Vrba and his colleague Wetzler crawled into the hole in the woodpile. At eight thirty that night, during roll call, the alarm went off, as they'd expected. From inside their woodpile, they listened to the sirens, the marching, the baying dogs. The noise would ebb and flow, with the two men scarcely daring to draw a full breath. Once, they heard some SS very close—*"Let's have another look in this woodpile."* They actually climbed up on it with their dogs—Vrba wrote that he could see their boots. But the Russian tobacco worked, the dogs didn't pick up their scent, and on the fourth day, the intensive search—again, as expected—let up.

That night, as soon as darkness fell, the two men crept out, put on the Dutch suits, overcoats, and boots stolen from the dead, and slipped out of Auschwitz.

They traveled 130 kilometers through the Polish mountains toward Slovakia, using a map from a child's atlas they'd found in a warehouse. Eleven days after escaping, they crossed the border.

Fantastic! Consie breathed to her dingy computer. A real "Fantastic!"

"*But,*" said Slyomovits.

Why "but"? They weren't caught—since Vrba lived to tell his tale, so why the but?

But "*But,*" Martin Slyomovits repeated, and then stopped talking again. Put his hands over his face.

There was a long pause. She held her breath. If he broke down now, she would still beat the traffic.

But he took a breath, pulled himself together—he was a soldier. You could see that it was true—if he'd gotten to the woods, they never would have taken him, or his mother, father, sisters, or brothers either.

But they never got to the woods, even though Vrba managed to get his warning to the Hungarian community leadership in time to save them, including "*a precise description of the geography of the camps, their construction, the organization of the management and security, how the prisoners were numbered and categorized, their diet, the selections, gassings, shootings, injections, and deaths from the living conditions themselves, as well as sketches and information about the interior layouts and operations of (and surrounding) the gas chambers.*"

Because the community leaders he had trusted to spread the alarm instead suppressed the report. It turned out that one of the heads of the Budapest Aid and Rescue Committee, the influential lawyer Rudolf Kastner, was deep into negotiations with Eichmann—

Was she hearing correctly? Eichmann??

—and thus instead of leaping with all urgency to spread the alarm, Kastner slipped the report to Eichmann and then boarded a Nazi passenger train to Switzerland, along with seventeen hundred family members and friends—the price of his betrayal. His reward.

"*They didn't tell us,*" Martin Slyomovits was sobbing to the camera. His mother and sisters had been sent straight to the gas that summer, when they were killing so many that human fat had to be used to accelerate the burning—

She clicked, she knew that, but instead of turning off, the picture froze. The funny thing was that she'd read something about Kastner once before, in Hannah Arendt's *Eichmann in Jerusalem*; but that was a book, so when she got to that part, so disturbing as to be unbearable, she could still slam it shut and put it back on the shelf.

Still tell herself that it wasn't really true, just Hannah Arendt trying to turn the narrative away from the fact that she'd been in love with Heidegger, her professor, a Nazi activist, and had helped to rehabilitate him when he came whimpering back to her after the war. Which proved that Arendt was human, but did that impair her judgment on this? Was she right about Kastner and the rest?

Was it possible? That there were members of the community who could have spoken but hadn't? That rather than warning every endangered soul from Prague to Budapest, they'd actively collaborated in the organization of their murder, 450,000 people that summer alone—including both Slyomovits's family and, now that she thought about it, Hermann's as well—in exchange for a train ride to Switzerland?

And then from there, they'd apparently gone on to found the new shining State of Israel, because that's who they seemed to be, the founders and early leaders of Israel—was it possible??

She stared at the screen—Slyomovits, frozen in mid-speech. She liked his looks, wondered what he'd looked like when he was young. Some of the speakers had shown early, lighthearted pictures, but Slyomovits showed no pictures.

A tap on the cubicle. "We're closing now."

She looked up. "What??"

"This room closes at five," said the woman.

Five? How could it be five?

She was screwed now, completely. Hers would be the mother of all drives, in the mother of all rush hours. She would sit through five lights just to push her way onto the freeway, to be followed by a slow-mo slog from the right lane into the left— twenty minutes or more, just to get into position to start inching west, and that only if it was a good day. If no one had texted into his or her predecessor's fender, which would bring the whole thing to a grinding halt while the backed-up masses swarmed around the malfunction, like caterpillars she'd once seen on a leaf in Brazil.

A broad leaf. Her husband had barely brushed it with his arm, which had been enough to send the caterpillars' poison shooting up to his lymph glands, where it nearly killed him.

She could try driving back on Venice—there were all the lights, but at least there was something to look at. First the Latino markets, the brides and the pawnshops, and the only real butchers left in town, and then the Indian shops with bags of curry and cardamom out front, along with bolts of raw silk, but where do you find a dressmaker out here? And then the nice Tibetan place where she might stop for some so-called yak milk tea, or the bright Brazilians next door for a real coffee, and then after that, the strip malls giving way to the quirky little theaters, and finally, the beach.

Though that would take an hour, at least.

"Just one more minute?" she begged the librarian. She suddenly had to hear the end of the Slyomovits tape.

He was saying that Vrba's report finally came to light anyway, but three fatal months late, and only after 450,000 people had walked, utterly unaware and in orderly fashion, onto the trains in Budapest and into the Auschwitz gas. She even knew what they looked like—some arty SS guy had taken photos of their arrival. Well-dressed people in coats and hats, looking worried but still trying to understand. Strong young men and women who could have fought in the woods had they known.

Had they been told. But the first account of the Auschwitz death camp was broadcast only on the fifteenth of June by the BBC, followed by the *New York Times* on the twentieth. This led the Hungarian government to panic, fearing that they might be held responsible for the whole thing. They insisted that the Nazis stop the transports, which they did on July 9, 1944. Voilà.

. This saved the last 200,000 slated for the gas. And the Swedes, under Raoul Wallenberg, managed to shelter another 33,000, until January of 1945, when the Red Army got to Budapest and liberated the town.

What was left of the town. Some of those who could have spoken and hadn't, defended themselves afterwards saying that if the truth had gotten out and there'd been an uprising or people had tried to flee, more of them might have been killed in the process. But Hannah Arendt had done the math on this one too: of those who resisted the Nazis, about fifty percent died. But of those taken to Auschwitz, it was a clean ninety-five percent.

"*Thank you, Mr. Slyomovits,*" the Australian was saying. "*It's so important to hear from the survivors—*"

Slyomovits cut him off. "*I don't like to be called a survivor,*" he said. "*I'm not proud of that. I'd rather be a victor.*"

But that had proved impossible once he'd gotten on the train. Anyone who still asks why people walked like lambs to their deaths in Auschwitz clearly hasn't read any one of the extant accounts of the logistics, how death in the gas chambers started in those boxcars. Because once on, once locked inside, deprived of food and water, unhinged by this, there was no chance of resistance when those doors were finally opened on the dead and the still-living. And the prisoners in Auschwitz knew this, which was why they collaborated on Vrba's death-defying escape, which against all odds succeeded—only to be sabotaged by the very ones to whom it was entrusted.

"Four hundred and thirty-seven thousand and four hundred and two"—Slyomovits knew the exact numbers, precisely how many unsuspecting Czechs and Hungarians were shipped out in the months after Vrba's warning had been given to the community leaders.

Was it *possible?* Consie gathered up her things and walked outside. It was still lovely, with the sun getting lower, cutting flat across the diagonal pathways where the carefree boys and girls in sandals strolled to and fro. There were bikes lying about, unlocked—free bikes, she realized, for the lucky students. Did they even know how lucky?

Though if they knew, would they be quite so lucky? She too had had her American time in that bliss, unawares.

It would take an hour at least for the roads to clear a bit. In the meantime, what was she supposed to do? Stroll around with the golden horde here? Her nice suit was rumpled. She felt old. Less chic in gray than lay nun.

There was a small outdoor not-quite-café. More like an airport stand. What do you get in these places? A few kids were sitting at the little tables, loners all, eating yogurt and cups-o'-noodles. Ramen. She knew that from her own children. She got a tea and sat under a tree.

Could she use the library? The regular library likely

required an ID, but no one had stopped her from walking into the Doheny. She gulped the rest of the tea and went back inside, and immediately found a free computer that someone had left online, password and all.

Fine. She had a fact for which she'd lost the source: "Each individual was worth precisely $745 to the German government, counting his or her bones, hair, and teeth, and deducting the costs of food, transport, and poison gas." Even figuring low, at about 1.5 million at Auschwitz alone, you could see how the death camps fell into place, from the banker's point of view.

She'd been careless with the source, though, and what she should have done with this dead time was type in "Auschwitz" and then slog through the data till she found it again. But what she typed instead was "Kastner," which led to another "Closing time," and another dazed "What?"

"We close at ten."

Ten? She looked up. When had it gotten dark?

"The Leavey is open, though."

"No, that's fine, sorry, uh, thanks"—she staggered to her feet.

She had to hand it to Kastner. He'd gotten her kicked out twice in one day. She walked outside into the darkness—there was the fountain, and still some of the kids, and all those bikes, left out. Her Ohio upbringing balked at this, but after all, there was no need to put things away out here. It wouldn't rain for months.

Kastner—bloody Kastner. Her research had confirmed what Slyomovits had said, made it worse. Kastner had had what you might call a special relationship with Adolf Eichmann, the high SS officer who'd come to Budapest to ensure that what even the Nazis saw by then as their final act was all that it could be.

What they didn't want there was, as they put it, "a second Warsaw." Resistance in Budapest would slow them down, now perhaps critically. Time was running out, but the death camps were primed. If things went smoothly, the Nazis could still rid the world of at least half a million men, women, and children, Eichmann figured, before the Russians came over the mountains and shut them down.

To this end, the Nazis plastered the walls with the usual posters—YOU WILL BE RELOCATED TO A FAMILY CAMP, YOU WILL BE SENT TO PICK GRAPES IN TOKAY—replete with the usual lies. And then they called in Kastner, the community leader, to grease the wheels.

Eichmann had liked Kastner from the start, he told *Life* magazine in an interview in the 1960s, liked his style. *"This Dr. Kastner was a young man about my age, an ice-cold lawyer and a fanatical Zionist. . . . While we talked he would smoke one aromatic cigarette after another, taking them from a silver case and lighting them with a little silver lighter. With his great polish and reserve, he would have made an ideal Gestapo officer himself."*

It didn't take them long to reach an understanding: Kastner would help Eichmann *"keep the people from resisting deportation and even keep order in the collection camps if I would close my eyes and let a few hundred emigrate.*

"It was a good bargain," Eichmann felt. *"You can have the others,"* Kastner had told him, *"but let me have this group here."*

Eichmann admired this, Kastner's willingness to sacrifice half a million people to his own ends. *"As a matter of fact, there was a strong similarity between attitudes in the SS and Kastner's,"* he concluded, *"and because he rendered us a great service, I let his groups escape."* These would be the founders of a new country, *"biologically valuable blood,"* Eichmann said Kastner called them, *"human material that was capable of reproduction and hard work."*

Eichmann could relate. *"As I told Kastner: 'We, too, are ide-*

alists and we, too, had to sacrifice our own blood before we came to power.'"

The two men shook hands, and thus it was that Kastner and his list were boarding their passenger train to Switzerland while Slyomovits and Hermann were allowing themselves to be shoved into boxcars to Auschwitz, under the logical if false assumption that they were being tapped for their labor, and that this was the best way to keep their wives and children alive.

Kastner—she could picture him smoking with Eichmann. The studied cool, the thrill of this pas de deux with the devil. Hermann had probably had a silver cigarette case, too, though his would have been long gone by that time. Stolen or bartered right off, traded for nothing, a loaf of bread, an invalid permit, maybe even in Budapest itself, and it wasn't beyond the realm of possibility that it had found its way to Kastner. After all, theirs was a small world, and the market for luxury goods would have been yet smaller, since the SS and the Gestapo presumably would have arrived already supplied with silver cigarette cases. They'd have had them for years, since the "happy days" of the early war, all that beautiful loot in Vienna or Berlin.

Had them so long they would have come to think of them as their own, think that they'd been born with silver cigarette cases, those Nazi prestidigitators, but who would have gotten Hermann's? One of the Hungarian Nazis, the Arrow Cross boys? But they were thugs—she couldn't see them affecting a cigarette case. And Kastner had money, though how or whose remains a mystery. Plus, he was still permitted to stroll about like anyone else: Eichmann had exempted him from wearing the yellow star. Free from this, he could still enjoy an elegant public smoke.

She could see it—Kastner with Hermann's cigarette case.

Anyway, with someone's. Kastner had not been born to silver. His father had a small shop, which he'd neglected. Kastner's mother had struggled to support the family. She wondered if Kastner had taken his cigarette case on the train, but why not? You could smoke on a passenger train to Switzerland in those days. Kastner would have smoked very comfortably, in the dining car as he supped. *"One after another, just like an SS man."*

And then perhaps, just as Hermann and his wife, both of them shocked by the violence and half-crazed with thirst and hunger, were being shoved out of their boxcar and getting their first dose of Auschwitz on that Stygian platform, the guards, the stripes, the dogs, the separation from each other, the longing looks that would turn out to be the last ones in this world; maybe even at that very moment, in one of those synchronisms that happen from time to time, Kastner too was stepping from the train he'd bought with their lives, at a nice clean Swiss station, Hermann's cigarette case tucked in his tweed.

Or linen, for it was summer by then. Nor was it possible to continue this exercise, because Hermann disappears at that point. But Kastner's life, au contraire, is part of the public record. He lived out the war the way people did in Switzerland; and afterwards, he, along with his wife and daughter, and all of his family and friends, took their places among the elite in their new world, the new State of Israel.

He lost his bids for elective office there, but received an appointment, as spokesman for the Ministry of Trade and Industry. That was in 1952. His colleagues in government seemed to have put the Budapest of May '44 behind them. *"Let the dead bury the dead,"* as people in that part of the world had been saying for almost two thousand years.

But every party needs a pooper, or maybe it was just that

Malchiel Gruenwald was having trouble with transition. His entire family had been shipped from Hungary to Auschwitz and gassed while Kastner was smoking with the Nazis. Only Gruenwald had made it through, and now he lived in Tel Aviv, alone, except for the mimeograph machine in the back room of his little café. Which he used one day to publish a three-page pamphlet, which he handed out for free.

"I have waited a long time," it read, *"to expose this careerist whom I consider, because of his collaboration with the Nazis, an indirect murderer of my dear people."*

And collaboration wasn't the only charge. Gruenwald went on to accuse Kastner of using the money of those sent to Auschwitz, *"millions for which no accounting is given,"* to pay to save *"his relatives, and hundreds of his friends . . . people with connections, [making] a fortune in the process."* But as for the rest of the people—*"these, Kastner left in the valley of the shadow of death."*

The pamphlet burned through the city, and calls went out for Kastner's head. The Labor government sued Gruenwald for libel on Kastner's behalf, which turned the thing from brush fire to conflagration.

The trial dragged on for two years, as every Hungarian not on Kastner's train stepped forward with their own "J'accuse." Even the mother of Resistance martyr Hannah Senesh made the long trip out to charge Kastner with complicity in her daughter's death. When Senesh was arrested at the Hungarian border, her mother had begged him to intervene, since he was known to have influence with her captors and even access to her prison. *"But he did nothing,"* she sobbed on the witness stand, and meanwhile, her daughter was tortured for months, and finally shot by the Nazis in November of 1944.

The crowd was horrified, the headlines black, and the

judges ruled against Kastner, for Gruenwald. Kastner had *"sold his soul to the devil,"* they concluded. Kastner resigned from his government position and withdrew from public life. He compared himself to Dreyfus, and lived with a loneliness *"blacker than night, darker than hell,"* he told reporters.

The Labor government managed to get the verdict reversed on appeal, but even those judges conceded that Kastner had in fact served the Nazis, *"expediting the work of exterminating the masses."* And by then, the damage was done. Labor fell over the affair, and Kastner was shot on his doorstep on March 3, 1957. He died twelve days later.

"Good," she blurted out loud, even in the library.

But was it good? It turned out that his killers weren't avenging Hungarians, but rather connected to the far-right terrorist Stern Gang, who then formed the new government. The one who'd pulled the trigger had once worked as a paid informer for Israeli intelligence. So instead of vengeance, was it a silencing? And why had the secret service wanted Kastner dead?

SHE WALKED SLOWLY toward the parking structure. She had no recollection of where she'd left her car. Maybe she'd never find it, maybe the car was gone, or covered with the dust of decades. She suddenly understood what the historian Raul Hilberg had been after. He was quoted extensively in the French film *Shoah*, and had seemed half-mad, poring over all those minuscule train schedules, as if to pinpoint the evil. But now it seemed to her that he was right. Death here was in the details.

One man facilitating, working with the Nazis for whatever reasons—they all had their reasons. The German engineer "following orders," Kastner serving his vision of a new land—and there it was. The trains arriving, the trains pulling out, people showing up peaceably for deportations, all the little bits coming together and then you had it, the working death camps.

Kastner was one of the best of them, but there were plenty more, all the mini-collaborationists. Hitler couldn't have done it without them.

As for her, she felt like Bluebeard's bride, who'd opened one room too many and now couldn't get the blood off the key. She'd come here this morning looking for good news, Hermann's escape, but what she'd found instead was the precise mechanism of his probable death.

There was her car—she ran.

"Everything okay?" A guard came to the rail. There behind him, bright in the night sky, was a gigantic Felix the Cat, terrifying, horrible. It's just an ad, she told herself, a billboard, but even as a child, she'd felt there was something about him. Something bad.

"Yeah, fine," she said to the guard, fumbling for the key, the lock, pushing the button, pulling the door, pushing again. It opened. She fell in, then took off, down around the infernal circles, into the weird, deserted streets. No wait at the lights now, no one on the freeway. It took the classic LA twenty minutes, or must have, because suddenly she was home. Where was the ocean? How had she missed it?

She got out and looked up at the sky. There was the moon, rising late, it was waning. "Weak," as they say in Brazil. "*Cold*," as one of the French Resistance women wrote, about Auschwitz. Cruel, it had seemed to them, as it shone down upon them, night after deadly night, and did nothing.

19

She sat up that night reading *Eichmann in Jerusalem*. What was there to be afraid of now? The story had burned into her mind, into her soul.

And she'd come to love Hannah Arendt, loved her clarity, her tough, direct gaze, loved the way she smoked, and the way she talked, the way she wrote. But as she read her analysis of evil, she got the feeling that Arendt had gotten that wrong.

Not about everything. She nails the *"elation"* of easy confession—young Germans in the sixties confessing to guilt without any indignation, or the Protestant churches admitting to a lack of *"mercy,"* when what is really lacking was and is justice. An accounting, say, from the princes of commerce, most of whom profited from slave labor. Bayer, Siemens, IG Farben, Krupp, Mercedes, Volkswagen, who built their factories right next to the death camps and signed contracts with the SS, who would provide a specified supply of guards, dogs, and whips, along with steady replacements for prisoners who would, it was understood, be worked to death.

Hannah Arendt is good at this, but then, watching the little man Eichmann in his glass booth for months on end, she concluded that evil was banal.

But what was banal was the man, not the evil. Eichmann was like someone who'd woken up from a dream. Banal, perhaps, as he sat there, captive, in Jerusalem, blinking, in isolation, facing the full turn of the tables, human, all too human, and completely alone.

But when the Nazis were in full swing and Eichmann was in full step, figuring out, day and night, how to stuff their ovens with ever more live people—where was the banality there? It was, rather, the wild beast incarnate, the blinding blue-white light, the mouth of the wolf. *"Amidst a Nightmare of Crime,"* was what one of the SK prisoners called it, who left notes buried for after his own predetermined death.

It was only afterwards, when the trains stopped and the ovens went cold, in that stunned silence that followed, then there came that glance around—*Did I? Did you? What happened? And who can we blame?*

And that's when the banality came in—the attempts at flight, the lies, the excuses, the long, talkative explanations. "I didn't," "I was only," and the rest of it, all of it banal in the extreme. Boring, predictable—excuses we all know from kindergarten, when we might have used them ourselves.

And even the retribution turned out to be banal—since it was so useless, so disproportionate, a grain of sand in that vast sea of crime. Yes, Eichmann was hanged, but he was only hanged, and hanged only once. For it to work at all, he would have had to be hanged a million and a half times.

Or at least hanged Nazi-style—a little bit, so their victims felt it, and then stopping for a moment, and doing it again. Or hanging them not quite high enough, so it took a very long time—and was that banal?

Was it banal to transport people for days with no water, having calculated the precise effects of extreme thirst on the human being's capacity for resistance? Banal to strip them bare and then push them, men and women with their own small children whom they loved, into a room without enough poison gas to even kill them quickly? Where death would come in such a way as to cause them to tear their own flesh? Bring blood from the eyes and ears?

Banal to force other prisoners to then pry the bodies apart, the bodies of people they'd seen alive a few minutes before, sometimes people they knew, sometimes even people they loved, and cut their hair if it was lovely and pull out the gold in their teeth, which went to the Central Bank in Berlin? And how banal was even the Central Bank then, and how banal those gold teeth in its coffers? How banal were all those jewels flooding the Swiss markets, or the baby clothes handed out for free in Berlin?

Nothing about it seemed banal to her. She even knew some of the faces, from the SS man's photos, one last look at the Hungarians coming off the trains. Nice people, mostly old-fashioned looking, some with head scarves, most with good coats, and lots of children, very nice children, in coats and hats, sitting with their mothers, their aunts, their grandmothers, each one "*a world*," as one of the prisoners who worked in the ovens managed to write, "*and in twenty minutes, that whole world will be transformed into ashes. No trace of them will remain.*"

They must have gone straight from the trains to the little grove of trees, where they sat and waited, with the worried faces you see in the pictures, but some hope that maybe it wouldn't be so bad after all. The people who first saw those photos after the war knew them as archetypes—the tall woman, the boy in the sailor suit, the girl with the braids—but then someone who survived filled in the names. This somehow made it worse.

THE NEXT DAY, she scanned her list again—"Escape References, Auschwitz"—and saw there was another testimony probably worth the drive, a man who'd landed there about the same time as Hermann. It was easier this time—the traffic meant nothing, and the computer remembered her. She too was in jeans, no longer hoping for a civilized word from an assistant curator.

The testimony she'd come for was from a Greek, named Morris Venezia, whose family had been in Thessalonika, he said, for five hundred years before they were seized and sent to Auschwitz. They had come from Venice in the Middle Ages, hence the name. He and his brothers were put to work in the gas chambers—"*You know why they chose the Greeks?*" he asked the interviewer.

Why? she said aloud in her little cubicle. She had wondered, often, listening and reading.

But the interviewer stopped him with one of those "*Wait, before we get to that,*" and then never did get back "to that."

So why the Greeks were chosen she would probably never know, although there was a reason, and Venezia would have been the one to tell it. He was not an intellectual, but a man who saw clearly nonetheless. Almost poetically—he got the blood-red poetry of the whole thing. He said when they first got there, they still didn't know. They were taken to the building with the huge chimneys, and still didn't know. But then they were given huge scissors, "*like sheep-shearers,*" and taken to the door of a big room, and when the door was opened, they knew.

There were hundreds of women lying there, "*like sardines, like alabaster, all beautiful, all dead.*" He and his cousin were still terrified of dead bodies that morning. They handled them gently at first, laid them carefully on the floor, holding their heads so that they didn't hit the cement, till a guard came and struck them with his cane, so hard they saw stars. "*Like this!*" the guard screamed, and threw the women on the floor, "*like junk.*"

"*Faster!*" screamed the guard. Another blow. They were assigned to cut the long hair off the dead women with the shears, as an introduction. Later they would graduate to throwing the bodies into the ovens. Three at a time, two men with one woman in the middle, to speed things along. "*Since fat burns,*" said Morris Venezia.

She knew that by now, didn't have to hear it again. But the reason she knew that truly incriminating piece of testimony, that undeniable detail of the death camps, is that men like this one had lived to testify. He had been in there with his brother and his cousin, which is probably how he survived, and he was clever—he learned the ropes. Learned to shield himself from the horror just enough to stay sane. He was supposed to wait just outside the door, but from there you could hear the people inside "*praying,*" said Morris Venezia, "*calling on God.*" He soon learned that he could run and hide himself away during that part, so as not to have to hear it. As long as he was back when they opened the doors.

Once, he said, after they had pulled some men from the gas and had them stacked up, waiting for the lift to take them up to the ovens, one of the dead men suddenly sat up and started to sing.

Everyone stopped, transfixed, and stared, even the guards, even the SS, froze for a moment, silenced. The man's eyes were shining, and his face was lit by a beatific smile. A man who'd just been through the gas and hadn't quite died. "*He was singing like this*"—Venezia hummed a few bars of "Eine kleine Nachtmusik." Mozart. "*He looked around, not really there. Happy.*

"*But then an SS drew his gun and shot him in the neck.*"

Not that it mattered perhaps, because here was a man who

must have been beyond bullets. He had breathed poison gas
and woken up singing. Was it possible that that's what they all
did, just before they died? Went to that place, wherever Mozart's
music takes one? A lovely meadow, with their own mothers and
fathers, their own children, happy at home?

Could that be? Since it happened this once? Since there is
this one, detailed firsthand account? An unknown man who
stopped between life and death, in that inferno, that *nightmare
of crime*, with a smile on his face and Mozart on his lips. Morris
Venezia and his cousin Dario were there. They saw it and heard
it and lived to tell. Took the trouble to tell.

A GREAT GIFT, THAT. One of the few, along with the docu-
mented escapes. And she felt lucky that she'd gone back and
played that tape that day, lucky she'd heard that story, for the
sake of everyone the Nazis had killed, not just Hermann—who
could have been that man, actually. The timing was right, late
May or early June 1944, during the Hungarian transports.

It occurred to her that maybe that was the best she could
do for Hermann, because as far as that quest went, she had to
admit that she was coming to the end of the line. True, there
was her uncle's letter—the nieces who had seen Hermann "*at
Auswetz Concentration Camp.*" Strengthened that claim with the
assertion that "*he was very strong and healthy,*" further evidence
that they might in fact have seen him. And all this back in 1945,
unaffected by a future in which he never came back.

"*They do know that he escaped from the Concentration Camp*"—
but not formally, she was forced to conclude. The histories seem
to have those names.

Unless the girls meant later, in the chaos that swept over
the place in the fall, as the Russians closed in. The problem

with that was that Hermann's nieces hadn't said when they left Auschwitz themselves—or rather, they probably had, but Consie's uncle hadn't written it down. *"They told me the same stories I had heard the night before from the other refugees,"* was what he wrote instead.

Which left her crying over an old letter. But history, real history, is like that. Everything there but the one thing you want.

Although on the other hand, that left open the possibility that they were still there, in Auschwitz, those two girls, Klara and Alice, in October of 1944. Because if that's the escape they were talking about, there was still a chance.

20

It was near the end, with a little hope in the air, even in Auschwitz, which is what people needed to find the strength to act. "*You must be strong to wish to escape*," wrote the French Resistance prisoner Charlotte Delbo. In 1942, when she was taken in, "*no one dreamt of escaping*."

But by the fall of 1944, the Nazi Reich was no longer infinite. On a good day, you could hear the Russian tanks from Auschwitz. Allied bombers flew over regularly, though always on their way to somewhere else.

Still, they were the future, and everyone knew it, including the SS, who were suddenly facing a very big problem. The trains were no longer arriving day and night with a prodigious number of new victims to be processed, which left eight hundred strong, tough SK prisoners standing around with nothing to do. The strongest and toughest of the prisoners, the gas and crematorium workers, the men the Nazis had forced to do the worst work since the beginning of time.

No one was going to trick these guys into the gas. There wouldn't be any "Tie your shoes together" or "We've got a nice white coffee waiting for you afterwards" for them. On the other hand, they couldn't be allowed to live, they were never allowed to live. The system had been honed over the years: the groups worked for two or three months, meanwhile always training a new group to replace them, so that on the day they were suddenly surrounded with no warning by the SS in force with machine guns and dogs, and shot down, there were new men standing by to throw them into the ovens that they'd taught how to operate by then.

A neat trick, the SS congratulated themselves. They even showed these prisoners their lighter side on the subject. *"Your path to Paradise is assured,"* they liked to tease them.

The prisoners got the joke, but might have questioned the concept of "Paradise." "Inferno," they knew —as Zalmen Gradowski, the SK worker who managed to leave a written record buried in the ash, put it, *"The dark night is my friend, tears and screams are my songs, fire my light . . . Hell is my home."*

These men were kept completely segregated from the other prisoners. Once in that door, there was no way out. In compensation, though, while they were working, they were permitted to eat some of the food the dead left beside their neatly tied shoes, and even to wear their sweaters under their own stripes. In the few pictures, there are boots on their feet, instead of the deadly wooden clogs.

All of which made them even more of a problem for the SS by late summer of 1944—men who knew, men accustomed to looking death in the face, straight on, but who were neither starving nor hobbled nor confused. It had always required some skill to kill them, but the momentum of the whole death apparatus had kept things moving forward, and the numbers had always been kept under control. Before that summer, there were only about two to three hundred active crematorium workers at any given time in Auschwitz-Birkenau, half of whom were always slated for slaughter themselves.

But the Hungarian transports had required more workers. The ovens had to be kept fired round the clock, and the gas chambers running as well. There were always people outside, waiting for their "showers." Standing quietly and waiting, hand in hand with their own children, still oblivious to the fact that they were queueing for their death.

The summer of '44 had been a sort of apotheosis for the SS, who had risen with flying colors to the epic demands placed upon them. They were, after all, the incarnation of the Third Reich here. Their führer in Berlin was the one who uttered the stirring words—"Send the Hungarians"—but it was the SS who had to make them flesh. And Eichmann in Budapest, in an organizational exaltation of his own, was rounding up and shipping out more people faster than ever before and without stop. This meant trains pulling up to the platform at Auschwitz day and night, with too many people for the gas, too many for the ovens, which broke down continually all that summer from overuse, and it was left to the SS on the ground there to find the way.

And they had. They had dug pits for outdoor burning when the ovens were on the blink, and shot people one by one when there was no room for them in the gas chamber. They even managed to keep the thing tidy. Having discovered that a man shot in the neck tended to fall backwards and splash blood on shiny SS boots, they trained prisoners to hold them by the ear and then thrust them forward as they fell, into the pit that had been dug precisely first to catch and then to burn them.

Fine. The SS did all that and whatever else Berlin required of them without complaint, and they got through the 450,000 sent to them by June. But to do it, they'd had to more than double the number of prisoners working the gas and the ovens, to eight hundred, and bring in the Greeks with their strength and the linguistic divide, the fact that they didn't speak or understand Hungarian. Clever, that, but once the transports started tapering off, these men became redundant. There was no further work for most of them, nor did the SS see the sense of allowing eight hundred eyewitnesses to the logistics of the Final Solution to survive the camps, particularly with the Russians already outside of Krakow.

They considered lining them up and shooting them, but feared that sort of action could engender an uprising, or a hand-to-hand scuffle that the SS, though armed, weren't sure they would win. Creative solutions were called for, and the first thing the SS came up with was to retrofit a legitimate delousing station into a gas chamber, bricking up the windows and then covering them with sandbags. In this way, they managed to trick the first three hundred prisoners inside, on the twenty-ninth of September 1944. The gassing went smoothly, and the SS were pleased. There were five hundred left now, a more manageable number. These the SS thought they could handle with the more routine method of selecting them out, group by group.

But there was an underground in the camp by then, several undergrounds in fact. There were the Polish partisans, who had the weapons and the connections; the Russian POWs, who had the guts and the skills; and these crematorium prisoners, who had the least to lose. Since they had always been killed off like clockwork after only a few months, they'd never been able to organize anything among the different crematoria before. But these men had already lived longer, and the SS too were slipping. There was a new overseer of the gas chambers, SS Staff Sergeant Busch, brought in to replace the staunch Otto Moll.

But Moll proved irreplaceable. He'd been one with the

place, had flinched at nothing, even went beyond, occasionally selecting pretty girls to shoot himself, and leading the way
when it came to throwing live children into burning pits. But
poor Busch had to get drunk to effectuate these duties. This
meant the crematorium subversives could work around him
more easily.

And an uprising was finally in the works, a serious plan,
coordinated throughout the camps. For months, some young
women prisoners, working in an ammunition plant just outside
the gates, had been risking their lives to smuggle little bits of
gunpowder to the prisoners, who'd been fashioning hand grenades out of shoe polish tins. Another of them, a welder working for the SS, managed to make four bombs in oxygen cans
with acetylene. One girl stole diamonds from the dead women's
corsets she was sorting, and traded them to corrupt guards for
keys to the sheds with rakes and hoes, axes, tools that could
be turned, French Revolution–style, into weapons. Still others
filched wire cutters to cut through the triple rows of barbed
wire, along with the tools needed to slash the SS tires. Some
even managed to hide a few guns taken from wrecked planes
hauled back from Stalingrad for dismantling. Something akin
to hope was in the air.

The plan was that on a given day, at a given signal, the prisoners throughout the various subcamps in Auschwitz would fall
upon their guards in unison, seize their machine guns and kill
them, set off their home-made bombs, cut the wires, and liber-
ate the camp. Even the half-dead among them thought the plan
was good.

But the problem was when? The Greeks claim they were
pushing for action, with the Poles stalling for more weapons.

The crematorium prisoners were complaining that the partisans wouldn't arm them. But when they got word through the underground that another selection for the gas was imminent, they resolved to act on their own, without the Polish partisans if they had to. And on the seventh of October, they did.

Some say it started when a guard overheard the prisoners plotting and threatened to reveal their plan to the SS. In this version, one of the men seized him on the spot and threw him alive into the burning oven, and the action commenced.

Another prisoner, Filip Müller, says it started with a selection that day, at Crematorium IV. "*Towards mid-day*," he says, the SS staff sergeant, Busch, "*along with several other SS men and guards, arrived in the yard in front of the crematorium. All prisoners were ordered to line up. Then Busch began calling out the first few numbers on the list, starting with the highest and working his way down to the lowest. Those selected for transfer were made to stand on the opposite side of the yard.*"

Everyone knew what that meant. Those with the least to lose now had nothing to lose. One of those selected, Chaim Neuhof, a Pole who'd been at Auschwitz since 1942, approached SS Staff Sergeant Busch, said something low, and then shouted out the password, "Hurrah!" and struck him with a hammer.

Or shovel, some say. The rest of the prisoners then "*set up a loud shout, hurled themselves upon the guards with hammers and axes, wounded some of them, the rest they beat with what they could get at, they pelted them with stones without further ado*," according to Salmen Lewental. The prisoners dug up the hidden munitions, tied up the SS men who were nearby, and grabbed their weapons.

Jukel Worona, a glazier from Czeconau with "a thick black beard," led a group back into Crematorium IV with bottle

bombs and handmade grenades, and blew it up. The crematorium burst into flames.

At the sound of explosions and fighting, the prisoners at
Crematorium II joined the revolt. The *Reichsdeutsche Oberkapo*
and one SS man were thrown into the burning furnace alive,
and another SS man was beaten to death. The rest of them ran
for help, blowing their whistles, while the prisoners cut the
barbed-wire fence, at the women's camp as well, and escaped
into the woods.

AND HERE'S WHERE IT should have ended, where it could end,
if someone makes the movie. The crematorium in flames, men
in stripes, and some women, with hair grown in just enough to
look like Mia Farrow in *Rosemary's Baby*. And all of them running into the woods and then stopping, at least one pair of them,
to embrace. The Russians, anyway, are coming. The worst was
behind them. Last shot perhaps of Allied planes, overhead.

Which actually did happen. There was an Allied air raid
that night that prevented the SS from further pursuit, and that
was good, for a while.

But this was Auschwitz and what happened next was what
happened there. There were about two hundred and fifty
unarmed prisoners on the run, and three thousand SS men with
two machine guns each against them. Even so, if the prisoners
had turned northeast, toward the Vistula River, then maybe.
But they turned southwest, and thus hit an Auschwitz subcamp
and were trapped. Some of them took refuge in a barn, which
the SS set on fire. The ones who ran out were shot. Most of the
organizers of the revolt were dead by then.

Twelve others who did get across the river were hunted

down with dogs and shot. Their bodies were dragged back to the camp. All in all, two hundred and fifty rebels were killed, along with another two hundred prisoners.

But this was not the worst of it. The worst of it was what happened to the four girls, the ones who'd smuggled out the powder, some of which the SS found and traced. There were only the four who worked in the small room in that particular munitions factory. They were arrested at once.

They were held for a few months and tortured beyond reason. They were young, in their teens and twenties, Estujsia Wajcblum, Regina Saperstein, Alla Gaertner, and Roza Robota. Despite the torture, none of them said a word.

There was hope that those girls would be saved by the Russians. The New Year came, even in Auschwitz, January 1945. The Germans were burning papers and dynamiting the crematoria in an absurdist effort to hide what they'd done. The camp commanders seemed to have lost their appetite for hanging. One of the men in the underground managed to ply the SS guard with liquor and sneak into Block 11, the punishment cell, to see Roza Robota in prison.

"I descended the steps, led by the guard, until we reached Roza's cell," wrote Noach Zabludowicz. He *"opened the door, led me inside, and disappeared. When my eyes became accustomed to the dark, I made out a figure wrapped in rags, lying on the cold cement floor. The figure turned its head in my direction. I barely recognized her. Her face was marked from endless pain and suffering. After some moments of silence Roza began to tell me about the sadistic means that the Germans had used against her during the interrogation and she said that she had accepted total responsibility without naming anyone else."*

"I knew very well what I was doing and I know what is in store for me," she told him, and asked that the comrades continue their work. *"It's easier to die when you know that your work continues."*

He told her to take courage, that the Russians would save her. "*Maybe*," she whispered, and closed her eyes.

And they almost did, the Russians; they would have, except for a special order, radioed from Berlin, to execute the four girls immediately by hanging. On January 6, 1945, gallows were erected in the women's section of the main camp at Auschwitz. All the women remaining in the camp were forced to witness. The girls who'd known them best were ordered to the front.

The SS commander, Hössler, read out the sentence, screaming that all such traitors would be destroyed in this manner.

But the last word went to Roza Robota. "*Revenge!*" she shouted, just as they hung her.

And three weeks later, the Russians were there.

LATE, THOUGH. For Roza Robota, for all those millions, and maybe for Hermann too. One man, plucked from the uncountable heap of stiff gray bodies by a line in a letter. There was a footnote to the mass escape in October of 1944, though, that seemed to offer one last chance for him.

"*One group, numbering twenty-seven prisoners, moved westward under the leadership of a prisoner, reached as far as Germany. They were apprehended by the 'Volkssturm' (German Civil Defense) and jailed in a small German town.*"

There had been an all-points alert by then, about the escaped prisoners, but these men "*were saved by their claim to have escaped a transport on the way to Dachau. It was not possible to refute their claim, as this was a throughway of prisoner transports, and the transfer lists were by that time in utter disarray. The prisoners were sent to one of the remote camps in the area and remained there until the day of liberation.*"

They would have the names of those prisoners, somewhere.

Consie figured she could write, delve further, but she wouldn't. Hermann hadn't come home. Unless she wanted to put him in some Polish hut somewhere with a new wife, permanent amnesia, and a faraway, puzzled look in his eyes every fall during plum season, it was better to leave him shot outside of Auschwitz, in the uprising. Give him that moment of absolute triumph over the Nazis, just before a bullet grazed his head and left him facedown in the Polish mud.

Which, she knew from her dreams, would be better than the gas. She walked outside. Scorpio was rising. It was the one Zodiac sign she knew, although one clear night somewhere out west, she'd looked up and seen them all, circling in the sky, and gotten it. Got the whole turning of the cosmos, and it made the night even more wonderful. As it must have been for Greek shepherds, ancient night hunters, everyone, really, from the beginning of time till now who had cause to venture out into the real dark. A dark with great beauty twinned with terror, packs of wolves and lions, leopards in the trees, grizzly bears rampant. Which meant you didn't go out without some cause. Food, your animals, and once in a while, love. In the spring.

She read the philosopher Jean Améry, who'd been in Auschwitz: *"I do not have [clarity] today, and I hope that I never will. Clarification would amount to disposal, settlement of the case, which can then be placed in the files of history."*

Yes, he was right. He knew, he had been there, lived it, died it too, though years later, by his own hand. But he was right. She too had no clarification, no "disposal," nor should she.

SHE LET IT GO. Moved on, as they say. She had other work, neglected too long, going nowhere. She had lost, even almost forgotten, that feeling of dawning astonishment, even joy, when she'd first read the letter, read what had seemed to her the only good news from that world that she'd ever come upon. That her grandfather's brother, a man whose picture had smiled out at her from the pages of their own album, had escaped—might have escaped—from Auschwitz.

Which is where she figured she could leave it, at "might have escaped."

But one evening, months later, she found herself leafing again—how? why?—through her grandmother's old address book, and noticed a number she hadn't seen before. She dialed and got a distant cousin in New York who remembered her family, and gave her a name and a phone number.

"I'm not sure it will work," said the cousin.

Consie hung up the phone and dialed with shaking hands.

"... BUT MAYBE A THREAD"

The Letter

21

"You take the D train," they'd told her, and get off at Church Avenue.

She'd lived in New York in the seventies, but had never taken the D train beyond the Village in those days. To her it was the unknown. Bob Dylan. *All-night girls. Escapades out on the D train.* But this was nothing like that.

For one thing, it was four in the afternoon. For another, it was ninety-six degrees in the shade. The train was packed with tired-looking persons of all description except all-night anything. Blacks, Asians, bearded white men in baggy black suits who looked like they'd gotten dressed last January in one of those villages in Poland that had wiped the slate clean of men like them seventy years ago.

And yet, here they all were, as if nothing had happened. All those millions killed, and yet, here they still were, their doubles, their clones, as if they'd come back up the chimneys, fully clothed, to ride the D train with everyone else back to Brooklyn.

She got off where they did. The place looked rough but not exactly dangerous. The billboards on the main street were in Spanish, the usual 1-888 affairs, giant lawyers, smiling tutors. LOSE YOUR ACCENT! BEEN IN A CRASH? PODEMOS AYUDAR!

She ducked into a florist shop—mostly funeral wreaths draped with ribbons, also in Spanish. VAYA CON DIOS! WE WILL NEVER FORGET YOU. A few teddy bear arrangements for kids shot in a schoolyard.

A Korean girl, still in her Catholic school uniform, was hard at her books. "Don't you have anything more cheerful?" Consie asked her.

The girl looked up with math in her eyes, and then blinked and went into the back and came out with a bunch of yellow mums.

"Nothing pink?"

No, there was nothing pink. This wasn't the Upper East Side for peonies and tulips.

"Can you wrap them? It's a present."

An offering really, and in fact, a garland from a sacred bull or a burnt sacrifice would have been more to the point. She was going to see Klara of "Klara and Alice" of her uncle's letter, who it turned out was still alive.

It was hot but Consie was cold. She wasn't expecting anything, not even for Klara to live to the meeting. She'd taken the first plane she could get, and then hopped on the D train, but if someone met her at the door with the news that Klara had died that morning, she wouldn't really be surprised. The whole thing already felt outside of the realm of possibility.

How could Klara still be alive? And if she was, since she was, how had Consie never heard her name till she read the letter? The only possible trace she had found was one picture from the fifties, of a glamorous couple, the woman with her hair up, the man with one of those pencil-thin European mustaches, sitting at a table full of flowers—"On the Danube," someone had written in German on the edge of the photo. And beneath, in another hand, "Klara," but followed by a question mark.

Living in Vienna, it had been assumed, and yet all the time, she had been in Brooklyn? Was that possible? Without giving any sign?

Or had she, to Consie's grandfather perhaps, or her uncle? She hadn't talked to Klara herself, but to her son's wife, who sounded like people she'd known on the Lower East Side. Could she come? she'd asked.

"Yeah, sure," the daughter-in-law said, nicely. "Klara's old, though. Too bad you didn't call before her stroke."

Yes, too bad, so much of it, but what about Wednesday?

And now here she was, like Orpheus, on a trip down to all those dead. Shaking in the heat, walking the two blocks as instructed, and then turning off the main drag in Borough Park, onto a street with good-sized sycamores where suddenly everyone was dressed like the Amish.

Women with longish skirts and thick stockings, herding groups of schoolchildren, laughing and playing in the street like children anywhere. The girls had on skirts and blouses, though, and the boys long trousers, no shorts or T-shirts in this 'hood, but still, they looked happy. A few men passed, some more fully costumed than others. But it didn't matter, because this was their world.

In fact, she was the only civilian, so to speak, on the street. It was a curious place, but not without its charm. The buildings were what you get in the New York boroughs, brick, three, four, six stories at most. Some trees, but nothing great, since this was Brooklyn, not Locust Valley. Still, there were more trees, sycamores, in the direction toward which she was walking, which she took as a good sign.

When she got to the address she'd been given, however, she started to wonder. It was a run-down, flat-faced building with two sets of doors. Metal doors, multifamily maybe—was Klara poor? This hadn't occurred to her.

She rang. Nothing. Was this how it would end, then? She had traveled a lot in the Brazilian outback. They call it a "disencounter" out there.

But then the door was opened by a woman dressed like the ones in the street—a long dowdy skirt, almost a head scarf.

"Oh," said the woman. Klara's daughter-in-law.

"Yes, we'd spoken—"

"Yeah, but when you didn't call—"

Of course, she should have called again, called twice, three times. She'd thought maybe it was better not to bug them, push her luck, that sort of thing.

But she should have. And now—

"Well, come in." She was ushered into a hushed, darkened house. Was Klara sick then?

But it turned out Klara didn't live here.

"Oh."

She lived close, though—

"That's great!"

"—if she's home."

The daughter-in-law took her up a flight of stairs, and then another. The house was echoing, empty.

"Do you have children?" Consie asked, and then instantly regretted it. There were no signs of children anywhere, nothing cooking, no toys or schoolbooks or jackets slung about. The terrible word "barren" flashed across her mind, from Sunday school days.

But "Yeah," Klara's daughter-in-law answered.

Relief. "That's great! How many?"

"Fourteen." She was dialing and then waiting—a long time, too long. "I don't think Klara's home."

Breathe deeply, Consie told herself. It was true that she'd put a lot into this trip, everything she had left, in fact. Charged the flight with the last of the credit.

But it's not Auschwitz, she told herself. Funny, though, how that didn't help. Just increased the proportion of bad to good in life.

But then the daughter-in-law was saying hello, and it didn't sound like to a machine. Had someone answered? There was a pause and then she said something else, not in English, but at least it was a conversation, which boded well.

"Yeah, it's okay," she said to Consie, and a few minutes later they were being driven by a bearded man with a hat to another brick building, where Klara lived.

Her apartment was nice, comfortable, everything you need. A sofa in the living room, a TV, a few armchairs off to the side. Even a nurse, a nice Hungarian woman, but it turned out that Klara was—of course—no longer the girl in blue from her uncle's letter.

As soon as she walked in, Consie realized her mistake. Realized, that is, that she'd been expecting to walk into her dream of a girl in her early twenties in a blue dress, who would look a bit like her handsome young uncle, and tell her how Hermann had escaped. And then maybe introduce her Romanian fiancé.

Husband, in the end—Klara's first husband, it turned out. Who'd died young, she was told, from a transfusion of the wrong type of blood, not long after the war, in all the confusion over there, behind the Iron Curtain.

It wasn't quite clear—nothing was. Klara didn't speak English, or much of anything else anymore. She asked several times who Consie was. The daughter-in-law would shout something to her, the old woman would nod and smile, and then ask again.

Consie moved closer, and asked about Hermann.

More nods, more smiles.

"But he was there with you? In the camps?"

The daughter-in-law translated, but Klara just looked puzzled.

"He was strong and healthy—"

More translation, though she didn't hear the word "Hermann," just her uncle's name and her grandfather's.

"Did you ask her about Hermann?" she said to the daughter-in-law.

The daughter-in-law turned to her, not unkindly, but definitive. Like explaining to her eleventh child that there would be no puppy.

"Hermann died," she said.

"But Klara told my uncle that he escaped!"

From Klara, a "*Vas?*"

"She said she *knew*."

"People didn't escape from Auschwitz," said the daughter-in-law.

No, no, they did, Consie said. Six hundred, and some of them lived, and when exactly was Klara in Auschwitz with Hermann? She leaned closer to the old woman.

"When?" she asked her.

"During the war," said the daughter-in-law. She got to her feet. "Klara looks tired—"

Consie took Klara's hand.

"When were you there? Did you see him? Or just hear?"

From Klara, a nod, a smile. "Good night, Ma," the daughter-in-law was saying. The nurse came in.

It was over. Consie leaned in to kiss the legendary Klara in the old woman. She studied her face, but couldn't see her uncle there at all. Still, she whispered, "Did you know, really?"

But there was no answer, and they walked out.

IT WAS DARK NOW, a nice night, summer, but soft, not too hot. The car service man with the beard was delegated to drive her back into Manhattan. Afterwards, she couldn't remember if she'd said good-bye to the daughter-in-law. So overcome was she with a sense of loss.

"Fuck," she said aloud as they drove toward the bridge, away from her last chance here.

"What?" said the driver.

Was it a stoning crime for a woman to blaspheme in this neighborhood? "That truck—" she mumbled, and slid down in her seat.

And even if he didn't stone her, he could take her to the Women's House of Detention instead of the Village.

Still, it was a miracle, after all, that this man, this driver, was even here. A miracle that she was here too, but lesser. There hadn't been an all-out campaign to keep her from walking the earth or breathing the air, but much of Europe had joined arms to kill this man's parents, and yet, here he was, driving her in a comfortable old car back to the city.

People could debate the causes, say this, say that, cite historical precedents or psychological proclivities. Speak of "projection," mold on bread, World War I till the cows came home.

But she had finally ended up with the historian, Raul Hilberg—there were no explanations, he'd concluded. The whole thing was *"the culmination of a process that in retrospect had emerged from an inner logic not recognizable even to the perpetrators. It was primal, beyond rationality and irrationality . . . a 'reckoning.'"*

NOT THAT IT WAS, in the end, a reckoning. It was all for nothing, after all. The people whom Hitler had wanted off the earth were still driving through the warm summer night, and meanwhile Poland lost 17 percent of its populace, the USSR 13.7 percent, Germany itself 8.6 percent.

And as for those dead, the loss is already mostly statistical. There are few hot tears still shed for any one of them. "Life carries you along," as a Hungarian countess who'd washed up in Brazil and survived by reading palms once told her. She herself had boarded the D train earlier that day, driven by what? Something to do with Czechoslovakia, a place she could barely find on a map? An attempt at resurrection, as much of her uncle as of anything? Mixed, perhaps, with a half-memory of her own grandfather, in the middle of America, eating the purple plums he got every year from one far-flung farmer, way out somewhere, farther than people would usually drive in those days, into the next county, farmland still, where people wouldn't change their clocks for daylight saving.

She remembered him sitting with them on the front porch in the evenings, at the end of summer, and cutting the plums in half with his thumb. He was a formal man who would have used a knife for an apple or a peach, but this was something else, something he did the way he did it, something from a world that wasn't theirs.

He never spoke of the plums, never linked them to his childhood, but they were special to him, sacred, she would say in retrospect. They were golden on the inside, with the skin almost navy blue. She never asked, and he never told her. Just gave her pieces, by the half, and seemed pleased that she liked them.

Fine, let it be. It turned out that she was no raiser of the dead.

THE CAR STOPPED—they were in the Village. "This okay?"

"Where are we?" She'd once lived here, but had lost her way.

"Seventh and Bleecker."

"Sure, fine—"

And then of course she had to pay—did she have enough? She'd forgotten that, hadn't thought to ask the price. She'd somehow assumed that even this ride from another world was included.

And now he could hold her up, but he asked thirty dollars, which seemed reasonable, and she had the cash, and paid him, and watched for a minute as the car turned off to head back. It wasn't a bad life over there—Klara's daughter-in-law's children all lived around her. Some worked for her husband, some were still in school, some were already devoting their lives to finding the one letter in an obscure text that held all of life's secrets, but just down the street.

Whereas her own children lived far away.

What is life? she wondered.

She walked along Seventh Avenue and turned down West Fourth. She used to live on this street, used to walk every day on these same cracked pavements, under these same trees, much bigger now—another miracle. There'd been a Japanese woman at the Santa Monica Farmers' Market selling purple plums last season. "Italian plums," said the little placard. They were ridiculously expensive but she'd bought them anyway.

You couldn't split them like her grandfather's, but they were very good. So good that she hoarded them, until they got too soft to eat, and then she cooked them and watched as they turned from purple to dark magenta. They were having people to dinner that night—she'd serve them with vanilla ice cream.

But in the end, she couldn't do it. She'd tasted them, and they were sublime, deep and sweet and a little bit bitter, like nothing else in the world, and she couldn't bring herself to share them. Maybe in the light of day, with one or two friends who would pause over the color. But no one would be able to see it in the candlelight, or at least not without ceremony and a certain ado. And could she ask the young Hollywood producers her husband was courting to cry over purple plums?

She realized as she walked her old streets that it could have been worse with Klara, much worse. If she'd found her ten years earlier, "before her stroke." Klara would have shaken her head sadly and revised her testimony, the way witnesses do, in the light of new evidence. Hermann never came back, so therefore, in retrospect, she and her sister Alice had never seen him. He wasn't in Auschwitz with them after all, nor was he "still healthy and strong."

But as it was, the good news still stood. For what it was worth, because the truth now was that though she had taken much trouble to save Hermann from the gas and preserve him as a hero, she found she no longer cared about that.

Because she'd come to see them all as heroes, and had also learned that how one dies might not matter. That all deaths might carry within themselves their own escape, touched, possibly, with light, with something freeing. That what we see is only the external, nothing to do with what is happening inside. That a man screaming for air in the gas might be singing "Eine kleine Nachtmusik." That a child thrown alive to burn in a Nazi pit could be smiling in its own mother's arms.

She remembered the last time she'd seen Magda, about five years ago, not long before she died. The old people, "Uncle and Auntie," were long gone, but Magda had few cousins, and she made the journey to California to see Consie and her mother, and once there, had taught them to make crêpes suzette. She

had learned, she said, in Vienna, where they called them something else, but "it's all the same!"

She laughed—"Vienna!" Shook her head. Consie didn't
know then to ask her any questions, just took her down to the
sea, and they walked slowly along the sand, into the sun. It was
one of those golden evenings, like nowhere but California. There
could have been nothing there to summon Magda's old world.

Still, she smiled and mentioned how her father had loved
"bathing," and taught her to swim when she was very small. He
had a navy blue "bathing costume, or *svim*suit as you say."

Consie smiled. The *w*'s. The *v*'s.

"And he bought me one, like his—navy blue too, which I
loved, and we *svam* in the little pond by the orchard. It was the
end of the day, and the sun came over the water."

And now, looking back, she saw another way to make peace
with Magda's Hermann. Not only as a hero, but as a man who
had loved, deeply. A good father who'd bought his daughter a
blue bathing "costume" and taught her to swim.

"And it seemed to me so big, that pond—" Magda had continued, then broken off. A silence. "Of course, he would be dead
by now, anyway."

Long dead—all of them, almost everyone the Nazis had
killed, certainly all the old ones, and by now, most of the young
ones too. Magda herself was in her eighties that day, as was her
sister Gabi. They lived near each other in Toronto. The youngest sister, Vera, had died in her forties, of what they called natural causes.

Consie had walked on with Magda in silence. The waves
broke on the beach, the shorebirds ran forward and back, peck-
ing the sand crabs. The "corps de ballet," as she called the sand-
erlings, swept in and out together.

All life was a mystery, but Magda's was touched with something else, and the light that afternoon had come off her head like a halo in a quattrocento painting of the saints and angels. She and Consie had turned and smiled at each other, and then walked slowly in their silence, back, away from the sun now, into the blue.

CONSIE WENT BACK to the small hotel in the Village where she was staying and dreamed that night of the camps—some version of the camps, with death in the offing. In the dream, there were many men, great men, Freud, Jung, friends, others, all threatened with imminent murder. But three gray cats came in, to lead them to freedom. Not to safety, she remembered knowing, but at least out.

They were beautiful cats—when she awoke, she remembered the gray cats of Freya, the Norse goddess. The Norse myths were different from the Greeks', or for that matter, the Hebrews'. Harsher, with their storm gods, and evil elves, and in the end, all-out destruction, as Hitler should have known from the start.

But there was beauty, too, stark and stirring—that whiff of cold, fresh air, clean from the mountains, and the horns, the bells, the music in the wind. The gods drank their mead, and you could hear them forging magic tools in their caves, hear their hammers ringing through the mountains. Sometimes they unleashed terrible storms on the world, but Freya was beautiful and, come spring, Heimdall would blow his magic horn, and then men—yes, Hitler, men like Hermann—could come out again and plant their plum trees in the sun.

O fim

ACKNOWLEDGMENTS

First, I should like to acknowledge the witnesses whom I was lucky enough to hear tell their stories, at great cost to their own peace and comfort, at the Museum of Tolerance in Los Angeles, in 2009–10. They were mostly old then; many of them are no longer with us. But a few remain, and in tribute, I will say that if you ever have a chance to hear one of them speak, run, fly, ride, speed-walk to wherever place on this earth that they are still gracing. Like Magda, they have been touched by the angel. The light comes off them, and you will find yourself in awe.

I also thank Dr. Crispin Brooks and the Shoah Foundation at USC, where, thanks to the vision and generosity of Steven Spielberg, a whole archive of testimony exists for anyone to access.

As for my editor at W. W. Norton, Starling Lawrence, as I was filling this page with words of praise and gratitude, I suddenly heard his voice, his dread: "Must we?" So rather than presuming and beginning, I shall simply say thank you. But *moltissimo. Muito.* Very, very much.

Many thanks as well to Nneoma Amadi-obi, also at Norton. And last as always, first as ever, to J.P.

NOTES

THE LETTER

35 "...our radio, our government": Otto Friedrich, *City of Nets* (Harper & Row, 1986), 51.

55 "they don't treat people like this for nothing": Incident from Hélène Berr, *The Journal of Helene Berr* (McClelland & Stewart, 2008).

58 through the deep Polish woods: Mike Popeck, testimony, Museum of Tolerance, Los Angeles, 2009.

68 at least nothing with pictures: Marthë Kardos, private conversation, São Paulo, Brazil, 1985.

78 Wotan, had thundered through the land: See Carl Jung's essay "Wotan," *Essays on Contemporary Events* (Princeton University Press/Bollingen, 1989).

81 people were eating stinging nettles: Irene Firestone, testimony, Museum of Tolerance, Los Angeles, 2009.

82 that it had a lid: Agnès Humbert, *Résistance: A French Woman's Journal of the War* (Bloomsbury, 2008).

84 "...Russian edifice will come tumbling down": Quoted by Peter De Mendelssohn, *Design for Aggression: The Inside Story of Hitler's War Plans* (Harper & Brothers, 1946).

84 Shostakovich's Seventh Symphony: Ed Vulliamy, "Orchestral Maneouvres (Part Two)," *Observer*, November 25, 2001.

88 rather than to minor Hungarians: On the fate of the Weiss steel mills, see Cathy Weiss, testimony, Museum of Tolerance, Los Angeles, 2009.

89 just laughed and walked away: George Konrád, "The Crown Prince of Frivolity," excerpt from *A Feast in the Garden*, translated by Imre Goldstein (Harcourt Brace Jovanovich, 1992).

"THE WITCH'S KITCHEN"

97 **when the train stopped:** Godel Silber, interview no. 2226, Visual History Archive, USC Shoah Foundation Institute.

100 **"My mother!":** Arrival accounts from Magda Ruzohorsky, Elisabeth Mann, Mike Popeck, etc.

100 **". . . Neither food nor water was plentiful":** Oliver Lustig, text presentation of photographs from *The Auschwitz Album: The Story of a Transport*, Holocaust Survivors and Remembrance Project, "Forget You Not," http://isurvived.org/Survivors_Folder/Lustig_Oliver/Commentary -PhotoAlbum-1.html.

101 **". . . Germans are barbarians, madame?":** Rudolf Vrba, *I Escaped from Auschwitz* (Grove Press/Black Cat, 1986).

107 **took out his gun and shot her:** Klara Aardwerk, interview no. 67515, Visual History Archive, USC Shoah Foundation Institute.

112 **". . . maybe they won't cut it":** Cathy Weiss, testimony.

115 **". . . your parents, your children, your friends":** Ibid.

121 **"death" here . . . "can start with the shoes":** Primo Levi, *Survival in Auschwitz*, translated by Stuart Woolf (Simon & Schuster, 1995).

123 **like an old woman's with the palsy:** Mary Nata, testimony, Museum of Tolerance, Los Angeles, 2009.

126 **like crazy women:** Terrence Des Pres in *Anatomy of the Auschwitz Death Camp*, edited by Yisrael Gutman and Michael Berenbaum (published in association with the United States Holocaust Memorial Museum by Indiana University Press, 1994), 130.

128 **". . . and it just hurts you":** Irene Zisblatt, interview no. 7832, Visual History Archive, USC Shoah Foundation Institute.

130 **Shakespeare's sonnets:** Lidia Rosenfeld Vago, "One Year in the Black Hole of Our Planet Earth: A Personal Narrative," in *Women in the Holocaust*, edited by Dalia Ofer and Lenore J. Weitzman (Yale University Press, 1998).

138 **quickly shut the door again:** Sophia Litwinska, from the Belsen trial, September 1945.

140 **large number of baby carriages:** Accounts of Guiliana Tedeschi and Danuta Czech, quoted in Richard L. Rubinstein and John K. Roth, *Approaches to Auschwitz* (Westminster John Knox Press, 2003), 239.

144 **his uniform splattered with blood:** Edith Singer, testimony, Museum of Tolerance, Los Angeles, 2009.

147 **to fill his slots:** Edith Singer, *March to Freedom: A Memoir of the Holocaust* (Impact Publishing, 2008), 61–62.

151 **extremely painful:** Vago, "One Year in the Black Hole of Our Planet Earth."

THE PINK TULIP

165 **behind them as they went:** Marie Glasser, testimony, Museum of Tolerance, Los Angeles, 2009.

173 **years ago from Prague:** Joel Sayre, "Letter from Berlin," *The New Yorker*, July 28, 1945.

178 *... reap the whirlwind:* Hosea 8:7.

182 **"... in vain anyway":** Mado from Chalotte Delbo, *Auschwitz and After* (Yale University Press, 1995), quoted by Lawrence L. Langer in "Gendered Suffering? Women in Holocaust Testimonies," in Ofer and Weitzman, *Women in the Holocaust*.

182 **all they had:** Anonymous, *A Woman in Berlin* (Picador, 2005).

182 **simple chance:** Langer, "Gendered Suffering?," 245.

183 **"... no one knows it":** Ibid.

183 **he'd laughed:** Ibid., 356.

"FOR NOTHING IS RESOLVED, NOTHING IS SETTLED . . ."

193 *"but not unknown":* Otto Friedrich, *The Kingdom of Auschwitz* (Harper & Row, 1982).

194 *"... tremendous hope":* Ibid.

194 **not far from the Czech border:** Gutman and Berenbaum, *Anatomy of the Auschwitz Death Camp.*

198 *"... holding their little hands, five in a row":* Chaim Feig, interview no. 34315, Visual History Archive, USC Shoah Foundation Institute.

203 **instead of being turned into gloves:** Irene Zisblatt, interview no. 7832, Visual History Archive, USC Shoah Foundation Institute.

209 *"... Don't let them take you alive":* Vrba, *I Escaped from Auschwitz*, 214.

213 **it was a clean ninety-five percent:** Hannah Arendt, *Eichmann in Jerusalem* (Viking Press, 1963), 125.

216 *"... an ideal Gestapo officer himself":* Eichmann interview, *Life* 49, no. 22 (November 28, 1960).

220 **in the French film Shoah:** *Shoah*, documentary by Claude Lanzmann (New Yorker Films, 1985).

224 *"... No trace of them will remain":* Zalmen Gradowski, *From the Heart of Hell: Manuscripts of a Sonderkommando Prisoner, Found in Auschwitz*, quoted in Gutman and Berenbaum, *Anatomy of the Auschwitz Death Camp*, 482.

225 **seized and sent to Auschwitz:** Morris Venezia, interview no. 20405, Visual History Archive, USC Shoah Foundation Institute.

229 *"no one dreamt of escaping":* Charlotte Delbo, *None of Us Will Return* (Grove Press, 1968).

230 *"... Hell is my home":* Nathan Cohen, "Diaries of the SK," in Gutman and Berenbaum, *Anatomy of the Auschwitz Death Camp.*

233   **to effectuate these duties:** Kitty Hart-Moxon, interview no. 45132, Visual History Archive, USC Shoah Foundation Institute.

233   **in oxygen cans with acetylene:** Godel Silber, interview.

233   **the Poles stalling for more weapons:** Morris Venezia, interview.

234   **and struck him with a hammer:** Filip Müller, *Eyewitness Auschwitz: Three Years in the Gas Chambers* (Routledge & Kegan Paul, 1979).

235   **The crematorium burst into flames:** Dario Gabbai, interview no. 142, Visual History Archive, USC Shoah Foundation Institute.

237   **just as they hung her:** Gutman and Berenbaum, *Anatomy of the Auschwitz Death Camp*, 157.

237   **"... *until the day of liberation*":** Ibid.

238   **"... *be placed in the files of history*":** Jean Améry, 1976 preface to *At the Mind's Limits: Contemplations by a Survivor on Auschwitz and Its Realities*, translated by Sidney and Stella Rosenfield (Indiana University Press, 1980).

". . . BUT MAYBE A THREAD"

249   **"... *beyond rationality and irrationality... a 'reckoning'*":** Raul Hilberg, *Perpetrators, Victims, Bystanders* (Harper Perennial, 1992), 16.

Levi, Primo. *The Drowned and the Saved*. Translated by Raymond Rosenthal. Abacus, 1989.

———. *Survival in Auschwitz*. Translated by Stuart Woolf. Simon & Schuster, 1995.

———. *The Periodic Table*. Translated by Raymond Rosenthal. Schocken, 1995.

Müller, Filip. *Eyewitness Auschwitz: Three Years in the Gas Chambers*. Routledge & Kegan Paul, 1979.

Ofer, Dalia, and Lenore J. Weitzman, eds. *Women in the Holocaust*. Yale University Press, 1998. See esp. Lawrence L. Langer, "Gendered Suffering? Women in Holocaust Testimonies," and Lidia Rosenfeld Vago, "One Year in the Black Hole of Our Planet Earth: A Personal Narrative."

Rubenstein, Richard L., and John K. Roth. *Approaches to Auschwitz: The Holocaust and Its Legacy*. Westminster John Knox Press, 2003.

Vrba, Rudolf. *I Escaped from Auschwitz*. Grove Press/Black Cat, 1986.

SELECT BIBLIOGRAPHY

Améry, Jean. *At the Mind's Limits: Contemplations by a Survivor of Auschwitz and Its Realities*. Translated by Sidney and Stella Rosenfield. Indiana University Press, 1980.

Anonymous. *A Woman in Berlin: Eight Weeks in a Conquered City: A Diary*. Picador, 2005.

Arendt, Hannah. *Eichmann in Jerusalem: A Report on the Banality of Evil*. Viking Press, 1963.

Berr, Hélène. *The Journal of Hélène Berr*. Translated by David Bellos with notes by the translator and an afterword by Mariette Job. McClelland & Stewart, 2008.

Borowski, Tadeusz. *This Way for the Gas, Ladies and Gentlemen*. Penguin Books, 1967.

Delbo, Charlotte. *None of Us Will Return*. Grove Press, 1968.

———. *Auschwitz and After*. Yale University Press, 1995.

De Mendelssohn, Peter. *Design for Aggression: The Inside Story of Hitler's War Plans*. Harper & Brothers, 1946.

Friedrich, Otto. *The Kingdom of Auschwitz*. Harper & Row, 1982.

———. *City of Nets*. Harper & Row, 1986.

Gutman, Yisrael, and Michael Berenbaum, eds. *Anatomy of the Auschwitz Death Camp*. Published in association with the United States Holocaust Memorial Museum by Indiana University Press, 1994.

Hilberg, Raul. *Perpetrators, Victims, Bystanders*. Harper Perennial, 1992.

Höcker Album. United States Holocaust Memorial Museum.

Humbert, Agnès. *Résistance: A French Woman's Journal of the War*. Bloomsbury, 2008.

Jung, Carl. "Wotan." *Essays on Contemporary Events*. Princeton University Press/Bollingen, 1989.

Lanzmann, Claude. *Shoah*. New Yorker Films, 1985.